SPEAK LOW

Also By Lynn Galli

<u>SCOTTISH CHARM</u>
Speak Low
One-Off

<u>VIRGINIA CLAN</u>
At Last
Forevermore
Blessed Twice
Imagining Reality
Wasted Heart

<u>ASPEN FRIENDS</u>
Life Rewired
Something So Grand
Mending Defects

<u>OTHER ROMANCES</u>
Winter Calling
Out of Order
Clichéd Love
Full Court Pressure
Uncommon Emotions

SPEAK LOW

Lynn Galli

Penikila Press

ISBN: 978-1-935611-27-1

Printed in the United States of America.

Synopsis

Taking a job in Scotland shouldn't be any different than Zoey's other jobs. Three months to dive into the intricacies of a university, find its shiny component, flaunt it to the world, and move onto another university. Her niche occupation has served her roving lifestyle well. Just because this job is in another country shouldn't affect her in any way. She doesn't count on liking it so much, on reconnecting with a friend from grad school, or on meeting someone like Celia, who puts up with all her quirks. Celia is sensible about love and knows that taking a risk on someone unaccustomed to permanence is probably a bad bet. Will the cynical wanderer and the reluctant romantic set aside their ingrained hesitancy to take a chance on love?

Speak low if you speak love.

— Don Pedro, *Much Ado About Nothing* (2.1.99)

ZOEY

1

SIDELESS AGAIN. THE ONE HUMAN IN THIS world who thought as I did about this archaic, often misogynistic practice has just taken a healthy swig from the tainted punch. A true cult indoctrination under the guise of a happy event, and I was here to witness it. My friend—the only other soul on this planet who understood my view on this—was getting married.

Married. When she said she didn't believe in it. Like I didn't believe in it. Only clearly my belief system was different from her belief system; otherwise, I wouldn't be here watching this happen. In Scotland. With sheep and kilts and plaid everywhere.

Had I not already been deciding between a job request from an employer here and another in London, I probably wouldn't have come. Okay, after hearing her story, I might have come to help out even without the need to be here for a client. But it helped that my next project would be an hour away from this beautiful little farmhouse and I hadn't seen Skye in two years and Ainsley in over fifteen and their asshat photographer turned out to be a homophobic prick and the wedding was small, and well, it was Skye. Skye, who'd always listened and understood and didn't think me a freak for believing the way I do and seemed to agree. Skye, who'd not only kept in touch after graduation when none of the other people in our study group had, but also worked to maintain an actual friendship no matter the miles between us at times. Skye, who, let's face it, after years of building my business and accommodating clients all over North America, was one of only three friends I had. So, yeah, even if I felt like she'd gone to the dark side with her choice to be married, even if she ditched me to flail as the one and only remaining member of the anti-marriage-institution league, of course, I'd be here for my friend. And I really liked her partner, too.

My hands reached for the SLR 35mm camera I'd set on the table next to me. The strap around my neck pulled tight as the digital camera I'd been using settled back against my chest. Through the viewfinder, I spotted Skye and Ainsley standing together away from the partygoers. I twisted the lens to zoom in on their expressions. Joyous. Pure and powerful joy. So, yeah, it wasn't like she didn't have a reason to go to the dark side. She definitely did. I'd never seen her this happy.

Ainsley, too. I didn't know her as well as Skye, but I'd gotten to know her a bit back at Columbia where I'd been in the MBA program with Skye. Ainsley was one of her three housemates, and our study group would often meet at their place. Since Ainsley and I shared history as our undergraduate major, we'd spend time chatting before and after the group got together. I'd always liked her. Skye hadn't shared that opinion of her. Well, that's not entirely true. Skye didn't dislike her. Their entire communication pattern centered on debating. Didn't matter the topic, choose one, and they'd instantly take up opposite sides. They were always picking at each other. Never anything too personal, which was how I realized they didn't dislike each other. The rest of the study group thought they couldn't stand each other, especially since Ainsley always seemed annoyed when we were around. Not to me. She liked me, and wow, did she know a lot about European history. Still, with Skye, she was standoffish. Some in the group thought she was snippy, but I thought she had a right to be annoyed that our group would crash her apartment two or three times a week. We had to meet somewhere, but it didn't always have to be at Skye's. It helped that her other two roommates were never there, so we could move to Skye's room and close the door if we really got on Ainsley's nerves. But their little battles of will served as amusing study breaks for our group from time to time.

My finger poised over the shutter release. I was waiting for another special moment. They'd given me a few dozen throughout the evening so far. I'd caught most with my digital camera, but this was film. Film would allow me to develop it just right.

Skye brushed aside a blond corkscrew curl from Ainsley's forehead. Ainsley's fingers slid along the dipping neckline of Skye's pink chiffon blouse. Their gazes never wavered from each other, despite the distracting revelry around them. Click. There it was. That look I'd been waiting for. The one that explained why this friend of mine, who'd always told me she didn't believe in marriage, hated weddings, didn't think love could last, would stand in front of family and friends and promise to love this woman for the rest of her life. Then, legally sign a paper to that effect. The lemming.

But yeah, that look. This was the first time I captured it on film. Digital, sure, all evening, but not on film. Big breathy release. I'd gotten the picture. If all the others I'd taken were just okay, this one would make up for everything.

"Zoey!" My five-year-old apprentice shouted as she approached. The compact digital camera I loaned her for the evening was outstretched toward me. "It's full again."

The camera dropped into my hand. Poppy was the only child at this affair and got bored right from the start. I'd fished out my traveling camera and asked her to help me take some wedding photos. That kept her busy, darting around Ainsley's parents' backyard, snapping pictures of anyone and anything. When the digital card fills up, she comes back to me to change it out.

"I got some good ones this time," she proclaimed proudly and climbed up onto my knee as I took a seat to swap out the SD card.

"Bet you did," I praised and clicked the blank card into place. Most of her photos were blurry portions of people, but she was loving it.

"Poppy," Morgan called in an exasperated but loving tone only mothers possessed. "Let Zoey do her work, honeybun."

"I'm helping." Poppy was as certain of that as she'd been when she told everyone she'd helped her florist mother put together the tasteful flower arrangements for this ceremony.

"She's fine," I assured Morgan.

"I think Alastair is looking for a dance partner, sweetie," she told her.

Poppy's blond head came up from watching me snap the cover of the digital card holder in place. She swiveled to find Ainsley's father chatting with his brother. He didn't appear to be looking for a dance partner, but that didn't stop Poppy. "Papa Alastair!" she called, making his name sound more like "Alster" than Alastair.

"My wee bairn," he called back and opened his arms, unbothered by the interruption. "Where have ya been all eve?"

Poppy jumped off the perch on my knee and raced toward him. "I help more later," she called to me over her shoulder as she launched herself into Alastair's arms.

"I'll try to keep her out of your hair." Morgan sat heavily on the seat next to me.

"She's fine," I repeated because she looked like she needed a break.

"I think you've turned her into a photographer." Her smile was tired. She'd done the flower arrangements on her own. The requested small, simple job turned more elaborate with every stem she insisted she add to the arrangements for her friends. Skye and Ainsley were thrilled, but I could see the evening starting to wear on her. Running around after her energetic kindergartner added to her fatigue. Thankfully, Ainsley's parents, Alastair and Elspeth, absolutely adored Poppy and were taking on much of her attention.

Turning my laptop screen her way, I clicked through several of the photos Poppy had taken in the last round.

Morgan's face went through a variety of expressions as we clicked through the photos. At the end of the card, nothing but pride showed.

"She's having fun and some of these are good," I spoke the truth.

"Thanks for indulging her." She stood and reached a hand out to squeeze my shoulder before making her way over to Elspeth, who was laughing at the twirling dance her husband and Poppy were putting on.

Moments later, Skye slid into the vacated seat next to me. "Put the camera down. You've got enough pics."

I chuckled. Skye hated being in photos. Enough so that hiring a photographer, even if it was a standard at all weddings, surprised me.

Her multi-colored hazels stared me down. I took my hand off the camera to make her happy. "Thank you again for doing this."

"I hope they turn out well."

"They'll be great." She looked out past the makeshift dance floor and found her bride chatting with Colin, Ainsley's cousin slash best friend. Dressed in a kilt with a black shirt and vest, Colin looked good next to Ainsley in her beautiful white strapless dress with a pink ribbon lace up back. Anyone looking might think they were the wedded couple. Until Skye stepped into the frame. Then, no one would mistake which couple was the one in blissful love.

I glanced again at the woman next to me. She was done up in black trousers and a formfitting three button black jacket over the pink blouse that peeked out from beneath. Ainsley's choice for colors. I expected a tux, but this outfit, custom made for her, looked so much better and more feminine. More like a stylish jumpsuit than a two-piece suit. Her dark red hair stood out nicely against the black of the jacket but blended flawlessly with the blush pink of her blouse. Last time we saw each other, she had her ginger locks in a trendy asymmetrical bob. For her wedding, she'd made the wise choice to let the cut even out, giving her a more timeless look. Both flattered her face, but this style wouldn't be dated whenever she looked at the wedding photos.

Her eyes dragged themselves away from her spouse and focused on me again. A slight lift of the shoulder explained a lot, but she spoke anyway. "She wanted a wedding." Her lips spread into a smile as she tipped her head in Ainsley's direction. "And I love her with everything that I am."

I matched her smile. Yeah, that pretty much said it all. How someone so adamant about not marrying could find herself married.

"Did you get lots of pictures of her?"

"I did."

"Isn't she the most beautiful woman in the world?" Her breathy sigh made me laugh.

"I think I told you something like that back at Columbia." I probably hadn't used the whole world as a sample size, but I'd commented on how attractive Ainsley had been.

"You did not," she huffed as much as someone ecstatically happy can huff.

"You didn't see anything but your books and job back then. You had the most beautiful woman in the world living in your apartment, and you didn't even notice."

"I noticed," she admitted with a small grin. "I was pretty focused, but I noticed."

"Too stupid to do anything about it," I joked.

"You're right about that." She gave another breathy sigh as Ainsley let her cousin swing her onto the dance floor. "But I'm glad it worked out this way. I would have screwed it up back then."

"Everyone would have screwed it up that young."

She laughed and patted my shoulder. "Did you get something to eat? And put the cameras away. You're done. You've got enough photos. Please act like the guest we intended you to be."

I tipped my chin up, knowing I wouldn't be listening to her. This was supposed to be a small wedding. Family and their two closest friends only. They even scheduled it on a Thursday evening to ensure extended family wouldn't be interested in attending. But when Skye's two remaining elderly Scottish relatives weren't up to traveling from western Scotland, she extended an invitation to a close friend from work and sent one to me. I hadn't planned to attend since my trip to the UK was scheduled for next month, but her call for help changed my mind.

"Eat, lass," Elspeth ordered, setting a full plate on the table beside me. "You're nothing but a slip of a thing."

My head shook. "I've been tasting all evening. You're a wizard in the kitchen."

Her beautiful face, so like her daughter's, showed the same kind of pride I'd seen on Morgan's. "Anything for my lassies."

It warmed my heart to hear her call both Ainsley and Skye her daughters. Skye needed that now that she'd relocated from Washington, DC to Scotland, thousands of miles away from her mother, her close friends, and the job that had kept her so busy she hadn't realized she wasn't living.

"Thank you again, love." Elspeth placed an arm around me.

"Think nothing of it," I repeated what I'd said several times over the course of today.

"I'll think everything of it, thank you very much," Elspeth said with another motherly squeeze of my shoulders. "I could just give that photographer a good walloping."

I could, too. Ainsley and Skye had left the finding and hiring of a photographer to Elspeth, who'd been as involved as they were in planning the wedding. Too busy wrapping things up at work to prepare for an extended honeymoon, they hadn't gone with Elspeth to interview potential photographers. Last week was the first time they'd all gone to meet and discuss the shooting schedule for today. The photographer got a surprise when she realized that neither Skye nor Ainsley was a man. I'd never known either name to be unisex, but the photographer thought one of the names was. She used some pretty colorful language to let them know she didn't do gay weddings. That left them without a photographer for a wedding in less than a week. Several calls later, they were still stuck until Skye remembered about my hobby. When she called, I was happy to help.

"Are you getting everything you need?" Elspeth tried not to be too curious.

My fingers automatically started clicking through the first few digital photos downloaded to my laptop. Her face broke into a smile that matched her daughter's as if this were her wedding day.

"Oh, darling, these are wonderful. They'll be so happy." Her hand came up and stroked my cheek. "We're so lucky you could change your plans to make it. That Skye has some amazing friends."

I glanced over at Skye. She was in a small gathering with some of those amazing friends. Her best friend, Dallas, along with Dallas's husband, Colin, her good friend Morgan, and a close friend from work, Celia. A mixed group at first glance, but that was Skye's specialty: getting people to mesh together. I picked up the camera and snapped a quick photo of them.

"Please, love, eat something. Start enjoying yourself. You're not here only to work. Be a guest for a bit." Elspeth stood and stretched out her hand to get me to follow her.

I smiled and shook my head, indicating I'd join the party in a minute. I wouldn't; social gatherings were difficult for me. Even if this wedding hadn't been in another country, I wouldn't have come. Not unless my friend needed me to. Which it turns out, she did. So, my cameras and I made the trip a month earlier than I planned. Didn't mean I could miraculously become a socializing wunderkind in a day.

Slipping the SLR over my neck, I grabbed up the digital camera and wandered the outskirts, snapping selectively to catch every guest, at least three times. I'd try for a couple more before the evening ended. It kept me busy and away from needing to make small talk with some of Ainsley's more rowdy relatives.

Skye's mom waved at me from across the patio. I'd met her several times when I visited Skye over the years since grad school. Nice lady, worked really hard and passed that on to her daughter. When Ainsley joined her, I snapped a quick picture of the two of them. Skye didn't like photos of herself, but she'd want one of the two women she loved most in the world.

"Damn, girl, I keep forgetting how tiny you are," Dallas exclaimed as she wrapped an arm around me. Tall and beautiful, she thought anyone under five-five was tiny. We'd gotten to know each other when she and Skye worked together in DC. "Do you even have a size?" She giggled at her own joke, pausing only to take a sip from the wine glass in her hand.

"Like you can talk," I shot back to the television-ready beauty. She might not be a size zero—okay, often size double zero—like me, but at five-nine, her size four made her look plenty skinny and camera-perfect for her job as a news anchor in New York.

"Isn't this just the best wedding?" Her head swiveled in all directions. "For my best friend, the best wedding."

The wine was getting to Dallas, but not nearly as much as some of Ainsley's wedding crasher cousins. They were drinking Skye and Ainsley out of their entire liquor supply. My hand came up to beckon her husband. Colin made a nonchalant show of joining us and sweeping his wife under his arm to guide her to a chair near Ainsley's mom. I grinned at the covert maneuver.

Through the viewfinder, I found several other good shots of Ainsley's family members to take. Unlike Poppy, I was selective with my shots, a skill learned from my father, who'd been a professional photographer for many years until he'd found his passion as a cinematographer at a movie studio.

The wedding guests stopped noticing me around the half-hour mark. No longer did they halt their conversations to pose in my direction. My lens focused on Skye's work colleague, Celia, approaching one of Ainsley's cousins a few feet away. One of the obnoxious cousins who'd crashed the wedding. He'd declined the invitation—meant only as a gesture of politeness—then turned up and started eating and drinking his way through his uncle's backyard. I'd avoided him and purposefully taken only one photo of him, knowing Ainsley wasn't happy he'd shown up.

"Shall we dance?" Celia asked the guy. Throughout the evening, she'd struck up easy conversations with everyone. A talent I coveted. She'd danced with many of the guests, so it shouldn't be surprising that she'd kindly offer to take the almost plastered cousin for a spin on the floor before he obnoxiously interrupted another gathering.

"You joking?" the guy responded. "I can't be dancing with a dumpy cow like you."

I sucked in a breath. Asshole! Who the hell did he think he was? If Skye had heard that, she'd give him a right earful. Dallas probably would've taken a swing at him. So what if Celia carried a few extra pounds? She had a lush figure with curves in all the right places and evenly proportioned throughout. She wore her blue dress well and didn't try to squeeze into a size too small or wear the trendiest styles just because they were popular. She knew what flattered her full shape, and if it weren't for how gorgeous both brides looked, she'd be the prettiest here.

Her expression fell at his unkind remark. All night, she'd been wearing a genuine smile. Like she could find joy in the simplest things. This was the first time the smile failed. That could have been what made me react.

I took four strides forward and asked, "May I have the pleasure?" in a perfect Scottish accent. I had an ear for accents and could mimic several. This wasn't a time to be interrupted by the standard reaction to my American accent. I wanted this to be about getting that easy smile back.

"Now, you're definitely my type. Where have you been hiding all night?" Asshole cousin leaned toward me. The scent of scotch seeped from his pores. "Let's boogie."

"I was asking the lovely lass." My eyes flicked away from him and caught Celia's again. "If you don't mind dancing with another woman, that is. It's a gay wedding, after all."

Her brow hitched up, eyes wide and moving from mine to the dickhead's and back. I assumed she wouldn't object to a turn around the dance floor with a woman since she was at her lesbian friend's wedding, but I hoped I hadn't shocked her.

"Love to. Thank you for asking." Her voice was smooth and nicely toned. She must use that voice as a tool in her work. It was practiced, rehearsed, like how a singer works on her voice. Skye hadn't said what she did at their work, but if Celia was on camera, then the rehearsed voice would make sense.

"What?" The idiot cousin couldn't seem to grasp what just happened.

I lifted the first strap over my head and set the camera on the nearest table. The second joined it before I could talk myself out of this. Dancing in lesbian clubs was fine, but this was my friend's wedding. We'd be the only other same-sex couple dancing tonight.

My hand gestured to the dance floor to get us moving before coming to rest against my thigh to mask the tremor. Maybe this was a stupid idea. I was here mostly to work. I shouldn't be dancing with someone, a woman someone, taking notice away from my friend.

Celia turned and faced me on the dance floor. Perhaps she'd been reading my mind or had similar thoughts. "We can sit this out if you'd rather. It was kind of you to step in like that."

I shook my head and stepped toward her. I couldn't let her think that. If we'd been at a lesbian club together, I would have asked her to dance. She didn't fit my usual type, so maybe not, but she was beautiful and she needed to feel beautiful, especially when someone went out of his way to be cruel.

My hand slipped around to rest on her back. The other went up for hers to clasp. Soft and warm, her palm skimmed mine and fit into place, fingers curling to lock our hands together. It was a more formal stance than I'd take in a bar, but I wouldn't put a straight woman into a more intimate embrace. She was progressive enough to take me up on my offer, possibly as a graceful exit from the asshole, but that didn't mean she'd be comfortable with a clinging hold.

We swayed slowly at first, taking more certain strides as the song went on. She danced well. She spoke well. She smiled beautifully. People liked her. She had a lot going for her. No one should make her doubt that even for a moment.

"I have a feeling you'll be pestered for dances the rest of the night." Celia's smile had returned.

I glanced up at her. That trouble-free grin reached her eyes. We both had brown eyes, but hers were tinged red and mine with honey. Same with our hair. Chestnut described hers best, while mine was more golden brown. She had five or six inches on me. I was used to that. At five-two, pretty much everyone had inches on me, but it didn't feel like a huge chasm with her.

"You've been hiding behind that camera all night. Good job that or you might not have caught any pictures of Skye. She hates them, you know."

I did know. Skye didn't like weddings and photos, and yet, here she was being photographed at her wedding.

"I was thrilled to be invited. They said they were keeping it to family, but Skye surprised me with an invitation." Her eyes left mine to glance around the backyard. "They did all the decorations themselves. Tasteful, don't you think? And the weather was perfect for them. They deserve it."

"Yes," I agreed. With everything actually. I liked the sound of her voice, and she didn't seem to mind that I didn't have much to say.

I scanned the beautifully appointed yard. Skye and Ainsley, along with their best friends, had turned a nice backyard into an expensive looking wedding venue without the expense. What they'd managed to do with twinkle lights hanging between the trees surrounding the cottage garden, a few linen-draped tables, a couple dozen ribbon-tied chairs, and elegant but minimal flower arrangements was remarkable. I admired them for not going crazy on the costs. Handmade invitations by the brides, a two-tier cake baked by Ainsley's grandmother, hors d'oeuvres prepared by Elspeth and her sister-in-law, and a cousin with a loaded iPod and speaker system kept their costs to a minimum. Their biggest expense was the open bar, served by a rotating shift of Ainsley's aunts and uncles. Not that they couldn't afford a lavish wedding, but the outrageous cost of weddings was something Skye and I always objected to. At least she hadn't taken a complete one-eighty on all her views about weddings. The only professionals they'd hired were the officiant and a string instrument duo for the start of the ceremony. They'd planned to hire a photographer, but that went bust. They offered to pay for my flight, but I wouldn't think to charge them. They were my friends, and this wasn't my profession.

"Thank you." Celia smiled as she stepped back. We'd somehow reached the end of the song without me noticing. She released my hand after a long moment, bringing it up to brush back her shoulder-length hair for something to do with it now that we weren't dancing anymore. My own hand flexed, seeking an occupation as well. I gripped my thigh before my hand decided to follow hers through her silky strands. "I quite enjoyed that."

I gave her a return smile, agreeing without having to say anything. As much as Skye and Ainsley appreciated me helping them out, and as many times as their parents kept thanking me, I felt most proud of helping Celia get that smile back.

It was a great smile.

2

AS AN ALARM CLOCK, SHEEP WORK PRETTY well. My eyes blinked open as the sheep bellowed again. Do sheep bellow? Whatever noise they make, they sure make a lot of it in the morning. In cities with fire engines, police cruisers, motorcycles, trucks, and all manner of rude neighbors not caring how loud they are when they leave every morning, I could sleep through basically anything. But take away all the usual city racket, add in only one sound, and it's like a dentist's drill in my ear.

I stumbled into the bathroom and avoided turning on the light. Mornings take a little while for me to get up and going. My squinty eyes took in the renovated space. Everything else about Skye and Ainsley's stone cottage was retro. That the bathroom was renovated was a welcome surprise since I'd be housesitting for the next month while they were on their honeymoon. Sheep sitting, actually. It sounded great when Skye proposed the idea.

After an amazing shower under some fancy deal that shot water at me in massaging spurts both to warm me up and loosen my tense muscles, I ran a comb through my wavy brown hair. I'd planned to use the month before my next job to continue growing out the short, sharp cut I got before my last job to a collar-length shag style. Taking this job early meant I was in public during that not exactly attractive stage of going from precisely cut shorter strands to carefully shaped longer layers.

I applied some styling cream to keep the wisps from flipping this way and that. Depending on how well it dried, I'd either add more product to tame it or a headband to hold down some of the wilder wisps. I didn't bother with makeup yet as my presentation wasn't until this afternoon. Sheep don't care about makeup.

My phone rang as I was pulling a t-shirt over my head. "Hey, Dad." I didn't need to check the display first. He always liked to check in whenever I went to a new city. The fact that it was after midnight his time didn't matter to him.

"Hi, sweetie. How was the wedding?"

"Fun."

"Anything good happen?"

I laughed. "Other than my friends getting married?"

"That was a given. I meant drunk relatives, long-standing feuds, cops called, you know, the basic foundation for a good wedding."

"Dad," I gave my combo amused-exasperated reply.

"I'm glad it was fun. Did you take good photos?"

"I hope so. I'll do some developing soon."

"I know you did. You're just as talented as your father." He bit out the last word. Thinking about my other dad still got to him. When your spouse leaves you for another man half your age, yeah, it irks. Even twenty years later.

"Thanks, Dad."

"Maybe I'll come for a visit. I haven't been to Britain since the last time you were there."

I intended a semester abroad as many of my friends were doing, but it turned into a year abroad. I knew my dad wouldn't be able to resist coming for a visit. We had a nice time touring London and other parts of the UK during my time as a student at King's College.

"You'd be welcome anytime, but if you hold off a month, you'll be able to see Skye again."

"Good idea. She's a doll. My favorite of your friends."

"Shouldn't you be getting some sleep?"

"I wanted to check you're all set there. Are you ready for your day?"

"The sheep made sure. I'm going out to visit with them, then I'm off to prep for the presentation."

"Good luck, sweetie."

"Goodnight, Dad." I hung up and shook out the sudden onslaught of nerves. My introductory presentation was always the hardest, even if I knew every word and gesture by heart. I should have chosen a profession that allowed for silent communication. Instead, I went for one that forced me to speak publicly on occasion.

Using the back door, I headed outside into the chilly morning air. I'd most recently been in Louisiana, helping a smaller university establish itself among its competitors. Chilly didn't appear as a word in dictionaries there, but in Bathgate, Scotland, at eight a.m., even in July, it was chilly.

Skye and Ainsley only had two sheep, which in my opinion couldn't qualify as a flock, but I liked the idea of tending to the flock for a month. Their house sat on almost two acres but was surrounded by a few hundred acres of pasture lands on each side and behind. One neighbor had a legitimate sheep herd. The other neighbor used his extravagant mansion and acreage as a vacation spot. Skye said she'd seen him twice in the year she'd lived with Ainsley.

Behind their detached garage sat a sheep enclosure. A livestock fence surrounded the border of their land. Skye assured me the sheep pretty much took care of themselves with grazing, but I could add hay and muck out the enclosure from time to time. Ainsley's parents would probably stop by to help out, leaving my only duties to stroll out and pet the creatures every morning.

The sheep trotted up to meet me as I unlatched the gate. The boy's little black head pushed into my stomach for some attention. The girl followed, staying close to his hip. They'd both just been sheered, their white fluffy bodies now looking quite svelte. We walked as a mob to the enclosure. Nothing looked disturbed, but I grabbed two slices from the hay bales and spread a little more straw on the ground for their comfort. I checked the feeders and trough but nothing needed to be filled. Their preference was to graze, so as long as the grass and clover were still plentiful, they wouldn't need any other additions to their diet. Pretty much maintenance-free as promised.

Back inside, I took a little time to wander the house. When I arrived yesterday morning, I barely had time to glance around before putting my camera to work taking photos of Skye and her mother getting ready for the wedding and then driving a half hour to Ainsley's parents' farm to get photos of Ainsley's prep and the transformed backyard.

The house was small by American standards. Two bedrooms, one bathroom, a living room and dining room with an eating nook in a small kitchen. They had plenty of room to expand into their front or backyard, but the house seemed to work just fine for them. Except for the bathroom, apparently, because that was a recent renovation. I stood back and looked into the master and guest bedrooms on each side. Space had been taken from both to accommodate a larger bathroom and master closet. Their bedroom still had plenty of room, but my guest bedroom had just enough room for the bed, one nightstand, and a small closet. The house was about two-thirds the size of Skye's last place in Washington, which had renovated everything. This retro classic didn't seem to fit Skye's ideal. Then again, neither did marriage, so apparently everything could change.

Back in the dining room, I brought up my presentation. Even knowing every word by heart, I had to practice. Once I got into the job and used to the people, I could allow myself to speak off the cuff. Until then, I contemplated every word used.

Giving myself plenty of time, I got ready to go into Edinburgh for the meeting. A tan suit would work for the anticipated heat that would eventually come today. It went well with my autumn coloring all year round, but for summer it was a must. I choose a cranberry colored shell and brown ankle boots to finish out the look. In the bathroom, I applied a light base of makeup. In my off hours, I didn't wear any, but in a career that relied on client contact and public interaction, makeup was expected. Glasses with maroon plastic frames finished out my look.

I preferred wearing glasses to contacts, and the extra bulk of the plastic frames always felt more like a shield against social interactions. First days always needed the extra shield. My standard wire-rimmed glasses could make an appearance next week.

At the college, I pulled into the parking lot reserved for the local television station that used the college's facilities. Skye ran the station, an affiliate of a national network. Their summer programming was turned over to the network, giving Skye the summer off for an extended honeymoon. It also kept the parking lot practically empty. Only two other cars were in the lot when I slid Skye's Alfa Romeo into a slot.

I was early, which allowed time to calm my nerves and explore the campus before the meeting. Set close to city center, the campus was compact but didn't feel cramped. Unlike its nearby neighbor, Edinburgh University, this campus wasn't architecturally substantial except for the one original castle on the grounds. The design lent itself more to a community college feel than a grand university. Of course, that's why I was here. Give it some presence.

Names on the buildings were a little hard to read, something I made note of, but I eventually found where the presentation would happen. Inside, it looked like any other classroom building. So far nothing about this place stood out. They definitely needed my help.

Voices got louder as I approached the end of the hallway. It sounded like a thousand people were talking at once, but no more than twenty people were expected in this initial meeting. I ducked into an empty classroom and began my relaxation technique. If anyone looked inside the room, they'd see me hopping as if on an invisible pogo stick. After five years doing this exact thing, I shouldn't be nervous anymore. Intellectually, I knew that to be true, but it didn't help with the nerves. Only exertion helped. Hopping in place for a minute was enough to calm my nerves, but not enough to start perspiring.

Suitably calmed, I exited the classroom and headed toward the noise. The door was open and all I could see were the backs of people. Lots and lots of people. Had the vice chancellor invited everyone? Only department heads were supposed to be in the meeting. This looked like everyone working on campus this summer.

I shuffled into the room, sliding between groups. Easily eighty people were crammed into this room. Capacity couldn't be more than sixty. Irritation also helped calm my nerves. An overcrowded conference room when there should have been a few open seats at the table served to irritate.

"...an American, if you can believe it," one of the louder voices said near the front of the room.

"American?" several voices repeated.

"Aye. He'll obnoxiously tell us what to do before recommending we be sacked."

"And be obnoxious about it," another voice added.

"Obnoxious Americans."

"Excuse me." I would need some of these people on my side and letting them continue on when they'd be embarrassed to be caught wasn't the way to do that.

"How many guns do you think he'll have with him?" another voice asked.

"Excuse me," I said again, trying to push my way through the throngs of people. At five-two and under a buck, I wasn't always heard or seen in groups.

"Cowboys."

"Ooh, will he be wearing a ten-gallon hat and spurs?"

"God, they're obnoxious."

"Two of the fattest tourists I've ever seen stopped me on the street last night to ask me where the nearest Dairy Queen was. Dairy Queen! Like this is America, and there's one on every block. Even if there was one nearby, I wouldn't tell them. They'd probably have heart attacks right after their meal and then sue me for giving them directions. You know how Americans can be with their lawsuits."

"Obnoxious," the one guy added again.

"Excuse me," I almost shouted. The two closest groups parted and turned to face me, which made several others take notice. I completed the journey up to the front of the room and spoke to the lawsuit commentary woman. "The obnoxious American is obnoxiously already here, being, of course, obnoxious."

Several chuckles sounded from the crowd. At least some of them got my humor. Pink tinged the cheeks of the woman in front of me. I gave her a disarming smile to show her I didn't take offense to any of their comments. Some of those views were highly accurate, but I could discern a person from the group.

I turned toward the large group, hoping to see the chancellor's face close by. Instead, I didn't recognize anyone. Was he not coming? All eyes were on me as I brought out my laptop and connected it to the room's projector. The tension in the air wouldn't allow for further delay.

"Hello, everyone. I'm Zoey Thais." Beyond the second row, my lack of height hampered my attempt to make eye contact with everyone in the room. This went over best with a school administrator smoothing the way first to settle everyone down. As it was now, several of the talkers started talking. Many of the accents were too heavy to immediately understand. The others just talked over themselves.

I rehearsed what to say to start the meeting without being introduced first, then spoke. "We'll get started without the vice chancellor and have you on your way in no time."

With a few clicks on my laptop, I started my presentation on branding. My specialty was branding educational institutions. In the corporate world, branding came with cutthroat competition. Not many branding specialists concentrated on the educational market, which allowed me to create a successful niche.

The chancellor came in halfway through, acting surprised that we'd started without him, but it didn't stop him from interrupting me to fumble through an explanation for my presence on campus. I'd been doing a fairly good job only to have him muddle it up.

"We have a marketing staff," someone, I assume, from the marketing staff spoke up.

"Aye, well, of course, we do." The chancellor looked to me to explain.

"Marketing is essential," I began. "It lets people know what you do. I'm here to find and then flaunt your brand."

"What's the difference?"

"Marketing gets your name out there. Branding is your identity." Still a lot of blank faces, so I asked, "Best medical school in the world?"

A few guesses, one of which was correct, before the majority settled on, "Johns Hopkins."

"That's branding," I pointed out. "You know Johns Hopkins is an excellent medical school. Some of you are convinced it's the best in the world. If I told you I went to Johns Hopkins, you'd likely be impressed. It wouldn't matter if my degree was in something unrelated to medicine. You're aware that Johns Hopkins is excellent at medicine. Therefore, it must be excellent, period."

"Of course, people will be impressed with the best medical school in the world, but we're not that."

"And neither is Johns Hopkins." That garnered a few wide eyes. "Depending on the ranking agency, Hopkins is anywhere from third to seventh, but it has amazing branding. That's what I plan to do for you."

That seemed to settle most of the crowd, but there were always the ones who would continue to think I was here as a consultant to recommend layoffs. "Do not be worried if your field of study isn't the chosen brand. I'm not here to make you feel bad or less than if—"

"Badly," someone interrupted from the back of the room. "Poor English might pass in your country, but in Britain, where English originated, do try not to murder it."

My eyes landed on the smug speaker. She wasn't an English professor because if she were, she'd know I used the adjective correctly. The interruption and the challenge made me falter, though. This was not part of any presentation I've ever given. No one had challenged me on something so petty before. I needed a moment to rehearse what I'd say in response. If I should say anything in response, that is.

Several of her colleagues looked satisfied that she'd landed her jab. If I corrected her, I would look like an asshole to her and possibly everyone else in the room who already thought Americans were arrogant assholes. No, I should just let it go.

"Quite," I acknowledged without specifying that I was agreeing we should use correct English, mostly because we were in an educational institution, not because we were in Britain.

"No, sorry, if one of our English lecturers doesn't speak up, I will." The people clustered around the conference table at the back let the speaker move forward. My mouth parted when I recognized Celia. "She's describing a state of being, not an action. That merits the use of an adjective, not an adverb. If you're going to correct someone's English, Sarah, make sure you're doing it correctly."

Several snickers sounded throughout the room. It felt vaguely like a high school lunchroom before a food fight began. Who would side with whom? My eyes found Celia's. She gave me an encouraging smile. If we were among friends, I'd run over and hug her.

"Go, Ceal," someone muttered to another round of snickers.

My face pinched at the shortened form of her name. It should have been "Cee," not "Ceal," and it seemed to have a double meaning among her colleagues. An unflattering double meaning.

I gestured back to the screen. "If we can continue, we'll all be back to the things you'd rather be doing soon enough." That settled everyone into audience mode again. Hecklers were now on alert. "Over the next few weeks, I'll be talking to your students, sitting in on your classrooms, and conducting surveys among the locals. All to find the right branding strategy for your school. My goal is to make you the university known for...whatever it is we decide to emphasize. Everyone's field of study will be bolstered by this brand as evidenced by the example I gave with Johns Hopkins."

"She probably went to some mail-order school," someone muttered loud enough for me and pretty much everyone to hear. I didn't rise to the bait. It didn't matter where I went to school as long as I did a good job.

"I'll expect you to welcome Ms. Thais into your classrooms and answer her questions openly," the chancellor instructed them while I was shutting down my laptop. He turned to me and shook my hand, apologizing again for being late. It didn't help me now, but some people seemed to think an apology made everything all right.

The room emptied fairly quickly. More muttered comments about Americans and useless this and pointless that. Other than the accents and the constant slam of my nationality, this could have been a meeting conducted in the States.

"Not a photographer, then?"

I looked up from putting my laptop away. Celia had stayed behind in the now empty audience. A smile tugged at my lips. She had on another pretty dress. Not as beautiful as the one she wore to the wedding last night, but a nice lightweight summer dress that did wonders for her figure.

My head shook once as my smile brightened. Knowing she worked here added a level of confidence over and above the basis established by my expertise. It was good to know at least one person seemed to be on my side.

"Not Scottish, either?"

"Obnoxiously, no."

She laughed, a surprisingly sharp sound. I jolted, not expecting the sharpness of it. It wasn't a bad laugh, just edgy. A laugh with personality. "Why?"

I tilted my head at the ambiguous inquiry.

"Were you making fun of our accents?"

My hand came up and waved that thought away. "No." Her expression remained doubtful. "No," I repeated and considered how to phrase this. "I thought if that jerk heard my accent...it would delay our trip to the dance floor."

A small twitch curled her lips. "Smooth."

I hadn't meant for it to sound like a line, but if it kept her from thinking I'd been mocking nearly everyone at the wedding, I'd go with it. "You work here?"

She gave me a look that said, "Duh, idiot," but was too polite to actually say the words.

"Not with Skye, I meant."

"Oh, yes. Well, I'm in the television program here. All of my students eventually end up working at her station. We work closely together, but not for the same employer."

At the risk of getting another "Duh, idiot" look from her, I asked, "You're a professor? Or a TA?"

Her hand reached out to squeeze my arm. "Bless you. I haven't been a teaching assistant in too many years."

Not that many. She couldn't be too far off my own mid-thirties. Younger, if I guessed correctly. "Television?"

"It's a legitimate field of study." This time, sharpness edged her tone.

My hands came up again. "I was asking you to expound."

She stepped back, a flush crawling up her neck. Someone in her life challenged her on her chosen field. Someone important to her. "You'll be sitting in, won't you?" She sent a playful look my way this time.

I gave a definite nod. "Looking forward to it."

Her eyes swiped over me before she turned and walked to the exit. With a quick glance over her shoulder, she said, "As am I."

3

HISTORY HAD NEVER BEEN MORE BORING. MY undergraduate degree gave me more knowledge than this lecturer. These poor students. History was so dynamic and engaging. The professor gave it her best effort, but it wasn't good enough.

I knew before arriving history wouldn't be the brand basis. It wasn't just the lackluster teaching style or minimal effort at compiling a more interesting take on this topic. This was Ainsley's subject, and she taught at Edinburgh. I wouldn't take her brand and place it here.

The class ended, finally, and I waited to gauge her approachability. Absolutely no students went up to talk to her at the end. She glanced at me a few times as she was saying goodbye to her students, so it only felt right to go up and give her positive feedback.

"Very interesting," I lied. It had been my most boring hour spent in Scotland so far. We talked about her other class offerings throughout the year and it was clear she liked to talk. Too bad she couldn't use that gift to come up with anecdotes to accompany the slew of facts and dates she'd spent the last hour giving out.

Once able to politely excuse myself, I headed outside and checked the time. A calculus class or sociology lecture awaited my attendance. Or I could use the actual lunch hour for lunch. Or my version of lunch, which involved keeping my sanity by taking a walk. Wasn't a hard choice, really.

"Escaping so soon?" Celia called out as she came toward me.

I stopped and let her catch up. She had on another dress, this one mostly purple with a delicate geometric design in silver and lavender. A hairband created a tasteful bouffant in her russet brown hair. Her tan skin glistened in the sunshine. I'd been stuck indoors at my last job to keep from melting in the heat and hadn't had time to get any color on my skin. While the summer here would be cooler, I planned to be outside often enough to keep me from looking too ghostly.

"Lunch," I replied as she fell into step with me.

"We have some wonderful canteens on campus." Her arm gestured back to the cluster of buildings I'd come from.

"I was going for a walk."

"Doesn't lunch usually involve food of some sort?" she teased.

"For normal people." I gave her my own teasing smile. We'd entered the parking lot, and Celia stopped as I approached Skye's car.

"That's Skye's—so, not a photographer, nor Scottish, and not just someone they hired to help out when their photographer ditched them at the last minute?"

"I'm a friend."

"A friend who is housesitting, perhaps?"

"Sheep sitting," I clarified. "In all my life, I never thought I'd say sheep sitting, and now I can't stop saying it."

She laughed that sharp laugh again. It didn't startle me this time. I'd been hoping for it. "They have a lovely place and wonderful sheep. Pets really, that's how they treat them, but it makes Skye happy to say she has sheep."

I nodded in acknowledgement. Skye felt more a part of Scotland to have sheep. Weirdo, but I still liked her.

"You're staying out there on your own?" The question was more than idle curiosity. As Skye's friend who just found out I was also Skye's friend, not just a photographer, she probably wanted to make me feel welcome. She shouldn't feel obligated. I did fine on my own.

"It's cozy." I reached into the trunk for my duffle bag and pulled out my sneakers. Swapping them out for my flats, I replaced my glasses with prescription sunglasses. My wire-rimmed glasses had transition lenses, but not these plastic frames. Finally, I offloaded my laptop bag and suit jacket.

"You're quite serious about walking, aren't you?" Her eyes watched every *Mister Rogers' Neighborhood* movement of mine.

"Clears my head."

"If you use your lunch break for walking, when do you eat?" This time her eyes swept over me from head to toe. "Don't tell me, you don't eat."

Yeah, I was short and skinny. To someone taller and fuller, it probably looked like I didn't eat. I didn't eat much, but I ate. It wasn't a conscious diet thing; it was a food thing. Nothing tasted so damn good I had to have a ton of it. My food intake basically kept me from passing out. If I liked food more, I'd weigh more.

"I brought from home." My hand gestured back to the bag in the trunk.

"A piece of fruit, probably?"

She had me there. Grocery shopping was low on my list of priorities and fruit never disappointed. It tasted good, didn't involve cooking anything, and was less labor intensive than making a sandwich.

"Do you cook?" She looked genuinely concerned. The same amount of concern Elspeth had shown every time I declined an offer of food at the wedding. "You'll have to come to mine for a proper Scottish meal soon."

My eyebrows spiked. That was kind of her, and I didn't think it was just because we had a friend in common.

"Aye, you'll come to mine for tea. This week, Thursday?"

"That's not...that's very...you don't ha-have—"

"It's sorted. We'll have a nice Scottish meal, and you can tell me all about your friendship with Skye."

I felt a bit steamrolled, but the good kind of steamrolled. She wasn't being overbearing. She was simply confident I would enjoy any meal she cooked and wouldn't mind eating it with her. My eyes drifted over her again, trying to determine her sexual preference. I usually didn't have a problem figuring that out, but some women in a professional setting were harder to discern. She could be asking me out, or she could just be taking me under her wing because she knew I was staying alone at Skye's and probably didn't know anyone else here.

"Are you sure I can't persuade you to join me for a real lunch?" She gestured back toward campus again.

I smiled and shook my head. "You're welcome to walk with me." Only she wasn't. What was I thinking? Chatting about a meal over dinner wasn't nearly as difficult as coming up with things to say while walking. Things not yet rehearsed. Any topic would be up for grabs. I didn't have go-to things to say on every topic.

Her face pinched in distaste as she looked down at her slightly heeled sandals. Practical for her work day, but not good for a walk. "Maybe another time."

Strangely, relief mixed with disappointment inside me. I was here for three to six months depending on how involved my client wanted to get with their branding efforts. I could use some acquaintances to avoid becoming a leech with Skye and Ainsley. Celia seemed like a good person to start with.

4

CELIA'S TOWNHOUSE LACKED THE CHARM OF Skye and Ainsley's cottage. Anything built in the past century would fall short when compared to their stone cottage, but it had a nice feel. Not overly crowded with furniture, it felt both lived in and like new.

"Make yourself to home," she said as we entered the living room. "Wine or something else to drink?"

I was in the process of waving off her beverage offer when a black and white cat stretched up from the sofa and peered at me with blue eyes, distracting me. My hand automatically reached out to scratch the mostly black head.

"That's Panda, she loves attention. Hemlock is shy. I doubt you'll see him." She headed into the kitchen and started pulling things from the narrow but tall refrigerator that made use of every vertical inch on the wall. "Let me get dinner started, then I'll show you around."

A tour wasn't necessary, but it would add to our catalog of topics for the evening. Talking wasn't really my thing. Over the past week, she'd catch me moving from one class to another or on my way to my lunchtime walk and engage in an upbeat, relatively easy conversation. She wasn't overly inquisitive, well, somewhat inquisitive, but she'd offer guesses to the questions, leaving me to either agree or disagree. It wasn't a challenge talking to her, but I still needed to prepare for an evening of talking.

"Is there something I can help with?"

"I'll let you know. For now, Panda needs a friend."

I sat on the couch where Panda decided my lap was the perfect place for her to resettle after her strenuous stretching. Petting a cat can be mesmerizing and calming. I wasn't even thinking about how to fill the next hour or two with conversation. I was thinking about how soft her belly was.

A movement caught my eye. I turned toward the back hallway and spotted Hemlock, a gray and black tiger striped cat with speckles of white dusting his coat. He darted from one obstruction to the next, curious, but too skittish to do anything about it. His chosen hides weren't doing their job very well, but I'd let him think he was being stealthy. He inched closer and closer. I didn't shift to follow his path toward me. He could be brave without an audience. It took ten minutes before I felt the brush of a passing kitty on my shin. When I didn't jump or look down or try to pet him, he came back for another drive-by brush, marking me with his scent. Cats were odd little things, but I related to Hemlock. He could take all the time he wanted to decide if I was worthy of his attention.

Celia came back into the living room, and Hemlock made a break for it. He wouldn't be caught sucking up to me when his person thought he was too good for visitors.

He had a reputation to keep. "She's never giving up your lap now, you know."

"Fine by me."

That earned me a smile. People and their pets. Too easy.

"I hope you like halibut." Celia said as she waved me into motion.

I didn't, but what could I say? That was always the tricky part about being invited to someone's place for dinner. Can't ask what she's preparing before accepting, and can't tell her whatever she's already purchased and prepped for dinner wasn't appetizing. I could eat whatever she made. I wouldn't like it, but as long as it didn't have too many different seasonings, my stomach wouldn't protest. Bland was usually the best option for me.

She showed me through the two-bedroom townhouse. Her second bedroom had multiple functions with a writing desk, bookshelves, a craft table, and a pullout sofa for visitors. The back window looked out onto the alleyway behind her building and the building opposite. Not exactly the view I was waking up to every morning. Her bedroom was slightly larger, and the view out the front showed the park across the street. Much better. It was always good to see a bit of green every day. No sheep, but green and a few trees.

Throughout the tour, she flitted from one subject to the next. It wasn't inane conversation. Everything she said tied to a previous subject and made sense. It didn't feel like excessive or useless drivel. She had interesting things to say, and either recognized I didn't talk a lot, or she was so energized by conversation she didn't notice how little I spoke. Either way, it was refreshing and very easy to be around her. Other than with my dads that didn't happen.

We ended up back in the kitchen. After some silent negotiations on my part, I helped set the table while she pulled pans from the oven. Nothing about the meal looked exclusive to Scotland, but I wouldn't question that since I knew very little about food.

By the time we sat to dinner, I hadn't needed to air out even one standard go-to discussion point. Celia knew how to carry a conversation. She was one of those people who knew a little about almost everything and a lot about many things. I barely had to prompt her for more information or clarity to keep her going.

If I lived here, I'd try a little harder to figure out her sexuality. Her eye swipes could either be appraising or, like many people fascinated with my size, worrisome. I didn't think I was that skinny, but I did prompt a lot of muttered comments about needing to eat another cookie. For someone feeding me a home-cooked meal, it seemed natural that she'd be concerned how well her guest liked the food. I wasn't enjoying the fish, but the veggies were nice. She'd made some sort of potato concoction that tasted very good. There was just too much of it. I'd tried to serve myself only what I'd eat, but she'd pushed for more. So now, either I ate until I was uncomfortable, or I left food on the plate and chance having her think I didn't like her cooking. I liked her cooking, I just didn't like the taste of certain foods. That didn't reflect on her cooking skills.

"Are you sure I can't pour you a glass of wine?" Her brown eyes searched mine, dropping once to the glass of water I'd been sipping from.

Doubtful my aversion to alcohol would be accepted any more easily in this country than in mine, I hesitated before shaking my head. Telling her could wait until the next dinner, or the one after. I was different enough, no need to pile on. Once people knew I didn't drink, they'd become self-conscious about their own drinking. She enjoyed the food and beverage pairing too much to miss out due to a misguided impression.

She tilted her head, accepting my decision before her eyes narrowed. "You don't like fish, do you?"

I'd eaten all of the serving I took. She shouldn't have any reason to think I didn't like it. Was she uncannily attuned to someone's eating habits? A dining whisperer?

"I should have asked. I'll make sure to next time."

"This was wonderful, Celia. Thank you for going to the trouble. I'm just not much of a foodie."

"I'll say." Her eyes ran over me again. Yeah, they were eat-lots-more-food-before-you-waste-away-to-nothing eye swipes, not you're-smoking-sexy eye swipes. Not that I'd do anything about it if they were. Over the past few days, I started wondering if I might be shallow in that regard. Never thought of myself as someone caught up in the superficial, but I'd never before dated a woman her size. It could be that no one with her figure had shown any interest in me, and therefore, never caught my attention. Or it could be that I was too shallow to have noticed anyone like her. Either way, it was troubling. I needed to work on that. Nothing about being shallow was commendable.

"Did you say how you knew Skye?" She brushed a hand through the air. "Of course not. I've done nothing but talk your ear dead all night."

"You're fine." More than fine, a blessing, really. It was rare to find someone who made it easy for me to participate in a conversation. Despite public speaking being a job requirement, in private, talking would never be listed as one of my talents.

"You know her from where?" she persisted.

"New York."

"Nice city, although I'm partial to the West Coast." Which made sense since she'd gone to USC for her MFA and PhD. Not that LA was worthy of partiality, but I could see where someone in the television field of study would appreciate that city more.

"As am I."

"Really? Where is your home?"

"Seattle."

Surprise registered on her face. "I saw you as someone from the East Coast. Not sure why. New York seemed to fit. I've never been to Seattle. Is it nice?"

"It is."

And she launched into a catalogue of a few places she'd visited in the States, saving me again from having to come up more to say on the topic. Two hours had passed, and I barely noticed. Normally, I'd be sweating about now, trying to think of what else to say and how to get out of here.

The drive-by brush was harder this time. I looked down and caught Hemlock's tail giving a last thrash against my shin as he walked past. I reached my hand down and let it hang there. Seconds later the cool swipe of his nose hit my fingers, and his body pushed against my shins this time. I'd been bagged and tagged by this shy cat. I smiled proudly.

"What's that about?" Celia pointed at my smile, taking delight in my sudden happiness.

"Hemlock."

Her eyes widened, and she ducked her head down to look under the table at Hemlock's tight circuit of shin and hand rubbing. "That's amazing, that is. He never takes to anyone. I'll have to make some of your favorites from now on to keep you coming back for his entertainment."

I shared a smile with her. All evening I'd been feeling more and more comfortable. Now I felt something else, which kind of amazed me. Perhaps I wasn't so shallow after all.

5

"OFF ON YOUR WALK?" CELIA CAUGHT UP TO me as I headed toward the parking lot. I was halfway through auditing classes and saving hers for last after doing my homework on this job. Her program would be one of the top contenders for differentiating the university from others in the country.

I glanced over, noting yet another dress. Did she own any pants? Not that the dresses didn't suit her, in fact, she made them look casual and classy instead of prissy or overdressed. I hadn't worn a dress since high school graduation when my dad begged me to dress up for the pictures. Since he was paying for most of my college, it was the least I could do to make him happy. He'd always wanted a little girl. He had to be horribly disappointed when his six-year-old started refusing to wear cute little dresses. I allowed it for a few special occasions, mostly to make him happy. To willingly wear a dress every day didn't seem conceivable to me.

"I might join."

"Please do." I glanced down at her shoes. No heels on her sandals today, but they weren't exactly great walking shoes. Zero arch support. Clearly, she'd never had problems with her feet.

"What did you sit in on this morning?"

I named three classes, all of which were interesting, but nothing stood out about them. I'd be hitting one of their other campuses this afternoon. Each campus had different specialties and might need separate branding, but that could complicate things.

"How long have you been at this? And when do the others from your team arrive? Or are they being extra stealthy?"

"Five years, and it's only me."

She stopped and turned to me. "You own the business? That's really admirable, Zoey. I couldn't imagine running my own business."

I couldn't imagine working for another marketing firm ever again. They'd been all about bringing in clients and compromising standards to make those clients happy. When I found my niche, I broke off on my own. Selling was hard at first, but only for the first few clients. No one else ventured into my specialty area until I'd already established a name for myself. Getting clients after the first few proved to be fairly easy.

We hit the entrance to the Meadows and meandered along one of the pathways. Celia talked about deciding on her chosen career. We walked at a slower pace. She probably wasn't used to walking her lunches, but it was enjoyable. The sun shone brightly today, heating up the path we were on.

"I've been talking this whole time," she said as we stepped out of the park's exit. Based on her heavier breathing pattern, I'd cut my usual walk in half to ease her into the whole idea of a walking lunch. "Prattling on, really."

"No," I assured her. She did move from one subject to another and sometimes back, but I could easily track the conversation. Being able to listen without the pressure to make some salient point or prove I was intelligent was so different than what I was used to. With this job, too many of the professors treated me as one of their students, constantly prompting me to add to their lecture. Celia didn't do that. She talked about the things that interested her and didn't constantly quiz me or seek my validation.

"Yes," she insisted. "I've been told that a lot. You're being kind." She blew out an exasperated breath. "You're just too easy to chat to. Tell me to stop next time. I am capable of shutting my gob."

"I li-like it," I blurted and cleared my throat. "I don't talk enough."

"I've noticed," she said with a gracious smile. "I wonder..."

We stopped to wait for the light at the crosswalk across from campus. I turned to face her and gave a head tilt when she didn't finish. My stomach clenched, worried about what she might say. She didn't seem the type to offer an unsolicited diagnosis for my lack of gabbing issue.

"I wonder if you simply take care with what you say." Her eyes searched mine. "Perhaps too much care?"

I swallowed the trepidation at what I thought she might say and tried to process her statement. I was careful but probably not for the reasons she thought. "I like listening to you."

Her hand came up and pressed against her sternum. "You must tell me if your ears start ringing from me chatting all the time."

"They won't." We crossed the street and stepped back onto the campus.

Her head turned back to look in the direction of the park. "I quite enjoyed that."

She'd used those same words after our dance together. She seemed surprised by her statement as much as she'd been at the wedding. Surprised but pleased.

6

SMALL IN SIZE, THE CLASSROOM WAS NO LESS noisy than the larger ones I'd visited. Seventeen students clustered into a few groups, chatting easily before the class began. A few heads turned my way, not entirely uncommon, but it was the only class where I was questioned one step inside.

"Can we help you find a classroom?" the tallest guy in the room asked.

I double-checked the listing on my tablet and shook my head.

"Are you transferring in?" This came from the woman standing next to him. She looked tiny compared to him but taller than my stunted stature.

My ears tingled at recognizing a north London accent from her. I weighed my options and decided to mimic hers, familiar with all the sounds after listening to so many classmates at King's. "Just observing for the day."

"Oh, a fellow Londoner." She came over and grasped my hand as several of her classmates groaned, obviously having heard her wax nostalgic about her hometown one time too many. It was the exact distraction I was hoping for by mimicking her accent.

They would have gone on and on about the England versus Scotland division had Celia not sauntered into the classroom. Her expression was open and excited to start her class. Within seconds, she'd caught onto the group discussion, then her eyes landed on me. She glanced back and forth between us with a warm smile.

"Have you met everyone already, Zoey? These kids aren't shy."

"She's from my hometown, Prof." The Londoner wrapped her arm around my shoulders.

"Is she now?" Celia asked through a soft chuckle. "Let's hear a bit of that hometown, Zoey."

A smile played at my lips. I was glad she didn't get upset about tricking her students. After three weeks in Scotland, I was getting really tired of the automatic, "Are you American?" question that came up whenever I opened my mouth. It was one of the reasons I learned to mimic my classmates during that year in London.

"University town, actually," I clarified. "King's to be exact."

"Really?" the student's eyes widened. "My sister was there forever. Took her ages to graduate. When were you there?"

"Many, many years before your sister," I assured the woman who couldn't be more than twenty-one.

The students laughed at my joke. Celia winked at me and told them, "Ask her if she can do a Scottish accent."

They looked at me with interest. As with most people upon hearing someone can mimic their accent, they encouraged me in various levels of excitement.

"Your professor thought me Scottish when we met," I told them in my imitation of the accent learned from Ainsley during grad school. It was crisper than several I'd heard around campus these past few weeks, but that could be attributed to her overseas and London educations, which sharpened the words. Similar to news anchors in America sounding generic rather than from a specific region where they might have been raised.

"Ha!" one of the Scots in the room declared. "That's dead brilliant. Listen to her."

"You have to teach me how you do that," another Scot made the demand sound like a request.

"Wait till you hear her American accent," Celia goaded and I laughed, shaking my head at her.

"Not possible, surely not," another of her students said.

"Absolutely possible, and don't call me Shirley," I quoted in my best Leslie Nielsen impression.

The kids laughed again. "What else can you do?" someone from the crowd asked.

My eyes flicked up to the clock. It was still a few minutes till class started, but I checked with Celia first. Her expression showed pure interest, not bother that I was riling up her students before class. I gave my version of Irish, Australian, Canadian, and New Zealand accents; the latter was my weakest. The only study I had of the Kiwi accent was from a wacky show on HBO about two folk singers living in New York. Celia's class erupted into applause when I finished. A good ear had served me well over my lifetime. It helped with my speech pattern at first and kept me from standing out in the many locations I'd visited over the years.

"That's brilliant, truly brilliant. You must teach us. Prof, make her."

"She's here to work, actually," Celia told them. "We've bothered her quite enough, I should think."

"But, Prof," several of them whined.

"But nothing," Celia told them. "We've had enough fun for today."

"Where is she actually from?" the Londoner asked Celia as they'd taken to talking about me rather than with me.

"Guess," Celia told them and shot me a smile.

Everyone tossed out their guess as to which accent they thought was most authentic. None of them chose New Zealand, which wasn't surprising, nor did they guess America, which was pretty funny. Celia glanced at me and waited.

"I'm from the States," I said in my normal accent.

"No!" several of them hissed, eyes rounded. "You must teach us. Every time I try an American accent it goes nasal instantly."

I nodded, agreeing that was the usual problem with people imitating an American accent. Even some of the best British and Australian actors sounded nasally when they took American roles. Others were so good it was a shock to find out they were British or Australian.

"Another time, kids," Celia said, clapping her hands to get them to settle.

"But why are you here?" someone finally asked me directly.

I blinked, surprised by the question. They'd been talking about me or requesting my standard imitations. I hadn't needed to come up with something original to say from the moment I'd walked into class.

Celia must have seen my fluster because she explained, "She's consulting for the university. We're to act as if she's not here, which will be impossible to do, I know, but do try."

With that, the class began. As expected, Celia's teaching style was as absorbing as her personality when in private. Today's lesson was on camera work. It made me wish I'd had film and television classes to take when I'd gone to school. I'd geared my distribution courses to things that would help my intended career. As much as I liked film and TV, it didn't fit with my career path.

"Did ya enjoy yourself?" Celia asked when the students filed out.

"You're very engaging."

She pushed out an amused breath as if she thought I was being polite. Surely, she'd been complimented about her teaching style before. "Thank you, and I had no idea you were so talented."

My head tilted in question.

"The accents. They're spot on."

"I have an ear."

"I should think you do." She shoved her laptop into her bag. "Are you walking today?"

"I am."

"Care for company?"

"If it's yours," I told her and watched a bright smile grace her lips. "One question first, and you're not obligated to answer." She gestured for me to ask. "Are you happy here?"

"That's a personal question." She didn't look like she minded, but she was curious as to why I was asking.

"It is," I agreed, but I couldn't think of another way to ask her if her career plans included staying on indefinitely here. "One you don't have to answer."

"I am happy here, but is that what you wanted to ask?"

I paused and thought about how to phrase this. "Generally, when I select a branding touchstone, personnel is often not a consideration." Interest brightened her eyes. "That's not the case this time."

"Are you saying you need to know if the department you focus on will keep its faculty?"

"The students talk about their instructors as much as they talk about the atmosphere and everything else college students usually love about their colleges. Many say they wouldn't hesitate to transfer if they lost their instructors." I spotted the pride as soon as it flashed in her expression. "So, yes, it's important to know the plans of those instructors before I make a recommendation. I can't tip my hand just yet, but if you told me you were contemplating offers at other universities, it might influence my recommendation."

Her eyes widened for a moment before a graceful smile lit her face. "I bet you say that to all the professors."

"Only the—" I stopped my automatic response to what would be considered a flirtatious statement if we were in a bar together. I had a plethora of automatic flirtation responses to help in those settings. It saved me from needing to rehearse whatever flirtatious thing I might want to say.

Her brow rose, waiting for my response. As I thought about what to say, a frown formed on her forehead. "Only the...?" she prompted.

"Only the best professors," I gave a version of my flirtatious response. In a bar setting I would have said, "Only the pretty ones." If I'd been trying to win a date.

"You flatterer," she kidded, nudging my shoulder when she came close. "Did you have any other questions before we take your walk?"

"My walk?" I echoed.

"Your walk. You're the one who got me hooked." She reached over and gripped my arm. "I've lost half a stone thanks to your walks."

"A stone?" My eyes flicked up in thought. "Right, that's Brit for something good, isn't it?"

Her grin flared again. "Very good. I keep this up and I'll be a quarter of the way to my ideal weight. Just from walking."

My eyes drifted over her. I didn't like that she thought her ideal weight wasn't where she was right now. Someone had made her think that way about herself. She looked good, not slender or slim, but good nonetheless. "Well, I've gained half a stone just from your wonderful cooking."

The look she gave was a mixture of pride and concern. Obviously, she thought gaining weight was a bad thing, but she was pleased I appreciated the dinners we'd shared at her home. "I should apologize for that, but I do so enjoy good food and great company."

"As do I. The company part, the food I never really considered before. And there's nothing to apologize for. I have more energy and feel stronger. I should have tried this eating thing a long time ago." Who knew what a few pounds would add to my strength and stamina? In high school I'd been this weight because I played a few sports. After college and into a desk job, I was too busy to eat or keep up with athletic workouts, which was the reason I started my lunchtime walks. Even then, I trimmed down too far, but now I felt really good, healthy, and ready to take on anything.

She laughed and squeezed my shoulder again. "I promise I'm not trying to fatten you up."

"And these walks are just walks, not a diet plan." I waited for her eyes to meet mine. "I like the way you look, half a stone less or not."

Pink blotched her cheeks. I'd bet money that no one had ever complimented her figure. Her face, her eyes, her sculpted cheekbones, her sleek hairstyles, sure, but her body, no, probably not, and that was a great shame. "You're being kind again. That's a thing with you. Something you share with Skye, I think."

I waved my hands in immediate denial. "Skye holds that title exclusively." Skye had an intuition for knowing when someone needed to be complimented or encouraged or flattered to give them an extra boost for the day.

Her eyes searched mine. "I think she might have competition with you." Her hand pointed toward the sidewalk. "Our walk awaits. Shall we?"

"We shall."

7

WE WERE HAVING DINNER OUT AS A THANK
you for all the dinners she'd made at her home. I missed
having Hemlock give me drive-by swipes under the table,
but it was nice to help feed Celia for a change.

"Did we find something else you might like?" Celia
paused before taking another bite of her salmon, an item
she'd kindly taken off the menu of her homecooked meals
for me.

I glanced down at the shepherd's pie she'd suggested.
A third of it was gone, and aside from the peas, it was bland
enough for my liking. "It's not as good as everything you've
made."

She gave me a wide smile. "You don't eat much of
anything I make either."

More than I was eating here. In fact, I wished we were
back at her place, trying something else she thought I'd
like. Since finding out I wasn't a foodie—barely even a
taster—she'd been experimenting with dishes she served,
taking flavors she knew I liked and coming up with dishes
to try for our weekly, sometimes bi-weekly, dinners. Every
dinner was followed by an introduction to a British

television show. I always thought I watched too much TV, but Celia had me beat. Of course, she had a professional reason for it, but for the first time, someone I hung out with didn't immediately shut down my suggestion that we simply veg out and watch some TV for our nightly entertainment. Celia was always up for that, and once she found out I'd only seen a few British offerings available on PBS back home, she aired out her DVD collection, and the marathon of whatever she thought would be good viewing for the evening began.

"I know, I know. It's not a reflection of my cooking," Celia repeated what I'd told her many times. "But there's always so many leftovers that you won't take home."

I chuckled at her exasperation. She didn't know what to do with my eating habits. It constantly amazed her whenever she found out I hadn't tried this dish or that one. She enjoyed trying to find something I would like.

Her eyes darted over my shoulder and widened. Distress crossed her face as she slumped in her chair and said under her breath, "Oh, no."

Flowery perfume filled the air beside me as I twisted to find out what caused her distress. The odor clung to a woman stepping up to our table. She wore her hair in a sharp bun of medium brown with zero variation in color that screamed home dye job. Her face was pulled tightly across her skull, eliminating the natural wrinkles that someone her age should have. She hadn't learned early enough that her hands and neck needed moisturizer as often as her face, nor could they be lifted like her face.

"You should be ashamed, flaunting yourself like this," were her opening words. "You know this is one of my favorite restaurants, and you came here to embarrass me."

I stared at her, wondering what the hell she was talking about. Was she rehearsing an improv scene or something? The man beside her, younger by easily fifteen years, shifted his gaze from the woman to us and back.

"Dinner out is the last thing you should be thinking about with your weight problem. Have you gained more weight? I think you have," she answered her own insult.

My hands gripped the table. She was talking to and about Celia. Some of the university staff could get a little petty with their comments to Celia, but they were indiscriminately petty with all their colleagues. Often academic greetings among colleagues included verbal sparring. Everyone else found Celia delightful. This woman was the complete opposite of everyone who spent any meaningful time with Celia.

"And who is this? No, don't tell me, I don't care. You're sinning here, that's all that matters." Her brown eyes shifted to me. Brown eyes that looked slightly familiar. If not for the tightened skin around her eyes, their shape would be identical to Celia's.

"Excuse me, but you're interrupting our dinner," I heard myself say, which was a great surprise to me since confrontation is my least developed skill. My mouth rarely managed to speak what so eloquently ran through my mind. Yet, here I was confronting this woman because Celia had yet to say anything.

"An American?" The woman's pitch rose as she swung her accusatory gaze at Celia again. "Really, Celia, you've embarrassed your family enough. You shouldn't stoop lower by gallivanting about with an American."

"Don't talk about Zoey that way, Mother."

The woman's head swiveled as if now realizing the diners around us could hear her, or more likely, hear Celia call this person her mother.

"A sinner, that's what she is. I've stopped wasting my prayers on you, but dragging someone into sin with you is deplorable, even if she is an American."

"Since when is dining a sin?" I asked Celia, ignoring the woman I refused to label as her mother. Mothers are almost always caring and loving and concerned. This woman doesn't deserve that title.

"Listen, smart mouth," the woman addressed me, or my mouth, I guess. "What you're doing here is sinful. There are children around. Jesus abhors homosexuality."

My eyelids flickered, giving away my astonishment. How did she know I was gay? Then my gaze landed on the red-faced Celia. Ah, got it. I glanced back at the bitchy parental unit and said, "Divorce, vanity, judgment." Her questioning stare tightened my stomach and rushed heat to my face. I should shut up. I was going to screw this up.

"What?" the woman demanded.

"Divorce," I repeated, waving two fingers between the woman and her boy-toy. "Vanity." I used those two fingers to swipe against my jaw and up toward my ear, indicating the tightness of her obviously surgically lifted face. "Judgment," I finished and pointedly stared between Celia and her. "Jesus doesn't much care for those either. And Jesus wasn't the one to say anything about homosexuality."

A small sound escaped Celia, but I kept my gaze on the woman. Her mouth pinched in distaste, color blooming on her stretched cheeks.

"Don't you dare presume to know the Bible better than me," the woman doing a lousy impression of a mother spat at me.

"Of course I do. I don't know you at all. I think you meant to say, 'Don't you blah, blah, judgmental blah, better than I.'"

A sharp laugh got stifled by her hand as Celia remained seemingly shocked by this conversation. I was rather shocked myself. I never managed to say all I wanted to say in an argument.

"I'll have you know that you're talking to an ordained minister."

"And you're talking to a friend of your daughter's, which is a far more important role in life. Or, it would be to most mothers."

Her eyes narrowed, and the flaming stretched skin grew blotchy. "You mouthy little—"

I pointed at myself and cut her off. "American. Obnoxious." Then I pointed at her. "British. Condescending." I pointed at the restaurant's front door. "Exit. Use it."

"Why you—"

"Let's walk away, my pet," the man spoke up for the first time, his gaze darting around the nearby tables and noticing all the eyes staring at us.

"You'll not hear the last of this, Celia. Shame on you." The woman hooked her hand into her escort's elbow and strode from the dining room.

I tracked them until they reached the door and swung back to glance at Celia. My heart was racing, and my stomach was roiling. Even being able to speak eloquently in an argument for the first time, it didn't help all the nerves and queasiness that cropped up every time I tried to avoid confrontation.

My dining companion, whose mother I just insulted, stared intently at me. I should apologize for interfering, but it might seem like I was apologizing for what I'd said to her mother. I wasn't sorry about one word. Yet, it was her mother.

"I'm so sorry," Celia said, taking away my need to say anything. "That was completely uncalled for, and I'm embarrassed you felt you had to get involved."

"Celia," I started but stalled, not completely sure what to say. "I didn't mean to intervene like that. I'm usually never..."

"So verbal? Yes, I nearly choked when you said more than a whole sentence." Her hand reached out and grasped mine, giving it a gentle squeeze. "And what you said, my goodness, I don't think she's ever been challenged like that before."

"She's your mother. I should have shown some respect."

"You were brilliant. Thank you." She squeezed my hand again, and a gratified ripple spread up my arm. "No one has ever been able to put her in her place."

"I take it," I paused, trying to find the right words.

"We're not close?" she guessed. "You'd be correct. They have been throwing Bible verses at me my whole life, but once I came back from grad school with a girlfriend, I was no longer welcome in their house."

"Oh, Celia," I whispered and placed my other hand over the one currently squeezing mine.

"Every time I think I've gotten past it, one of them shows up. Sometimes I think they drive past my usual haunts just to see if they can spot my car and have the opportunity to call me a sinner in public yet again."

"They?" I questioned.

"Everyone in my family except one uncle and his family." Her eyes flicked up from our joined hands and her grip loosened its hold. "They're all involved with the church in some way."

"How nice for them," I snarked. "I'm sorry they've made you feel like an outcast."

"It's been years. I'm used to it. I just wish they'd stop seeking me out in public to berate me. It's bad enough they make demands to keep up appearances with their congregation, and I have to play happy families."

"They shouldn't do that to you." My eyes went back to the exit.

"I'm sorry you felt you had to get involved. Usually, if I don't say anything, they find it embarrassing to prattle on in public places when I don't even acknowledge them. They'll just leave in a huff. If I'd had time to warn you, I would have, but I can't say I didn't enjoy what happened."

"I can't believe I said all that. I hope you didn't take offense."

"Absolutely not. I quite like having a defender." She gave my hands a final squeeze and let them go. "You're a wonderful dining companion. I may have to take you everywhere with me. If you don't mind hanging around a sinner, that is."

"I'd be a hypocrite if I did," I muttered, not realizing until too late that I just admitted to being gay as well. I never liked immediately acknowledging mutual gayness to someone who'd just admitted to being a lesbian.

Celia's eyes widened again, then her smile was back. "I wondered how well you knew Skye."

"Not that well. We were always just friends. I did crush a little on Ainsley back in grad school, though. Sophistical, smart, and beautiful."

"Aye, some of my friends have also been guilty of little crushes on Ainsley."

She'd invited me to a game night with her friends last week, but I didn't do so well in groups, so I declined. I might have to revisit that decision on the next invitation. Sounded like many or possibly all of them were gay.

"Well, if I overstepped tonight, I'm sorry."

Her mouth stretched wide. "I haven't enjoyed watching a conversation more in my entire life. Divorce, vanity, and judgment. I love it. You're a clever thing."

"A mouthy thing, apparently, and I've contributed to the whole obnoxious American stereotype, I'm afraid."

"I don't find you obnoxious at all." Her eyes slid over me from head to torso and back. Every bit of her gaze was approving.

8

AT LUNCHTIME ON MONDAY, I MADE MY WAY over to Celia's office. I'd taken Thursday and Friday off last week to get settled into my short-term rental after picking up Skye and Ainsley from the airport. They'd offered to let me continue staying in their guest room for as long as I wanted, but they were newlyweds and being a houseguest for a week was one thing. Being a houseguest for two months was entirely something else.

The branding presentation was set for Thursday. I'd be spending limited time on campus to prepare the slides at home, but I wanted to drop off this present for Celia in case I didn't run into her for the next few days.

The department assistant looked up when I walked through the office door. He smiled, a toothy grin, possibly a grad student. "What can I do for you?"

"Is Professor Munro available?"

"You're the consultant everyone's talking about, aren't you?"

I inclined my head, hoping my lack of a verbal response would keep him from asking any other questions. He wanted gossip to spread, and I didn't have the time or patience to deal with that.

"I've heard about you, pet. Stirring things up, you are."

"The professor?" I insisted.

"Zoey?" Celia called from a doorway down the hall.

I turned and held up the package I was holding. "Hi."

"Come back." She waved me into her office.

I followed her command and entered a cramped but clean office. Neat and tidy like her appearance. Wearing a skirt and sleeveless blouse today, she looked professional and fresh. "Nice," I commented on both her appearance and her office.

"It works for me. Keeps the students from staying too long. That chair isn't very comfortable." Her eyes twinkled, then landed on the package in my hand. "What have you brought to show me?"

"A gift, for you." I held out the wrapped box.

Her eyes flicked up to mine and back down to the box. My stomach tightened when hesitation entered her expression. I'd never known anyone to be hesitant about an offer of a gift.

"A gift?" She gave voice to her hesitation.

I considered my reply. "Not a gift, really, although I have wanted to thank you for the wonderful home-cooked meals you've made. So, yes, a gift." Weekly, sometimes biweekly dinners for a month, and invitations more often, a gift was definitely in order.

"We're friends, Zoey. I like to cook for my friends. I don't expect anything in return."

She was usually so easygoing. Most people would have snatched the package out of my hand before I'd even finished telling them it was a present. "This is...it's just...I thought...you might like it. That's all."

My stilted attempt at an explanation got through to her. She gave a single nod. I pushed the box into her hand and gestured for her to open it. She carefully tore through the wrapping paper and opened the top. When she pushed aside the tissue paper, her eyes went wide. Yeah, that's what I was going for.

"Zoey, is this from—my goodness, you're talented." She lifted the first framed photograph and studied it intently.

"It's just a hobby, and I had a great model." I stepped beside her and looked down at the picture of her at Skye's wedding. I'd caught her in a rare moment of downtime when she wasn't socializing, when she was standing alone and looking at the brides with a sweet smile. This was before our dance when I didn't know anything about her other than she was enjoying herself at her friend's wedding.

Her eyes roamed the photo, scrutinizing every inch. "I hardly believe this is me."

"It is." I'd given the same assurance to Skye when she looked through the photos. Ainsley loved them and the special developing tint I'd used on some of the photos for an old-fashioned feel with a hint of her favorite color. I'd framed several in color, black and white, and with the special tint for a wedding present. Skye's eyes kept straying back to the photo capturing that special moment of them alone. They looked beautiful, but Skye, like Celia now, didn't seem to believe she was the one in the photograph.

Her fingers brushed against the glass. "I look..."

"Beautiful," I supplied, hoping it wouldn't make her uncomfortable. We both acknowledged being gay, but we hadn't moved onto flirtation to throw us off this friendship track. My compliments shouldn't be seen as making a pass. One friend can tell another she looks beautiful and not have her think she looks hot, which she did. "I put the color version of it and more snaps of you in an envelope under the other frame."

Her eyes glanced up at me and back down to the photo before moving to the other frame in the box. A smile instantly formed on her lips. "Skye looks gorgeous, doesn't she? Has she seen this?"

"I had several laid out for them when they got back. She grudgingly admitted that she liked this one."

We shared a laugh at our friend's aversion to being photographed. There were many of Celia to choose from, but I thought she'd want a framed photograph of Skye and her together. This one in color, both turned slightly toward each other, laughing about something. They looked like the good friends I was certain they were.

"This is brilliant, both of them. Thank you, Zoey."

"My pleasure. I had them done weeks ago, but I wanted the couple to be the first to see their wedding photos."

She reached out and ran her hand down my arm. "Well done. Ainsley must be chuffed if the rest of the pictures look this spectacular."

I turned my head, feeling a flush hit my cheeks. Ainsley hugged me nonstop while going through all the developed photos and the digital slideshow. At one point, she'd held onto me for a good twenty minutes, praising every photo appearing on screen. Skye would cringe almost as often whenever she was in one of the photographs, but she was very pleased that her partner was so happy with them. And later when Ainsley's parents dropped by to welcome them back, we went through the whole photography show again. I was lucky to be able to leave as Elspeth and Ainsley didn't seem to want to let go of me.

"They're both pleased. Have you spoken to them yet?"

"Skye called last night. She's going to sneak into the office tomorrow while Ainsley and her mum are off to make the rounds to see some family members. We're having lunch. Would you like to join? Break your usual habit and actually eat with some friends?"

The regret felt like a burn to my skin. "I wish I could, but I've got meetings for most of the day."

Her eyes came back from the first photo to study me. "Another time?"

"Absolutely." I tapped the frame, studying the solo photo of her again. She looked ultra-chic and glamourous, and it wasn't just the elegance of the black and white finishing. "That's a killer dress."

She flashed a wide smile, and everything felt a little better at that moment. I waved and backed away toward the door, leaving her to enjoy the photos in private. At the doorway, another professor surged into the office, nearly mowing me down. I stepped to the side as we both made apologies for bumping into each other.

Her booming voice was easy to overhear as I sped into the hallway to give them privacy. "Can you take my class this afternoon, Ceal?"

"Which one?"

"After lunch. I've got to—what's this? You're really that much of a fan? I know she's a fab singer, best around, but a framed picture in your office? Did she autograph it or something? You could sell that, you know."

My feet stopped moving as I tried to recall everything in Celia's office. My perusal had been cut short by Celia's hesitancy at the offer of a gift.

"That's me, actually," Celia replied, obviously talking about the photograph I'd just given her. Did Celia look like a famous singer? Which one? The best? Well, that's subjective, it really depends on a person's music pref—oh, sure, that one. British, beautiful, hell of a voice. The photo was in black and white, which that particular singer seemed to prefer for album covers. Their oval faces did have similarities, but it was likely her zaftig body type that prompted the mistaken reference. Still, look for even five seconds and everyone would see it was a photo of Celia.

"You? Wow, you look posh. Where was this? Who's the photographer? You should hire him to follow you around constantly if this is the result."

How could some people be so clueless when it came to complimenting someone? Or perhaps she meant to sound backhanded. Celia looked beautiful in the photograph. Even if someone was surprised by that, a friend should have managed a legitimate compliment. I wished I could think of some retort to make that woman understand she was being petty to her colleague and let Celia know she was beautiful always, not just in a black and white photo when she was all dressed up. But I wasn't always great with retorts, and it would probably just embarrass Celia.

I continued on my way, several rejoinders running through my mind. All of which I rejected. Celia would be able to come up with something much better, and by the way some of her colleagues spoke to each other, I'd guess she had a lot of practice.

9

THE AUDITORIUM WAS BOOKED THIS TIME.
Smart, since everyone on the faculty, their TAs, and all
department staffers were attending this branding
presentation. I'd already had a dozen preparatory
meetings to lead up to this discussion. Often this meeting
didn't go over well with some of the more egocentric
personnel. Given that many still didn't appreciate me
being an American—read: obnoxious outsider—they
weren't happy I had the power to decide this about their
university.

My eyes scanned the crowd and found Celia easily.
Beside her was a smiling Skye, who'd snuck in to work
again and decided to support me by attending the meeting.
Ainsley was meeting with her publisher today about her
latest historical text, leaving Skye free to work when she
was supposed to be taking the entire summer off.

"Thank you," I interrupted the chancellor during
another convoluted attempt to state my purpose for being
here. "It's been a pleasure sitting in on your classes this
past month. I've learned a great deal about your fine
university and enjoyed my time here so far."

Muttering rose throughout the room. The "so far" gave them pause. They understood I meant to stay on when they possibly thought I'd be gone after giving them my recommendation on branding.

"After speaking with many of you, your students, your non-teaching staff, neighboring business owners, and area locals, I've made my recommendation to the university on which program to highlight as your unique identifier."

Audible breaths held in the audience. Many eager faces tried to hide their desire to be the chosen program. I clicked onto the next slide in my presentation and heard gasps sound throughout the room.

"The television program." My eyes found Celia's. I'd broken my usual protocol last night by sharing the news of this decision with her. There were a few other professors in her department, but as her friend, I didn't want to ambush her with the approved recommendation. It could overwhelm some of the department staff.

Incredulity added to the gasps in the crowd. The television program was a small subset of their creative media department and to single it out might not make sense to instructors in the more traditional programs. Several people shouted comments asking how and why I'd come to this conclusion.

"Your school is one of two in the country in partnership with a national television network. You house their local station. It's a unique setup that makes branding almost automatic."

"Surely you could select something with more academic substance," one of the professors spoke above all the rest.

Before I could form a more polite response than the one fighting to get out, one of the other television lecturers yelled back at him. I had to turn away to hide my smile at the colorful language he used.

"How are my literature students going to be taken seriously at a university known for television?"

"Or my engineering students?" another person called out.

I considered my response. "Do you think anyone hesitates when they get an acceptance letter from USC, Oxford, or Yale?"

"How is that relevant?"

"Those schools have excellent traditional academic programs, but each is in the top three for television, film, and drama. As I stated when we first met, branding doesn't diminish the other programs you offer. It simply highlights something that your school is known for, and therefore, makes your school stand out."

"But television?"

"Your entire creative media department benefits from this partnership. It's my understanding your advertising and marking programs have gotten involved in creating advertising content for the station as well." My eyes automatically flicked to Skye, who gave me a confirming nod. My conversations with her over the past week helped make this branding decision. "Several other programs could add television or broadcast-related classes to the mix."

"How?"

"Classes on script writing, the history of television, media distribution, psychology of television media, and many more to incorporate your other departments. These are all part of the suggestions I'll be making as we establish this branding over the next five months."

"Five months!" The rumblings grew louder.

"It will take that long to ready the new studio building across the street. The official branding launch will take place then."

"What building? Not the administration office?" A dark-haired man called out over the din of the room.

My head nodded. This had taken some arm twisting on my part. With Skye's help, we convinced her network and the university how mutually beneficial it would be to move her station's studio to a newly renovated space across the street. Passersby would see it more easily, helping to brand her station, and with the renovation plans, viewers would see the campus in the background with every news telecast through the window as a set backdrop. Also, the creative media program could take over the current studio as a training ground before placing their students and content at Skye's station. A singular experience for the media students not attainable anywhere else. The school administration staff would swap office space with Skye's station once the new building was completed.

"Currently, they only take up two floors of that building. There are construction issues with the rest." I stopped myself from pointing out that they'd discovered mold on the upper floor, had to seal it off, and would need to replace the roof. "A full renovation will make the station state of the art, bring in more notoriety for both the station and its university partner, and keep the non-academics across the street."

That generated some nervous laughter from the crowd. All universities were the same, no matter where. There were academics and non-academics, people who understood the world of academia, and people who didn't. A bunch of television executives and worker drones weren't considered part of the world of academia.

I clicked to the next slide showing all the steps the university would go through to implement this new brand. "Over the next five months as the renovation is taking place, I'll be working with your marketing department, webmasters, and communications teams to revamp your public image. None of the other departments will be downplayed. We are simply boosting the television and creative media department's notoriety. Your website won't be all television, all the time. However, it will place television prominently on the home pages and in SEO tactics. All marketing material for the university will mention the television program, but each department's marketing material will remain unchanged."

"Leave it to an American to think television is a significant academic endeavor." This from a professor in the science department.

"They have no culture, you know." A colleague spoke up.

"That's quite enough," the chancellor stepped in.

I held up a hand. These comments have been coming at me since I arrived on campus. It was time to set some of these people straight. "First, television is a significant academic endeavor, as much as art, or writing, or music, or any other creative academic pursuit. Second, the US might not have as long a history as your country, but it is jam-packed with conflicts, missteps, developments, and achievements, as any other country in the world. As to culture, it might not include log tossing, tartans, curling stones, kingdom toppling, and other colorful elements, but our culture has been world-changing and long-lasting."

My heart was beating far more wildly than in any other public speaking engagement. I've never had to defend my country before, even at the one Canadian university I'd helped where poking fun at their neighbors to the south was something they could earn a degree in.

"Oh, please, what culture?" snapped a woman in the first row as she glanced up from her phone.

I let my glance linger on her. "Is that the newest iPhone? Did you Google when it would be available in stores or did you just order it from Amazon? Does it play all your favorite hip-hop music? Can you watch the latest Marvel movie on it? Nice jeans, by the way. How's that elaborate five-pound coffee drink you have there? Taste good?"

She looked confused at first until my questions settled in. "Those are just technological advancements, and you Americans didn't create all of them."

"When those advancements become part of everyday life, they're no longer just advancements. They're a culture. We may not have come up with all of those, but we have made them essential to the way people live the world over. So, no, our culture didn't introduce golf to the world, but we did create the movie and television industry which brings golf movies and televised golf competitions to the world."

I caught Skye's laugh among the other nervous chuckles in the room. Celia's eyes were wide, but she wore a huge smile. She was likely shocked I'd spoken so much, but honestly, this constant attitude from some of these academics was wearing me down.

"She's made a splendid point, and it ties into the approved branding effort, might I add," the chancellor chimed in. "The US is ahead of us on television and film distribution and integration. Our program has lost out to second and third tier schools in the US because we are not yet known for producing the same opportunities here. With this branding effort, that stops today. Or, next trimester when we launch. Either way, having our excellent uni known for one prominent element will only draw more attention to all the other programs. Now, please, let's give Ms. Thais a round of applause for her presentation and throw our support behind her as she sets about accomplishing this task."

Half-hearted applause rang out as I disconnected my laptop and readied my bag to leave. With the embodiment of the school administration standing next to me, the most vocal opponent stayed quiet and skittered away through the auditorium rows to the exit. The chancellor shook my hand before taking his leave.

"I didn't know you were so patriotic, Zoey?" Skye kidded as she stepped through the remaining clusters of people near the stage.

"I'm not," I said automatically, drawing stares from everyone within earshot. I smiled and shrugged at their confusion. "I was an undergrad history major and got a little defensive."

The chuckles this time were genuine, not nervous. A few people added goodbye waves to their chuckles as they left the room.

"Well done," Celia complimented. "On both the presentation and the culture smackdown."

Skye laughed and nudged Celia's shoulder. Celia wrapped an arm around her friend as they waited for me to join them off the stage. "You should have heard the nerdy showdown she'd have with Ainsley every time she came over for a study session. You'd think she was in grad school for history not business listening to those two."

"You just liked that she wasn't picking at you for those few minutes every day."

She beamed and nodded. "Damn right about that. I used you as a human shield every time. Why do you think I always had the study groups at our place?"

"I think I better get Ainsley's side of this story before I believe anything you two say," Celia told us, amusement dancing in her eyes. They had an easy friendship, and I realized it didn't look so different from ours. We weren't quite at the stage where we knew how we'd react to everything, but I felt more comfortable with her than I did with many people I'd known for years. The realization filled my chest with warmth.

10

THE PARK WAS A LITTLE MORE CROWDED today. The Edinburgh Festival Fringe was in full swing, crowding every part of the city. My lunchtime walks involved a lot of darting to the side to avoid being run over. Celia suggested we just walk on the grass, but I refused to give up the paths completely.

I glanced up at her, my semi-regular walking companion. These walks were my favorite part of the day. Things were progressing nicely with the branding efforts. My supposition about which department to feature at this school before taking on this project proved correct and was making the implementation that much easier. Even the extemporaneous plans to supplement the branding efforts were falling into place. It would be a lot more work than a typical project, three months more time, and the first time I was choosing a non-traditional academic field to profile. I should be trembling with nerves, especially since Skye was having me speak to her executive board about the network's part in my project tomorrow. My afternoon and evening would be continuous rehearsals of the presentation. I really shouldn't have taken this break, but

Celia's call asking if I was walking today brought me to campus to meet up and enjoy this walk with her.

"You're exceptionally quiet today," Celia commented as we stepped out of the park and waited on the corner for the light to change. "Or I've been talking too much again."

I reached out to grip her arm and gave it a gentle squeeze. She'd been told she talked too much by more than just one person. It bothered me. Someone talks too much when they talk over people or talk about inane things that no one wants to hear. Celia did neither. If people couldn't appreciate that, she needed to ditch those people.

"Just thinking," I said as we crossed the street and headed to her office where I was stashing my bag for these lunchtime walks.

"About?"

A lot, actually. How much fun this job had been. How much I'd missed being around Skye. Why it had taken me this long to make it back to Great Britain. Could I find another university client nearby so I could extend my stay? I wasn't sure I wanted to take that London job after this one, if it was still available. I'd rather stick close enough to still see Skye, Celia, Ainsley, and her family on a regular basis. Other than Seattle, this felt the most like home.

"It's about time, Celia," a voice said as we approached her office building. A man stood from the stone bench near the entrance and walked toward us. "I don't have time for this today."

Celia stopped walking. Her vibrancy seeped out of her as she deflated next to me.

"You owe Mother an apology. You've been disrespectful and purposefully embarrassing."

My hand snaked out and grasped Celia's. Her palm slid against mine, warm and soft. My fingers curled around her hand and squeezed in support.

"Another lover? Didn't you learn your lesson last time? God doesn't want you in a sinful relationship. It's why your chosen lovers all dump you."

Students passing by paused before realizing it was just three "old" people, not any of their fellow students. Three old people weren't worthy of posting online.

"Excuse me," my mouth spoke for us again. It was a hell of a lot bolder than I realized. "This seems like a private conversation that should take place somewhere other than at Celia's place of work. Or perhaps we should go back to your office and have this conversation there."

"Who are you to speak to me?"

I couldn't help but laugh. This guy had delusions of grandeur. "I'm the person who will call campus security if you don't leave right now."

"I have business with my sister."

I tightened the hold on Celia's hand and wondered if her method of staying quiet was better than mine. Not that I could change anything now since I apparently had a hard time keeping quiet around people who attacked my friends. It was a new discovery. A little late in life to be making this discovery. And shocking, given my issues with talking.

"Let's go," I told Celia.

His hand came up in a stopping gesture. "You need to call Mum and apologize for your behavior."

"She has nothing to apologize for."

"This bird is feisty, at least." His eyes drifted over me. "Beautiful and fit. Nice pull. What's she doing with you? Is she slow?"

"Stop it," Celia ground out.

"You're a disgrace. If Jesus could see you—"

"Jesus has other things to do. As do we." I tugged on Celia's hand and took a step forward only to run into his stopping hand. "Do not touch me. Leave now, or campus security will escort you out, and don't return. Stop seeking out your sister to embarrass her, or I'll insist she get a restraining order against you." If that's what they call restraining orders in Scotland. They had their own unique judicial system, so they probably have a different name for it, but his narrowed eyes told me he understood my promise.

"You have no right—"

"To intercede? You're correct, except I did, so deal with it. Your sister is a wonderful woman. If you're too dense to see that, it's your problem. Please leave."

"What are you going to do about it?" He'd taken his hand off my arm but stepped up to me. Taller than his sister by four inches, he towered over me. Men always think this will intimidate a short woman. I'd grown up around tall men and their friends. Tall men didn't intimidate me.

I fished out my phone and dialed a number. I didn't know campus security's number, but I knew my voicemail number. He didn't need to know it wasn't campus security. His eyes widened when I started to report someone harassing a professor. He pointed a finger at us and said something stupid, then hurried away.

Celia turned to me, her expression unreadable. I'd gone farther this time. Probably too far. Her hand came up. She wouldn't slap me. Not here in front of her building. I was expecting a hard pat to make sure I kept my mouth shut the next time another of her family members decided to cast verbal stones at her in a public place. When her hand touched my face, it wasn't a threatening tap, it was a soft caress. Her fingers gentled against my cheek. As nice as her hand felt in mine, it felt even better against my face.

Her brown eyes twinkled at me. "Jesus has better things to do?"

My shoulders lifted and dropped. "That always ticks off the Christians. For some reason, they all think Jesus has time to be worried about whether they win a sporting event or a Grammy. I could have gone through the whole historical versus fictional figure argument, but your brother might have imploded right here."

"Do I want to know?" she asked.

"Not if you're a Christian."

"You're not religious?"

Before answering, I studied her demeanor. We'd been joking around, but she'd been raised as a churchgoer. Even with her family turning away from her, she might still be an active member of that or another church. She didn't seem offended by my comments so far, so I replied honestly. "Not even a bit."

She nodded once, no judgment or distaste flashing in her expression. Our acceptance of what others believed worked for them but didn't need to work for us was something we apparently had in common. She reached out to grip my arm, tugging us into motion into the building and up the stairs to her office.

"So, that was my brother."

I looked her over to gauge how she was feeling after this ambush. "Where does he work?"

She chuckled, her posture relaxing. "That's not a bad idea, actually. I wonder how he would react if I showed up at his office and demanded an apology."

"I'm sure you could find something about him that Jesus would have a problem with. Is he divorced? That's always my go-to."

She rewarded me with another sharp laugh, confirming my hope that religion was something we could talk about without upsetting each other. "Sorry you keep getting dragged into it. They assume any woman I'm standing next to is being corrupted by me. That always just adds to the embarrassing scene."

"Your family should be embarrassed, not you."

She blinked, processing, then thrust my bag forward. "Only a few more family members to meet, anyway."

"A few more to anger. Goody." I rubbed my hands together.

"Nothing fazes you, does it?"

I took my bag off her hands, pulled my flats from the bag to step into, and stuffed my tennis shoes into the side pocket. "A lot does, but homophobic family members, no. Perhaps next time, I'll actually shut up."

"It's definitely been more entertaining with you around."

I turned toward the door. She had a class in fifteen minutes, so I had to leave even if I wanted to stay. At the doorway, a thought hit me. For the first time outside of a lesbian bar, I blurted what I thought. "Would you like to go out?"

Her mouth nudged ajar, eyes widening. "Out? As in a date?"

Her shock gave me confidence. "Yes."

"Why?"

"Why not?"

She just stared at me. A simple yes or no question hung heavy in the room. I'd never asked out a friend. Usually, friends introduced women to me and after a short chat, I'd either be attracted or not. At a bar, I'd ask women to dance, maybe drinks another night, but within a couple of meetings I knew if I'd like to see them romantically. I'd never been friends with someone for four weeks and then decided to ask them out.

When she continued to stare incredulously at me, I let her off the hook. "People have declined my invitations before, and I still manage to trudge on under the weight of my disappointment."

A tiny smile formed on her lips, but her confusion remained. She must never have been asked out by a friend before either. Perhaps she thought I'd been pining for her all along rather than just wondering if we might have something more between us.

I shrugged as if it were no big deal. "I find you interesting."

"Everyone is interesting. It's just a matter of degree."

"That's true. But not everyone knows something about almost everything. I like listening to you. We get on really well, and I wondered if we could get on even better."

Her eyes flashed for a moment, attraction and delight making them dance before reason seemed to set in. "I enjoy your friendship, Zoey. I don't want to risk ruining that."

"Understood. Just thought I'd ask. I hope I haven't made you uncomfortable."

"No, just a surprise."

"So, we're good?"

She gave a definitive nod. "Aye."

"Still on for dinner and more of that TV series you showed me last time?"

Surprise flared again. Longer this time, relief and relaxation the overriding emotions in her surprise. "Looking forward to it."

"Me, too." I headed for the door. With a glance over my shoulder I added, "I like your hands, too." My eyes dropped to the hand I'd held as mine contracted at my side. They really were nice hands. Too bad I wouldn't get to feel them with anything other than friendly touches.

11

THE THWACK OF THE GOLF BALL WAS MORE of a grating thump than a solid thwack.

"We're aiming for that flag over there, love." Alastair pointed to a flag at a thirty-degree angle from the path the golf ball had taken.

"So was I," Skye said without an ounce of frustration. She'd been mishitting balls for eight of the last fourteen holes, but unlike most people who perform badly at a sport, she didn't throw a tantrum or pout or blame her equipment or the conditions. She blithely continued to try because, like with her sheep, she was convinced learning to play golf would make her more authentically Scottish.

I turned my grin away from Alastair, a former professional player, and his student, Skye, a hopelessly amateur player, to Celia, a surprisingly good player. They'd invited me to join their once a month threesome, probably to add another set of eyes on the course to help find all of Skye's errant shots. Even with the extra walking and occasional sly drop of a new ball so we could all stop looking for the one we'd never find, it had been a fun afternoon.

"Is this what it's always like?" I whispered to Celia.

"She's gotten so much better. I only started joining them recently, but I've seen a lot of improvement."

"You two don't have to whisper." Skye pointed an accusing finger at us. "I know what you're saying."

"They're complimenting your form," Alastair said and broke into a hearty laugh. It didn't seem to bother him that his daughter-in-law was an atrocity at golf, a sport he loved and made a living at. Over the last two hours, I'd gotten the impression he appreciated how much she tried and considered this bonding time with his new daughter.

"Ha!" Skye scoffed. "They're saying I shouldn't even bother playing golf."

"You're not actually playing golf, Skye," Celia joked.

"You're hilarious," she snarked back. "Just because we all didn't play for our college teams or professionally."

"You played in college?" I asked Celia, admiring her form anew. In a golf skirt and shirt, a sleek ponytail and visor, she looked like she belonged on the course every bit as much as the professional among us.

"For three years, then I realized I'd never be good enough to make any real money on the tour and got serious about my field of study."

"You're not bad yourself, lassie," Alastair complimented me.

"My dad loves to play."

"How is Priam?" Skye asked. "I haven't seen him in a few years."

"You'll see for yourself in a few weeks."

"He's visiting? That's great, Zoey. Alastair, would you mind if he joined us on the course? He really enjoys golf."

"Anything for you, my girl," Alastair replied easily and looked at me. "Priam? Is that Roman?"

"Greek."

"Aye, and is your mum Greek as well?"

My head shook. "I'm lucky enough to have two dads."

His eyes widened and blinked as he processed what I said. Without knowing him well, I knew he wouldn't be like the parents of many school friends who, upon learning I was the child of two gay men, told their kids they'd never be having a sleepover at my house. "Aye, lucky indeed," he agreed. "Although, my Ainsley would be lost without her mum. Even during her teenage years, she and Elspeth were the best of chums."

"I'm like that with my dad. My other dad wasn't a natural parent, but he was great just the same."

"Is your other dad also Greek?" Celia asked.

"He's a mix, some Scottish, though."

"Ah, you've got some Scots blood in ya, lass. That's good."

I winced, studying Alastair and wondering if I should bother correcting him. Alastair's patriotism and pride were obvious. "I'm adopted, actually."

He didn't make the typical embarrassed and awkward sounds of someone not familiar with adoptees. Most people immediately backtrack whatever they've just said and use words like "real" when talking about biological parents. "Blood or no, lass. You were raised by a Scot, you're a Scot. Am I right, Celia?"

She grinned at him. "You're right, Alastair."

"You can be Greek, too, but you'll forever be a Scot to me, love."

Tears pricked my eyes. No one had ever immediately accepted my situation as easily. No one other than Skye, I should say, and now it seemed, Celia and Alastair, as well. I'd learned over the years that people had different views of adoption. Some were like my parents and me, knowing adoption made no difference in a family unit. But a lot of people still clung to the idea of "real" meaning biological. Some refer to an adopted sibling or child as a stepsibling or stepchild. Or once the adopted child turned eighteen, they treated him or her like many kids are treated in a foster situation and cut loose from the family. I'd been extraordinarily lucky with my parents. It wasn't just that they were good dads, it was that they'd never made me feel as if I were anything but their much-wanted child.

"What's his clan?" Alastair asked of my other dad.

"He's got an English surname, actually."

"Oh-aye, we don't need to be hearing that, then." He beamed at his joke. A typical Scotsman's opinion of the English, it seemed. "My Ainsley can trace your clan. She's brilliant, you know?"

"She is that, yes," I agreed and shared a smile with Skye. His role of proud daddy could rival my own dad's. Both dads actually.

"Will Warner be visiting while you're here?" Skye asked.

Catching the curious look on Celia's face, I explained first, "My other dad, and he did just text he's in Ireland for a shoot, so he may pop over when they get a film break."

"Film?" Celia glanced over in curiosity.

"He's a cinematographer for a movie studio."

Her eyes widened, and I could see the request forming in her brain. "Do you think we could persuade him to chat to my class? If he has time and would want to. Don't pressure him, but if you think it might be something he'd like to do, we'd love to have him."

My grin got her to stop the over-explanation of her request. "I'll ask him."

"I'd talk to yer class, there, Celia. I may not be the professor my daughter is or the teacher my wife is, but I can talk golf all day."

We all laughed at his joke, but Celia's eyes moved up in thought. "You know, Alastair, it might not be a bad idea to have you in to talk about how sportscasters and television coverage have made a mark on sport. If you're up for it."

He took a step back, not thinking she'd take him up on what he thought would be a teasing offer. He looked at his daughter-in-law for help, but she just gestured for him to accept the invitation.

"My students are very inquisitive. You won't have to prepare anything. As long as you can tell a few stories about television crews covering your games, they'll carry the class."

"That sounds fine."

"I'd love to sit in, Celia," I said.

"You'd be welcome. And you, Skye."

She smiled fondly at her friend and her father-in-law. "Wouldn't miss it."

"You're a fun lot, you lassies are."

"When we're not getting lost in the woods searching for my golf balls, right?"

He wrapped an arm around Skye. "Even then, love. You've improved so much."

"You mean how they land somewhere on the golf course now?" she joked and turned to us. "When we first started, my swings took them into the parking lot and a few backyards of homes lining the course."

"A little more exercise is what I say," Celia told her.

She always had something nice to say. It didn't seem to matter if she was talking to her friend as she was now or to a stranger when we were out together. It was one of the many things I enjoyed about her. One of many.

12

AFTER A COUNTLESS NUMBER OF BUSINESS trips, I shouldn't have been surprised to answer the knock on my door and find my other dad standing on my doorstep. He did this sometimes. If he got a break in his filming schedule and I was somewhere he wanted to visit, he'd just show up.

"Dad!" I exclaimed and flung my arms around his neck. The surprise visits were always welcome, as soon as I learned to manage the surprises, that is.

"Heya, Zo-girl. You're looking good."

So was he. He ceased aging a decade ago. His dark blond hair fashioned another expensive cut, making the waves swoop perfectly to appear both casual and purposeful. His six-foot frame was as fit in his late fifties as it had been in his late twenties when I first went to live with him. "You're early."

"Surprise!" he said without an ounce of apology. If I dropped in on him a week early, he'd make me regret it by dragging me to all of his meetings on The Coast, as he insisted it be called. He loved showing me off and having people rave about how he looked way too young to be my father. Not that I looked old, but he still looked like a well-toned, youngish, surfer dude. His blond hair hadn't thinned, his dimples hadn't dug crevices into his face, and his twinkling blue eyes hadn't stopped twinkling.

"You've caught me on my way out."

"Lunch date?"

"With some friends, yes."

"Perfect timing, then. I'm starving, and I always like your friends."

I chuckled. This dad always invaded, never lacked for confidence, and just assumed he was invited. I stopped trying to reason with him years ago. He lived under a different set of rules. He was the Sun and the rest of us revolved around him. He'd adopted the self-absorbed attitude of most of his peers in Hollywood. Anyone outside of Hollywood wouldn't understand, but those of us who loved them let them be.

"C'mon, then." I led him back outside. He must have already stopped at a hotel and dropped his luggage. This dad never stayed with me. He was a bit of a pampered prince, and he loved having a job that allowed him to live out of hotels while on location. "You were supposed to talk to my friend's class next Friday, Dad."

"I know." He had the sense to look guilty, knowing it wouldn't sit well with me since I never asked him for favors. Now that I finally had, he was blowing it off. "We had a shooting change. I needed to get over here sooner or push off the trip for two months."

Celia would be terribly disappointed. She'd been building it up, getting her class prepared to talk to someone with American film and television experience.

She'd had other guest speakers in, especially with Skye's connections at her network, but this would have been the first time someone with film experience spoke to this graduating class.

"So, when does Priam get here?"

I sighed, letting the breath push out completely before I responded. This was how I managed his surprise visits. For the past several years, he'd been asking about Dad more often. At first, I was honest about his travel plans. Then, this dad had shown up at the same time twice. They were not the type of divorced parents who spent time with each other. They'd barely spoken to each other for the first four years after splitting up, using me as the point of contact. Priam was my custodial parent, the responsible, solid, loving father. Warner, the one who'd left for Hollywood and seemed to become carefree overnight, would phone and send plane tickets for me to visit but never checked if they coincided with school breaks. While I missed him and loved him, Warner was never the parent-parent. He wasn't the one I went to with problems or to ask for permission. He was the one that gave unsolicited advice, bonded over sports and fixing things, and tried to make every visit fun. It was why I always labeled him as my other dad when speaking of both parents.

"Soon," I replied vaguely. He'd probably called Dad's assistant, posing as a potential client, and found out when Dad would be on vacation. He liked to shock Dad, show him how good he still looked, and find out if he was seeing anyone because this dad was on the perpetual lookout.

"Thought you said it was this week."

"I didn't, and I don't appreciate you trying to crash his visits." I slipped my arm into the crook of his elbow and squeezed his forearm with my other hand.

"Who, me?" He gave me his best innocent look. This was probably how he'd charmed my steady and reasonable dad. They'd been good together while this dad decided to play house, in part to prove a point to his homophobic parents. But he could only live his life to prove a point for so long, and when he stopped being a respectable photographer and got his first job on a film, his true personality—a charming, happy-go-lucky type—took over. His wandering eye also kicked in, and he had an affair with one of the supporting actors. That ended the thirteen-year relationship between my parents.

"You're impossible. What happened to that buff gym-crazy dude you were with last time I visited?"

"Curbed him," he said as if it were nothing to be ecstatically happy one visit and completely over someone the next.

"Well, stop trying to mess with Dad. You know you don't want anything more than a fling for old time's sake. Find someone else to charm."

He stopped and turned me to face him, looking serious for the first time. "That doesn't sound like you have a very high opinion of me."

"I love you, Dad. I'm happy when you're happy with whomever you choose to be with. But I love Dad, too, and a tryst with you won't make him happy in the long run. Keep to your separate corners of the West Coast, okay?"

He sighed and slung an around my shoulders. "You're right. I was feeling nostalgic. He wasn't the reason I changed my travel plans."

"I know," I said because he was definitely more about convenience than a one-night seduction.

We reached campus two minutes early for my lunch date with Skye, Ainsley, and Celia. Skye was back to work, officially her first day, and we all thought she should be taken to lunch. I spotted Ainsley first, or her voluminous hair, I should say. She emerged from the studio building with Skye right behind her. They turned when they heard Celia call out as she traversed the courtyard to join them.

"Those your friends?" Dad asked of the trio across the square. "Which one has my girl's eye?" He loved getting the scoop on my dating life. That was another truth in his personality. As soon as he dropped the stable photography job and home life, he became less like a father and more like a fun uncle. "Tell me it's the redhead; she's hot."

"That's Skye. You've met her several times, Dad. She's recently married."

"The television exec? Wasn't she a brunette?"

"She let it go back to her natural color." A choice I wholeheartedly supported. The red was most definitely hot.

"The blonde, then. The hair's a bit out there, but she's damn fine."

Ainsley's hair, when she wore it down, was a billowy mass of curls that fell past her shoulder blades. For someone like my dad whose stylist took appointments months in advance, Ainsley's hair might seem a little out of control. To me, it was marvelous, made even better by the fact that she no longer felt the need to tame it into a braid as she'd done in college when I'd known her. "That's Skye's partner, Ainsley."

"Oh, well, have you got your eye on anyone here? It's been a year since your last relationship, hasn't it?"

Two and change since my last attempt at a long-term relationship failed. It lasted almost two years, but nine months had been spent long-distance with me on three different jobs. She hadn't liked that, but she held on, all the while telling me she was fine never moving to the biggest step. Yet, as with the one other serious relationship before her, as soon as the one-year anniversary hit, the pressure to marry began.

"You do. I can see it. Who's my Zo-girl after?" His hands squeezed my shoulders as he stared into my eyes. I felt them betray me and flick toward Celia. He turned back to the trio walking in our direction. "The chubby brunette?"

"Dad!" I hissed at him. "Just because she's not a flesh-wrapped skeleton like all those actresses you work with doesn't mean she's chubby."

His hands came up in defense. "You're right, you're right. I'm warped by the industry." He glanced over at her again. "She's very pretty."

From his tone, I could tell it was a careful but truthful admission. "She is, and she's a beautiful person. She's also the one you're letting down by being here early, so be extra nice."

"She's the television prof?" His brow pushed up into his perfectly swooping bangs. "Great, so I'm getting a dose of guilt with my lunch, huh?"

"Nobody's fault but..." I let him fill in that blank as my friends joined us.

"Warner," Skye greeted as they joined us. She stepped forward, her hand outstretched. "Good to see you."

"Nice to see you again, Skye." He wouldn't admit he hadn't recognized her, a trait he picked up working in his industry. He used to tell me to just assume you've met or recognize everyone to spare their fragile egos. It wasn't necessary here, but old habits.

"I don't know if you remember Ainsley. We were housemates at Columbia when you sat in on one of our study sessions."

"I'm not sure we ever met back then, but it's great to know you now."

Celia was looking at him, bewildered. This was the first time someone met my dad and didn't try to figure out why we didn't resemble each other. She was wondering what the hell he was doing here a week early. With a glance at my face, she knew he wouldn't stay around to keep his scheduled talk with her class.

"Dad, this is Celia Munro. Celia, my father, Warner Ellis."

She shook his hand. "Good to meet you. Weren't we expecting you next week?"

"You were, but the filming schedule changed." Remorse was clearly evident in his tone. "We're in Romania next week, won't be back for two months. Thought I'd stop in and see my girl before we headed out. Sorry about missing your class."

She smiled that dazzling smile, the one telling anyone who knew her she was going to get her way. "You won't be missing it."

I turned away to laugh. Dad didn't like being told what to do, but she had him cornered.

"I can't stay till next week."

"I gathered," she told him and winked at me. "But since your daughter didn't tell us you were arriving today, I assume it's a surprise for her as well. That means you haven't yet had time to make plans for today. You've got the afternoon free, and you'll spend an hour of it in my class."

He turned an incredulous look my way. I shrugged and went to stand next to Celia. "You did say you'd talk to her class." I knew it wasn't as easy as Celia was making it seem. She had lesson plans to rearrange to fit him in, but she'd do it because it was a big deal to have a guest speaker from Hollywood.

"That's sorted then," Celia steamrolled over his surprised expression. I was beginning to love that about her. She gave me a wink and gestured toward the street.

Skye and Ainsley laughed as we left my dad gaping after us. Skye looped her arm through his and got him into motion. Celia was now the only friend of mine not intimidated by his casual but sometimes cavalier attitude.

13

THE STUDIO BUILDOUT WAS GOING WELL. IT helped to have Skye keeping her well-organized eye on it at all times, but I was surprised how quickly the process was going. Never once had I shown up and not seen people working. Some of the renovation jobs I'd recommended at universities in the States would get bid out to the lowest priced contractor, who would promptly flake out after a week. So far, this crew stayed on time and on budget.

"Your dad's gone already?" Skye asked me as we walked through the second-floor studio, control room, and offices.

"He only had two days off before he had to get to Romania. He's like that if you remember."

She nodded and studied me. "Does it bother you?"

"Not anymore. He's a bit much to take at times, anyway. If Dad did that, yeah, I'd be bothered."

"That would be totally uncharacteristic for Priam. I'm looking forward to seeing him again. He'll stay longer, won't he?"

"A week, then he'll visit some family in Greece and stop back here before heading home." We had a few side trips planned as well. I was looking forward to it even more than my dad was. "It's going to be so good for him to take an entire month off for the first time in his life."

"I know exactly how he feels. I never realized how much having more than two weeks off a year helps to reenergize you."

"Did you even get two weeks in a row off at your last job?"

She shook her head and smiled. "I'm glad I had that job. It makes me appreciate this one all the more."

We glanced around the studio set, only one of two in the building. There were twelve studios in her last network building. She was responsible for content approval and budgeting on all of them. By comparison, this was child's play, but it was so clear how much she loved it.

"Must be nice to have a light summer schedule. Do you think you'll get to where you'll have original programming over the summer?"

"At some point, but the station is still fairly new, and I'm not in any hurry. Ainsley doesn't teach summer sessions anymore, so it's a nice break for the two of us. We can head to the US and visit my mom and Dallas and Colin."

Something she never would have considered at her old job. She wouldn't have had the time to consider it. She barely had time for a couple of dinners with me whenever I took a job at a university near her workplace, and that was over the course of three to four months. "I'm happy for you, Skye."

"Thanks. I'm happy you're here." She quirked an eyebrow. "You know there are several universities nearby that could use your help."

That very thought had been going through my head the past week. I liked it here, but I was still amazed by Skye's relocation. Shocked, really, which probably meant I wasn't ready for something similar.

"Ainsley's having a dinner party on Friday. Some of her colleagues will be there. We'd love to have you over."

"I don't know."

She stopped our progress to face me. "I'll be there and so will Celia. Say you'll come."

"I'll think about it."

"Good." Her eyes tracked the electricians pulling wire through the metal studs. "The network is getting antsy." A hand waved around us, indicating the unfinished space. "Two execs are going to make the trip in from HQ to have a look."

"If you need backup to convince them this is for the best, I'll be there."

She smiled at me. "They're going to want to meet you. I've talked you up. Don't be surprised if they offer you a branding gig."

"Television networks are out of my expertise." Definitely not my expertise, but it would be nice to have an excuse to stick around for a month or two longer. I gave her a noncommittal shrug. She knew me well enough to know not to push it.

"I've got lunch with three of our biggest advertisers. I'd ask you to join, but it would scorch a little bit of your soul."

I chuckled and gave her a parting wave. Even if she was lunching with Ainsley, I wouldn't have joined. The start of fall brought on regular rainy days. I planned to take advantage of any clear or light rainy day for a lunchtime walk.

"It's raining," Celia called to me as I crossed the campus square toward the exit.

"It's barely sprinkling," I responded with a smile, delighted to see she was carrying an umbrella. I never pressured her or asked if she wanted to go for a walk. If she did, she'd find me here at this time every day it wasn't pouring down rain.

She was wearing a fitted wool skirt and a cashmere sweater. She didn't wear suit jackets. They would box her in. If she needed to wear a coat, she'd wear a short trench with the ties in an elaborate twisty knot in the back. She had three that I'd seen so far. "Need an umbrella?" She thrust it toward me.

My face fell. She wouldn't be joining me. She came out to offer the use of her umbrella. We spent two nights a week together and saw each other often on campus, and still, I was disappointed she wouldn't be joining me for one walk.

"I've got a hood." I popped up the hood on my rain jacket to prove it.

"Always prepared. Will this continue in the winter or do you actually start eating lunch at lunchtime when it's too cold to walk."

"I take shorter walks."

She laughed and glanced away. This wasn't typical behavior for her. Perhaps she did want me to ask her to join me, even though she knew she was always welcome. "Would you like to brave the sprinkles with me?"

"Wish I could, but we've got a department meeting in ten."

"Fun," I commented, knowing how much most professors hated those meetings.

"You know a lot about academic politics. Are you sure you never wanted to be a professor?"

"Never."

She laughed again at my immediate response. "Will you be at Skye's on Friday night?"

I still hadn't decided. With Skye there, I wouldn't feel completely out of place, but I really didn't like groups. Especially groups who all knew each other and not me. "Maybe."

"Need a ride?"

My eyes searched hers. Hope peered through those eyes the color of burnt sienna. She wanted me to go. From what Skye said, they were Ainsley's friends from work. Celia might not know all of them, but she never had trouble in group settings. "Maybe. Thanks for the offer."

"Let me know." Her hand came up but dropped back to her side. She probably thought an arm squeeze might pressure me into agreeing. "Wish I had time for the walk."

"I can wait."

She smiled and a ripple rolled through my stomach. "You're sweet." She counted off on her fingers. "Department meeting. Television Production class. Office hours. Check-in with the department chair."

"I could find a van, black out the windows, drive it onto campus, and make a show of abducting you?"

She gave me the spine-tingling sharp laugh again. "Thanks, but it would just postpone the day."

The ripple was still rippling. Every time now, little swirls of heat fluttered inside me whenever I spent time around her. So far, it was easy to keep the flutters from developing into all-out tingles. I liked our friendship as much as she did. It wasn't an uncontrollable urge to push for something more yet, but I could give it another try. "You could let me take you out after your day? Celebrate being done with it." Her eyes brightened, clearly ready to accept when I clarified, "On a date."

The brightness dimmed, extinguishing any tiny flutters I might have felt. "I thought we agreed we should stay friends."

"Thought I'd see if you changed your mind." I kept my tone light. No pressure for either of us. No full-blown romantic feelings to make things awkward. I could stay her friend. If that's all she wanted, I could stay her friend.

Her head shook and an embarrassed smile curled her lips. "We're good as friends. Why would you want to change that?"

I made sure she was looking at me. "You're super brainy. I like smart people. Women especially."

She pushed an amused breath through her nose. "There are lots of smart women available."

"Not with your smile."

She studied me with curiosity and a hint of approval. These invitations for a date weren't how we usually communicated. I was a lot bolder when I was asking her out, but like with our first dance, I thought she needed to know how certain I was about wanting to take her out. "You are a charmer."

"Is that a yes?"

"That's an acknowledgement of your charm. We should keep this a friendship."

"Okay," I agreed easily to let her know I didn't harbor any hurt feelings. If I was going to keep trying, I couldn't get discouraged or angry, and these little flutters would make me want to keep trying. "How about take-out and more of that uncomfortable but strangely addictive detective drama you started for us after the last dinner?" The brightness returned to her eyes, but there was still some hesitation and maybe, regret. "As friends, like always," I clarified.

"That would make my day, Zoey."

"Mine, too." I gave a nod and smile before turning to start my walk. I could feel her eyes on me as I headed toward the campus exit. I wasn't sure I'd prevail before I needed to leave, but so far, it hadn't felt too bad when she'd turned me down.

14

HALFWAY THROUGH SKYE'S DINNER PARTY, I found myself outside talking to the sheep. Not so much talking to sheep as avoiding people. Ainsley's friends were a bit much. All were professors and all liked to make sure the two non-professors knew it. They didn't seem to be close friends of Ainsley's, more like friendly colleagues. People to say hello to, grab lunch with, share classroom horror stories. They weren't people to confide in. She had her mom for that. And now, Skye, for that and more.

"You're hiding," Skye said from behind me.

"I'm sheep bonding."

"That's not a thing." She slid a hand over my back and up to my shoulder for a quick squeeze. "They're exhausting, aren't they?"

I turned and grinned. Skye had no problem chatting with them. For someone who didn't know her, it would look like she enjoyed being with them. For someone who did, I recognized all of her invisible eye-rolling moments.

"We get together once every couple of months. This was our turn to host. I'm glad you're here. Celia, too."

"Celia can hold her own with anyone."

"She's special. Saw that the first time I met her."

"She is," I agreed.

"Helps that she doesn't have a bunch of stereotypes about Americans."

"Tell me about it."

"Better get back inside. You won't be able to hide from—"

"What are you two doing out here?" Ainsley called from the back patio. "Darling, if you're helping Zoey make a break for it, I'll break something of yours."

"Ah, my beautiful partner," Skye stage-whispered to me. Her eyes sparkled at Ainsley, so unlike their barbs back in grad school. Back then, Skye was convinced Ainsley couldn't stand her, and Ainsley acted pretty annoyed by Skye. Nowadays, Ainsley could trade every barb she'd wielded in college and Skye's eyes would only sparkle at her.

"In the house, please." Ainsley may have phrased it as a request, but we didn't kid ourselves that it was anything other than an order.

Skye's hand gripped my shoulder tighter and turned us back toward the cottage. My sheep break was over. The dinner party awaited. It couldn't last much longer, seeing as the dining part had been over for a half hour.

"There they are," Lilah exclaimed as we came back into the house.

They'd spread out into the living room and looked to be entrenched. Skye might never be rid of them. I silently started counting the seconds until I could politely escape.

"Sit here." She patted a tiny space next to her on the couch.

Within two minutes of meeting her, I knew she was a lesbian, single, and very available. I didn't want to know those things about her, but she wasn't going to let me just sit here all night and not know them. I'd been trying to figure out what Ainsley must have told them about me. She wouldn't have dangled me in front of them, so it must have been something I did that betrayed my sexuality and singlehood.

My eyes searched out Celia, but she was sitting in one of the two club chairs. I felt like going over and sitting on the chair arm, but it looked like my fate was set. Skye turned a grin away as I walked toward Lilah and squished down between her and Winnifred. Both were fairly attractive, slim, nice hair and smiles. If this were a lesbian bar, I'd probably ask one or both of them to dance. But this was a dinner party, and I'd gotten to know them first. No dance for either Winnifred or Lilah.

"How long did you say you were stopping?" Lilah asked.

"We're keeping her as long as we can," Skye spoke up, seeing that I was getting to my social end.

"Longer if we have to," Ainsley added and gave me a bright smile. "My parents are pretty enamored."

I blushed. The feeling was mutual. It was amazing to feel so welcome here. Feel like I had a touchstone at this house and as close to a family as I could get outside of my dads.

"We'll have to show you around town. Entice you to stay. How about tomorrow night? Do you like to dance?"

I glanced at Celia, my last dance partner. Her cheeks flushed when she met my glance. Dancing with Celia was enjoyable, but what to say to Lilah. "I'm pretty busy with work."

"Some other time, then."

I shrugged. It had been a long while since my last fling on a job. My libido arrived in fits and spurts. If it reared up when on a job, I'd head to a bar and dance with some women for a few nights. One of them might catch my interest for a four or five-week fling, and then I was slaked for months, sometimes years. In a place like this, extending my usual three-month project to six months, it would have been ideal. Perfect for a short affair. But, well...Celia. She had my interest now and a casual fling with someone else didn't appeal. It didn't matter that these two were definitely affair material. I just didn't feel it. Not with Celia still a possibility.

"Have you been to the National Museum yet?" Evangeline asked.

I couldn't get a read on her. She hadn't volunteered like Winnifred and Lilah that she was a single lesbian. Janet and Gail, sitting beside Ainsley, were both straight and married, both sharing their status within two minutes of meeting them as well. It always made me laugh when some heterosexuals claimed that homosexuals shoved their sexuality into people's faces. They never realized the moment they mentioned their husbands or wives in passing they'd just shoved their sexuality in our faces.

"With Ainsley last week. It's magnificent."

Her eyes dimmed. Clue number one to her sexuality. She'd wanted to take me. "There's the Castle?"

"Zoey's a history nerd. Ainsley's made sure she's seen everything noteworthy," Skye supplied.

"Have you taken her to our favorite bar yet?" Lilah asked Ainsley. "She'll be a hit there."

Already tired of where this short conversation was leading, I put an end to it. "This has been nice, but I've got a lot of work to do this weekend. Skye, could I trouble you for a ride to the train station?"

"I can take you," three people said, one of them Celia.

My eyes found hers and she added, "I've had a long day. I'm happy to run you home."

"Thanks," I said before anyone else could say anything. Ainsley had already offered to have me stay the night, but I was ready to leave this gathering. Lilah looked like she might rip Celia's keys out of her hands to keep her from driving me home.

"You'll have to give me your number so we can get together before you leave." Winnifred tried to sound casual.

I wasn't that much of a prize, but I'd never stayed in one place long enough to know what it was like when someone new and available showed up in town. In Seattle, I rarely went out to bars. Acquaintances would introduce me to people. Bar hookups weren't necessary there.

"We should all exchange numbers," Evangeline said.

"You can reach me through Ainsley. I only have my work phone with me here." A complete fabrication, but if it kept them from making unsolicited calls, I didn't feel sorry for lying. I glanced at Celia and tilted my head toward the door to get us moving. "It was nice meeting you all."

Ainsley came closer and wrapped me in a hug. "Sorry," she whispered, obviously not realizing her colleagues would descend on me like buzzards on a carcass. Almost as if it were a competition among them to see who could interest me, rather than a true desire to get to know me. Based on the competitive nature of most academics, it wouldn't surprise me.

I shook my head and chuckled to let Ainsley know I didn't hold it against her. These women were nice enough, but I wasn't into it this time. I politely but firmly resisted hugging the three suitors, and after a quick goodbye to the other two and a short hug with Skye, Celia and I were finally free.

In her car, we were quiet until we reached the M8. I needed the quiet, but it was uncharacteristic for Celia. I turned slightly to look at her. She'd been fun and chatty throughout the dinner, but she looked beat now.

"Did you have fun?" she asked when she noticed me staring.

"Ainsley's friends are a handful."

"That's a good description."

"Do you know them well?"

"Somewhat. It's a small academic world here. They're at fundraisers and university talks, and Evangeline is in a book club I occasionally go to. She's very nice. In the history department with Ainsley. You could do worse."

I blinked and wondered if she'd just said what I think she did. "Worse?"

"You had three admirers back there. They're all nice. Personally, I like Evangeline best, but you could have any unattached woman at that party."

"Obv-obv," I cleared my throat and considered what my brain was trying to stop me from saying. Then I went for it. "Obviously not."

She glanced over at me briefly before concentrating on the turnoff to the city bypass. After completing the congested merge and splitting off at the next exit onto Calder, she spared another glance. "You certainly could."

"Not the one I'm looking at, unless you've had a change of heart?"

"Zoey," she said in a tone that conveyed kind admonishment and modest embarrassment.

"I know." She wanted to be friends. I liked having her as a friend. Not sure why I was pushing it, except she made me feel good. Made me feel charming and liked and smart and not lacking. So, I'd ask until she made it clear she wanted me to stop asking.

"I don't understand why you're being so persistent. What we have is good."

"It is, and it's enough. I like being your friend." I reached over the console to grip the wrist settled on the gearshift. She didn't flinch or pull her hand away. We shared these little touches easily, which kept giving me hope she enjoyed some of the same feelings of desire.

"I do, too," she agreed, flipping her hand over to squeeze mine.

The move was likely unconscious on her part and didn't feel like the comforting squeeze of a friend. My touch sparked her to seek out something more. It encouraged me to give her a few more reasons why I was so persistent. "You're cheerful. You think the best of people. That's a rare quality."

She scoffed. "I'm not always cheerful."

"I meant you're not unnecessarily negative. These days, that's almost impossible to find in a person."

Her eyes found mine as she stopped on the street in front of my apartment. As usual, my compliment triggered a pleased look on her face. "Thank you."

"And you've got beautiful eyes."

She tried to scoff again, but the sound came out more pleased than exasperated. It almost sounded like a crack in her defenses.

15

BARELY FIVE STEPS ONTO CAMPUS, I SPOTTED my dad sitting on one of the stone benches along the courtyard where we were to meet a half hour from now. Leave it to my dad to be early and happy to wait without calling me to tell me he was early.

I was about to call out when he stood and went over to say something to a tall man who was talking to someone I couldn't see. My dad held up his phone and pointed to something, asking a question. The gentleman looked perturbed to be interrupted but supplied a response.

When a second question was posed, it looked like the man would bite my dad's head off, so I surged forward and called out to him. "Dad!"

He turned with a wide smile. "Zoey, my girl." His arms came around me for a brief hug. Then, he settled one around my waist to turn us to face the twosome.

My eyes widened when I saw Celia standing next to the tall man. "Celia, hello. Dad, how did you manage to bump into one of my two friends on campus without my help?"

"Just lucky I guess." He grinned, squeezed my side, and released me to shake Celia's hand. "Priam Thais, Zoey's proud papa."

She chuckled and returned his greeting. "Celia Munro. Lovely to meet you."

My dad and I turned to the man standing a few steps away. He still looked perturbed and a lot impatient at our interruption.

"My father, Donal Munro." Celia's hand gestured to the man.

I rearranged my features to show delight. "Oh, this is your dad? It's so nice to meet you." I reached to shake his hand. "Did Celia tell you that her department is the face of the branding efforts for this university? Probably not. She's too modest, and yet, she's the main reason her department was chosen. You must be so proud of her."

My dad's eyes grew wider the more I babbled on. It was so unlike me, but I could tell Celia's dad was no different than the other two family members who'd sought her out. Running the scene back through my mind, I also guessed my dad had intervened in his most unobtrusive way.

Celia's dad blinked, threw a glance at his daughter, and gave a slight nod. "Aye, well, I should be going. We'll pick this up later, Celia. Good day." His head tilted, considering us before he swirled and stalked away.

"So, this is Celia?" my dad asked me, reaching forward to grip her shoulder. "I've heard so much about you. You're a wonderful teacher and cook, or so my daughter tells me."

She smiled, a mixture of pleasure, pride, and relief showing through. "That's nice of you to say. I've heard quite a lot about you as well. It's so lovely of you to make the trip to see her."

"We're on our way to lunch. Please join us," he asked her.

Her hands came up. "I couldn't intrude on your first day here."

"It's not intruding," I assured her, knowing my dad wasn't just being polite with his invitation.

"Thanks, but I have a class soon. You two enjoy." She sounded nonchalant despite her rigid posture. Her father's encounter might have shaken her up if it was anything like her mother and brother's encounters. Anger licked at me. The more I thought about the differences between her parents and mine, the more riled I got. She was so thoughtful and kind, and her parents were constantly critical and cruel. Now probably wasn't the time to encourage her to join us when she'd witness the glaring dissimilarity between my dad and hers.

"We'll see you for golf on Saturday, right?"

"Aye, it'll be fun." She waved at us and turned to head into her building.

"She seems great, Zoey." Dad faced me, smiled that wonderful dad smile of his, and beckoned me back into his arms. "So good to see you, sweetie. Sorry for the short squeeze before. I wasn't sure what was going on with them."

I tightened my arms around him, happy my dad wasn't anything like Celia's. Their statures couldn't be more different. Where Celia's father was easily over six feet and portly, my dad was five-ten and slender. He was fit, but didn't spend time in the gym working on muscle groups like my other dad. At fifty-nine, his short black hair sported a few silver strands at his temples. Likely it would be another ten years before he went all silver. Like my other dad, he still had all his thick hair. He was attractive in a more refined way than Warner's overt California Dude look.

I studied his dark brown eyes. "You overheard something and stepped in?"

"I asked for directions to Skye's studio. Thought it might diffuse the conversation. It was less of a conversation than a berating. They don't get along?"

"Some members of her family don't approve, apparently."

"Ah, hence the 'you must be so proud of Celia' babble." He pulled back and bobbed his head. "Nicely done. I'm proud of you for standing up for your friend."

"She's worth it."

His brow went up as he considered me. I'd probably just given him a big clue as to my growing affection for Celia, but I didn't care. She was worth it.

* * *

Elspeth's arm came around my shoulders as we listened to her husband and my dad chatting as if they'd been friends for years. We were on the last hole of the course where Alastair worked as a golf pro. Skye and I decided to sit the game out so my dad, who was a good golfer, could enjoy his playing time with Alastair more. Even if Celia and Ainsley were giving them a match they clearly didn't expect. Ainsley was shockingly good, shocking because I didn't know this about her, not shocking because I didn't think her capable, or even expected with a pro golfer father who now teaches golf every day. Elspeth, Skye, and I were having a great time as spectators.

"Och, he's needed this," Elspeth said to me as her eyes tracked the hearty backslap her husband gave my dad. "He got a little pushed to the side with all the wedding planning."

"Oh, Elspeth, you should have said." Skye shot concerned eyes out to Alastair.

"No, lass, 'tis just Ainsley and I got a little caught up at times. He loved the wedding and helping out, but he was disappointed Conrad couldn't make it."

Skye saw my confused look. "Elspeth's brother-in-law, and Alastair's good friend."

"He hasn't had a friend to himself in quite some time. Priam is just the friend he needs right now."

"I'm glad," I confirmed. "And it's easy to see Dad likes him just as much." He'd already changed his travel plans to cut his trip to Greece short so he could join Alastair for a Pro-Am tournament in three weeks. For Dad to leave Greece early, where he'd be staying with my great uncle and some of Dad's cousins, said a lot about how much he liked Alastair. It helped that I was here and would be joining their fan club for the tournament. Dad didn't often do things just for himself. He had a set group of friends back home, but they all stemmed from his professional life and work took up a good portion of any discussions they had. This was a nice change for him.

"I hear your other father was in town briefly?" Elspeth asked.

"Yes, a couple of days. He was on his way to Romania. His schedule isn't as consistent as this dad's."

"I should think," Elspeth commented. "Movies, my goodness. That must be exciting."

"He sure likes it."

Skye gave a soft snort from the other side of Elspeth. She knew just how much the whole Hollywood lifestyle meant to my other dad. He lived for the excitement and drama and glamour and even the extremely long hours and hard work. It suited him perfectly.

"Will we get to meet him? He'd sure be welcome to tea at ours any time."

"That's very kind of you. He might come through on his way back to Ireland before the shoot ends. If I can pin him down long enough, we'll be there."

"Elspeth!" Alastair called over before Ainsley could line up her putt. If he didn't look so happy, it might have been gamesmanship to throw Ainsley off. If she sunk this, she and Celia would be in a sudden death shootout with them. "Priam's invited us to Greece."

"That's wonderful, darling, but Ainsley's about to beat you for the first time."

"Och, aye," he exclaimed and stepped back, remembering where he was. Ainsley flashed us a smile before lining up her shot again and taking a nearly perfect swing. It skirted just along the cup, looked like it might drop, and slid to a stop a centimeter from the hole.

Alastair and my dad gave excited yelps and high-fived as Elspeth leaned in and whispered, "She pulled that on purpose."

My eyes found Ainsley's. Nothing in them said she'd thrown the putt. She was congratulating her dad and mine and wrapped an arm around Celia in consolation. Celia didn't seem upset by the loss either, probably never thinking she'd be this close to winning a game against a former tour player. My dad was good, but both Celia and Ainsley were better as a combo.

Skye walked over to drop a kiss on Ainsley's lips and hugged Celia before shaking the hands of the winners. Elspeth and I gave out handshakes and pats on the backs and encouraged everyone to the clubhouse for a celebratory drink.

"Now, what's this about Greece?" Elspeth asked as we settled around a table.

"You're all invited if you can make it. My uncle's place has extra bedrooms and a guesthouse. We can find beds for everyone." Dad looked as excited as Alastair did. It would be a tight squeeze with me on the pull-out couch in my great uncle's living room, but it would be fun to have everyone see his olive farm.

"You've that school holiday coming up, Elspeth. We could make a mini-break of it."

"Brilliant. I'm on the plane already."

"Sweetie?" He turned to Ainsley.

"We'll have to check Skye's schedule, Dad. She doesn't get to loaf like we teachers do."

Skye smiled. "I'll see what can be arranged around the station's schedule."

Priam tipped his head at me and I gave a nod in reply. He already knew I would add the trip to Greece on top of the other trip we planned. Everything was so close here. It seemed a shame to pass up the opportunity to head back to Greece for the first time since the last of my generation of cousins graduated high school. They'd all scattered to other parts of Europe like several of his siblings or to America like my grandfather. Uncle Auggie was a farmer from birth and no one challenged his role as the one to carry on running the family's olive orchard. His home served as the homestead for everyone in the Thais family. It would be great to show it off to my friends.

"Celia, you're included in the invitation. We can show you the best city in Greece. Do you like olives? We'll get them right off the trees for you."

She chuckled and shook her head. I'd work on her over the next couple of weeks. Dad and Alastair would be occupied with fishing and farm activities while they were there. The rest of us could have a grand time looking around the seaside city of Kalamata.

"You had fun," I said to my dad as we followed Skye's car on our way to Alastair and Elspeth's house. We had planned to stay in a hotel near the Glasgow airport tonight to be close for our flight to Spain tomorrow morning, but Alastair put a stop to that. They were putting us up, and Elspeth had been planning our dinner for the last four holes of the match.

"I did." He grinned and turned wide eyes to me. "He played on the PGA Tour, sweetie! Can you believe I played with a professional golfer?"

"And almost got your ass kicked by two nonprofessionals."

"Oh, yeah, how great were those two? Ainsley probably could have made the pros herself, and Celia was very good. Did you know that about her?"

"I played with her, Skye, and Alastair once. She's very impressive."

His eyes flicked back to me from the road, a smile playing at his lips. "She is. Nice and super smart, too, not to mention beautiful."

"Dad," I said through a chuckle, not at all surprised he picked up on my growing attraction to her.

"And she's a talker." His eyebrows fluttered.

"Yep," I confirmed, pretty giddy about that quality.

"Best of all," Dad paused dramatically. "She doesn't seem to mind that you're not."

I let a breath push out. "Not yet."

"Oh, sweetie." He reached out and gripped my hand. My lack of gab had been interpreted by friends and girlfriends as noninterest on my part. He'd always been there to commiserate with me. "There's someone out there who loves to talk and has been looking for a quiet one her whole life. Celia might be that someone."

My shoulder hitched up, but a smile played at my lips. "Maybe." I could only hope.

"When are you going to ask her out?"

"Already have. Three times. She keeps turning me down."

His head pushed back against the headrest before he cast his glance my way again. "Three times?"

"Three."

"Hmm." He drummed his fingers on the steering wheel. "Did she give you a reason?"

"She likes us as friends. I think my temporary status unnerves her a little."

"It would be a little hard to understand at first, but you're one of the most present people I've ever met. When someone has your attention, it's all your attention. That outweighs any transitory status."

My head cocked, having never thought of it that way. I did focus easily when I was with people I liked. Even when I wasn't in the same city, if I was dating someone, I always made time to connect with them via phone, text, or video chat. "Well, she hasn't said yes."

He shot a grin at me. "But she hasn't told you to stop asking either, has she?"

I matched his grin. No, she hadn't. If she'd shown any indication I made her uncomfortable by asking her out multiple times, I would have backed off immediately. Instead, the requests for dates had been flirty and light. In no way desperate or creepy. I hadn't let her rejection get uncomfortable for either of us. I'd give it at least one more shot. Possibly, two. Yeah, definitely two, or more.

16

CELIA'S FRIENDS WERE MORE TOLERABLE
than Ainsley's work colleagues, but still pretty overbearing
once they got tipsy. She'd finally convinced me to
accompany her to a drinks hour out with her group. After
getting a promise that it wouldn't be drinks and dinner and
a dance club, I relented. She'd been asking for a while, and
I kept declining until Skye agreed to come with us. At the
last minute, Skye had to pull out because of some work
fiasco. For a split second I thought she might be fabricating
the excuse, but since it was Friday and Ainsley didn't have
classes, she had to ask me to take her to the airport for an
overnight trip to meet with her network president. Skye's
car was currently parked at my place, ready for the return
trip to pick her up at the airport tomorrow morning. From
what she said, they'd had to fire the guy running the
Glasgow station and needed help figuring out who to put
in charge there. When she got off the plane tomorrow, I
wouldn't be surprised to find out she'd been given the
double duty of running both stations, at least temporarily.

"I feel like dancing," one of Celia's friends, the
Irishwoman, shouted.

Rousing agreement sounded from everyone in the group. Everyone but Celia and me, which was surprising because she liked to dance. But she didn't seem to be having much fun tonight. I hoped I wasn't the reason. Sometimes it was really difficult for me to pretend to enjoy socializing as much as everyone else. I tried, really tried, but without a lot to say, people noticed and assumed I wasn't having a good time.

"Tell me you dance, sexy," the tipsiest of the group asked me. She was a professor of film, no, acting, no, advertising? Who knew? Celia knew everyone on the faculty at her school and at seemingly every other school in the city. It was hard to keep everyone straight here. The Party Drunk was about the best distinction I could give the short-haired blonde. She'd been reticent at first when she recognized me as The American Consultant, but with each drink, she'd become friendlier.

"Who cares if she can't dance? It's fun, let loose, we'll teach you," one of the three best looking women in the group told me. Her long black hair looked silky and touchable, and the caramel skin tone of her Indian nationality looked like it had never sported even one pimple in adolescence. She was the kind of looker who could make anyone wonder why she was single. She'd been an actress but retired early when she hit thirty and was unwilling to get the plastic surgery every agent and director told her she'd need in about five years. Five years later, as an acting instructor, she looked model gorgeous to me, but then again, I liked women who looked like women, not women who looked like they spent thousands on their faces.

My head shook, throat tightening. They'd each had a minimum of three drinks and should have been winding down by now. Instead, they were just starting up. This is exactly what I didn't want to happen tonight. I went to lesbian bars occasionally when looking for company on the road. Other than a few greetings, I was never expected to hold entire conversations while in that setting. These women had been getting bolder over the past hour, asking more and more questions, and if we changed settings, I'd be expected to participate or they'd wonder why Celia spent any time with a silent loser like me. She shouldn't have to defend me to her friends, but I couldn't just become a wild, fun gal with the snap of my fingers. These ladies certainly could.

"I've got an early morning."

"Calling bullshit on that," the most attractive one of the group said. Distractingly attractive, really. My eyes drifted to her time and again throughout the hour. She had loose black curls that brushed her shoulders and tapered back from her triangular face with big brown eyes in a large almond shape, perfectly proportioned arrow straight nose, and a mouth anyone could imagine kissing. Sexuality wouldn't be a factor with the promise of a kiss from that mouth. She was mixed race, not easily identifiable, and like the other two gorgeous ones, her complete package was eye-stopping, not just eye-catching. "No excuses, lass. You'll come with."

"No," I said without thought, then remembered I was in a social situation with people I didn't really know. "I really do have to pick up a friend at the airport first thing."

"Thought you didn't have a car?" one of the others piped up, her bright blue eyes shifting between me and Celia. A flush hit her pale cheeks as if she couldn't believe she might have accused me of lying.

"It's her car."

"Nice friend," the super-hot one said.

"She is."

"Special friend?" the blue-eyed one asked.

"Friend," I insisted. My eyes drifted over the group again. I liked that they all had different opinions, worked in different departments or not in academia at all, and didn't look like mirror images of each other. My group of friends, well, acquaintances because it took a lot to reach the status of friend, were like this as well. I liked variety. If everyone thought and spoke and acted and looked like me, I'd be bored out of my mind. I was glad to see Celia shared my view on this.

"Then you'll come dancing," the former actress stated, her tone assuming the matter was settled.

"No," I repeated. "But thank you." I rose from the table to five sets of wide eyes and one set of relieved eyes. Celia must want to go home as well.

"Next time," the gorgeous one said. "And I'll remember, so don't trouble yourself with looking for another excuse." She winked, kicking up a swirl in my stomach.

My eyes shifted to Celia's, and the swirl turned into a tornado. The gorgeous one may be gorgeous and flirty, the Irishwoman may be cute and charming, and the attractive actress may be pretty and funny, but Celia was beautiful and kind and brilliant and engaging and so many other ands. She didn't seem to get that, though. Or maybe she didn't believe me when I told her so.

"Are we still on for tomorrow?" she asked, a smile playing at her lips.

"What are you up to?" the drunk one asked. She'd been pretty relentless all evening with her questions, and had she not been another professor and known why I was in Edinburgh, she wouldn't have let me get away without putting me under a heat lamp.

"Golf," Celia told her, which was a lie. We were headed to the Royal Mile to walk, eat, and people watch, but she wasn't telling them for some reason.

"Meh," one of them groaned.

Ah, got it. They didn't like golf, and she knew that. They were the type to invite themselves along to anything they found appealing. They were Celia's friends; she should want to hang out with them, but for some reason, she was making up a reason why they wouldn't want to come along. For which I was grateful. I couldn't handle a full afternoon with them.

"Have fun, but remember our dancing date," Gorgeous said.

I swallowed and took one last look at that mouth. Dancing would be a lot of fun with her and that incredible mouth because I doubted we'd stick to dancing only. At least, that's what her eyes seemed to be telling me. All I'd have to do is show the least bit of inclination and that mouth could be mine to play with for an evening.

Outside, I sucked in a breath and let it out slowly. I'd managed to make it through without people realizing I never had much to say. These women filled conversational space easily, often talking over each other but were never bothered by it. That always took a lot out of me, even if I wasn't participating fully.

"Was that okay for you?" Celia's hand reached out to grip my arm. "They're a lot."

"They're fine," I assured her, and had it been one at a time, I would have really enjoyed myself. All of them together? Yeah, a lot.

"Not to overwhelm you further, but I was ordered by no less than three of them to give you their numbers. I'm sure the other two will text me and say the same."

My heart rate kicked up. They were all nice looking. Three of them were damn fine. I should call one of them, maybe all five and see if I connected with anyone. Three more months here, I should do that. Anywhere else, I would have.

"Have you..." I searched for the right words.

"Pulled any of them?" Celia's eyes twinkled as her head shook. "Maisie and I went on a couple of dates when I first started on campus, but we found out quickly we didn't have that thing, you know?"

A spark, connection, blistering lust, cherishing care, an undeniable pull? Yes, I did know. It's what I kept trying to tamp down around Celia so I wouldn't get hurt every time she turned me down. All of that simmered below the surface of our friendship, waiting for a fissure to open and overtake the friendship coating.

"I love them all, but none of us have what we need to be it for each other. We're happy as we are."

I nodded, understanding completely. It's what I had with Skye, had always had with Skye, even though she was smart and considerate and fun and hot and so many other ands. We should have hooked up in grad school or any of the other times I visited whenever I was on consulting trips in her area. But the "it" was never there.

"Not to say you couldn't, though."

My eyes shot to hers. Was this a crack in her resolution to keep us in the friends' box? We had three months to explore these feelings I was almost certain we both shared. If the secret glances she thought I didn't notice said anything about how she felt. We could start tonight.

"Any of them might be perfect for you." Celia's words, delivered in a tone devoid of envy, slapped away the tiny prickle of hope surging inside me. "I haven't seen Damisi show that much interest in anyone in a long time."

The gorgeous one. So, I wasn't imagining the interest in her beautiful eyes. And the fantasies featuring that mouth I'd allowed to run through my head while still trying to concentrate on the conversation around me weren't completely out of the realm of possibility. I should call her. I really should.

"Maybe," I murmured, not loud enough for Celia to hear, or so I thought.

"Yeah? I'll text you her number. She'll be thrilled."

And you? I wanted to ask. *Would you be thrilled if I went out with one of your friends and stopped angling for a date with you?*

"Maybe," I repeated. "She seems really together, poised, aware."

"Aware of what?"

"Of where she is in every moment of the day.

She contemplated my answer. "Doesn't everyone?"

I shrugged. "A lot of people don't give much regard for where they are sometimes. They'll blurt inappropriate things. They'll get petty or angry or exuberant whenever they feel those emotions, no matter the place."

"Oh, well, I can't guarantee she wouldn't express her feelings whenever she has them. She's quite passionate."

"I don't mind passionate. I mind inappropriate." The number of times I wanted to walk out of a public place because the person with me had gotten angry or pissy or overly giddy or any other excessive exuberance when the setting didn't call for it were too many to count. If they needed to vent that emotion, it should be done in a more personal setting rather than making everyone around us or the people serving us experience that awkwardness.

"Like someone laughing at a funeral?"

"Nothing that obvious. More like misplaced anger or misdirected moodiness."

"Ah." Her head bobbed in understanding as we reached her car. "I think everyone is guilty of that sometimes."

My lips curled up. "You're not. Or not that I've seen yet."

She pressed back against the driver's door, her eyes moving up toward the sky as if trying to recall a time where she might have disregarded her surroundings to show inappropriate emotions in front of or at strangers. She could think for an hour and she wouldn't come up with an example. I knew that from the way she handled her extremely tactless family members.

It took her a full minute before her eyes landed back on mine and her expression told me I was right. She also seemed to realize I was again pointing out another of her attractive traits. Something I usually followed up with a request for a date.

Unfortunately, she chose to ignore that. "You won't know for sure unless you get to know her better."

"Maybe," I said again, my eyes locked on hers, not once drifting back to the front of the bar where Damisi was still enjoying drinks hour. "Then again, she doesn't wear the hell out of a dress like someone I know. So maybe not."

I wriggled my brow playfully. If I gave her enough of these compliments, maybe she'd start to believe them and give me a try.

The tiny smile she couldn't hold back said it was still a possibility.

17

BACK FROM A WEEK IN GREECE, I HEADED UP the staircase of Celia's office building. Despite trying to get her to fly over for a long weekend with Skye, Ainsley, Elspeth, and Alastair, Celia didn't go for it. It didn't take a genius to figure out the way her family treated her made her a little reticent to join mine and Ainsley's on a short vacation. True, it would have been a little intimidating. My dad's uncle and cousins were a rowdy bunch but charming as well. Alastair had a grand time, my dad was thrilled to have his new friend around while he bonded with his father's side of the family, and Elspeth, Ainsley, Skye, and I must have seen every inch of Kalamata as well as several historical sites to feed Ainsley's addiction and a possible new book. It would have been more fun with Celia, but we enjoyed ourselves well enough.

"Hey there, Zoey," the department receptionist called out as I approached. While he'd been hesitant the first time I came by, now he turned on the charm to wheedle as much information as possible from me.

"How are things?"

"Things? You Americans." His exasperation amused us both.

"Celia in?"

"She's just finishing up office hours. I think a student's in there now." His gaze roamed over me. "You look tan."

"Back from Greece."

"Hard life you have there."

I winked in response. He didn't need to know I often put in sixteen hours days on these projects. I earned my free time.

A student surfaced from Celia's doorway, brushing past before turning and delivering a stunning smile that could have been for either of us, but I wouldn't let him know that.

"She's a bit of all right," he muttered and looked away when he realized I'd heard him. I nudged his shoulder and tipped my head in her direction, giving some encouragement to go for it. He was young, cute, and it never hurt to ask as long as he wasn't creepy about it.

I knocked on Celia's doorframe and her head popped up from glancing at her laptop screen. A beautiful smile graced her mouth, brown eyes twinkling at me. My heart tripped at how happy she looked to see me.

"You're back! Did you enjoy yourself?"

"I did. You missed a good time."

She glanced away, a slight shrug tugging at her shoulders. If the roles had been reversed, I wouldn't have gone either, but I was pretty sure she'd wanted to. She just didn't feel like she should bust in on the family reunion.

"I brought some of Greece back for you."

Her eyes narrowed, and I flashed back on the last time I came to this office bearing gifts. She hadn't told me yet what made her so suspicious of people bearing gifts. Probably something wrapped up with her family. Every gift having strings or some other nonsense, but it wouldn't deter me. I'd been out of town on vacation and was bringing back something to let her share in the fun. She'd just have to accept it.

"What sort of things?"

"Olive Oil and olives from my great uncle's farm." Her eyes lit up. This was the kind of gift she could get behind. She'd no doubt use them in our next dinner together.

"That's wonderful. Thank you so much, and thank your uncle for me."

"And...flip-flops." From the gift bag, I pulled a pair of flip-flops decorated in miniature Greek flags.

She smiled and reached for them without hesitation. "Flip-flops?"

"You missed out on possibly the last semi-warm weather dunk in the Adriatic Sea this year, so I thought I'd rub that in."

"How considerate of you." She fingered the touristy flip-flops with fondness.

"And," I paused and pulled a box with a ribbon from the bag.

She stepped back from the desk, distancing herself, but her eyes remained on the box in my hand. "That's not necessary. I'm very happy with the cooking supplies alone."

"I know." I walked around the desk to where she'd stood and busied herself with shuffling papers. "It's from all of us, the girls, I mean."

"The girls?" She smiled and her eyes flicked from mine to the box and back to mine.

"Elspeth and Ainsley wandered into a shop only the locals know about. In fact, the woman who owns it doesn't sell to typical tourists. She'll interrogate people before she finds them worthy."

"How did they convince her to sell to them?"

"Those two could beguile anyone into anything, but it did help when Skye and I came in toward the end of their interrogation and she learned my last name. Everyone in town knows my great uncle."

"Good to have connections."

"If she wants the best olive oil and olives, yeah."

She laughed that startling laugh again and my stomach quivered. "What did they convince the woman to make?"

I thrust the box into her hands, not giving her a choice but to take it or drop it. Her fingers plucked the blue ribbon from the white box. She flipped open the box and her eyes flared at the silver bracelet inside. Jewelry was a presumptuous gift, but it was softened by the group aspect of the gift.

"It's beautiful."

I brought up my wrist and jiggled a similar bracelet wrapped loosely there. "We all got one, or her version of what would suit us. We had to tell her things about us."

"Really?" Her eyes looked interested now. It wasn't just a gift; it was a story. "What did you tell her about yourself?"

"Ainsley and Skye did most of the talking."

"They are good at that, aren't they? And you never mind when others do the talking."

I sucked in a breath. "Does that bother you?" She never seemed like it did, but I'd been surprised many times before.

Her brow furrowed and a hand came up toward my face before moving to squeeze the side of my shoulder. "Are you worried about that?"

"I'm," I started and thought about what to say.

She waited and waited for me to think of what I wanted to say. That was also something different about her. She'd wait for me to say something, rather than try to fill in the silence like so many others before her.

I shrugged, not able to come up with words to describe what I felt. Too many people decided I was just too much work to be around because I didn't converse easily.

"You don't need to be concerned. I've told you that when you get sick of my chattering, you just need to say so."

My hand reached out to take hold of hers. "That wasn't my concern."

"I know." She placed her other hand on mine and squeezed. In that moment, I felt she really did know. Not all the reasons why, but she knew I wasn't a talker and she was and maybe what my dad said was true. She was as happy to have someone quiet to talk to as I was to have a talker talk to me.

"Don't you want to know what we all said about you?"

"You all chimed in?"

"We did." I smiled. "It's no secret what Elspeth and Ainsley think of you. They like to share. Skye was her usual considerate self."

"And you?" Her eyes twinkled as she squeezed my hand again. The touch sent a spark of tingles up and down my arm.

"I told her you're vivacious. Lively and cheerful and proud and riveting. Everything that is vivacious is you."

She stepped back, surprise registering on her face. I'd been slowly slipping in compliments ever since first asking her out. She seemed to brush them aside without much consideration, but this one affected her. Some of the others pleased her, but this one got to her. About damn time.

Her eyes dropped to the design and twist of the metal that made up her version of the bracelet we all got. "I don't know where you come up with these things. You're being incredibly nice."

"I'm being honest. Skye could tell you all the same things and probably has."

"No." She shook her head. "She's lovely, of course, and so very kind."

"But you brush off what she says just like you brush off most of what I've said." My hand came up to wave off her denial. "I don't know who made you doubt these things about yourself, but you should believe your friends when they tell you you're wonderful."

She studied me for a long time. Silence settled over us as her brown eyes searched in earnest. "Thank you." It took a moment before she nodded and tipped the box indicating her gratitude for the gift, and I'm pretty sure, the compliment.

"Let me put it on you." I reached to take the bracelet from the box and stopped. "Or," I realized I'd just forced her to wear something she might not like. I'd never seen her wear a bracelet, necklaces and earrings, but not a bracelet.

She thrust her wrist toward me at my hesitation. My fingers brushed her wrist to clasp the bracelet. They lingered on her incredibly soft skin while adjusting the clasp to the back. "It's lovely. Thank you."

"Everyone will be thrilled you like it. I'm afraid you'll have to wear it at the golf tourney when we all get together again."

She smiled and touched the metal reverently. "I look forward to it."

18

THE STUDENT BEHIND THE CAMERA SHOT ME
a familiar look. She and one of the other students who had
been helping me get this footage for weeks recognized the
carefully delivered huff that left the professor's lips. It
would be another ten seconds before—

"I don't see why this is necessary," the whine came
before the ten seconds were up.

"It's not required, but it is necessary," I replied,
motioning to the cameraperson to keep filming. We'd be
doing a ton of editing anyway, she might as well keep going
until I could get this man back to teaching.

"Why?"

"The website and social media pages need updated
content. A three-sentence class description and paragraph
bio next to your picture don't do you or the school any
justice. Nor is it fair to the students who pay tuition, not in
this era. Students need to see what it will be like to be in
your class, what your teaching style is, how the content will
relate to what they want to do."

"Show's how little you know. You're practically
wearing an American flag right now."

I glanced down at my dark blue suit. My silk shirt was light blue, my shoes were black. Red and white were nowhere to be seen on me. My eyes caught the camerawoman's again. She hid a grin as she recognized the look in my eyes. We'd been at this for three weeks and were nearly done getting the footage we'd need to make short clips for each professor's profile page.

"We told the vice chancellor not to hire an American, that you'd not know what we were about. That you could never understand our university or our country."

"I'm well aware that Scottish students get free tuition," I told him in a bored voice, guessing this bit of knowledge was what he was trying to flaunt. "But you have many other students who do have to pay tuition, and they'd like a preview before sitting through the first week of your class and dropping out because they didn't like it."

Students started pushing past us to get to their seats. Normally, this would have been settled and we'd be set up to the side of the room before any students made it inside, but he'd been a whiner, so here we were.

"No one drops my class." His indignation was comical. A design lecturer made the same laughable argument just an hour before.

My response was automatic, drawing on the research I'd done. "You average a 35% drop rate and have a waiting list of nearly that, but only a quarter of those end up adding your class during the add/drop period because the others have already found another class to add by the time everyone drops. Wouldn't you rather only the students who want to be here sign up?"

He blinked at me, incredulity warring with the indignation. "I should have expected nothing less than a cocksure American."

I blew out a long breath and collected my thoughts. "I apologize if I came across as cocky. You're the seventh professor in the last week with whom I've had to make this argument. As I mentioned when we came in here today, this is completely optional. You can continue with your photo and bio and class description in text and image form, or we can add a short video clip of you teaching to entice and assure potential students. It's up to you."

"My page would remain the same?"

"Mostly. We're adding student descriptors to every bio page. They best know how to describe their experience in your classroom."

His eyes widened. He probably wasn't the most popular faculty member on campus, and the idea of students dictating how he's seen to other students didn't sit well. "Very well then. Set up where you need to, but do try not to disturb my class."

"Of course." I swallowed what I really wanted to tell the guy.

Fifty minutes later, we had more than enough to use. Normally we would have quietly left after we'd captured something witty or engaging, but it would have irritated him, so we stayed for the full class. There wouldn't be time for a walk because I needed to get another five clips recorded before the end of the day as well as shots of students in several of the common areas. Celia's television students were providing much of the student-life content and would act as my video editors for the web and social media pages.

"What an astonishing knob," the cameraperson said as soon as we were out of earshot down the hall.

I gave a sharp laugh. "Funny. I've never heard that before."

"We've got a million of 'em," the sound tech guy added, slinging an arm around the cameraperson. If the body language said anything, it screamed how well their bodies knew each other. He had the same body language familiarity with two other camera people we'd used. Ah, to be young again.

"Sorry it took so long. I thought we could grab him and two others during the hour I had you, but I guess we're all an hour smarter about transport engineering."

"Like that'll do us any good," the guy muttered, waved, and wandered off with his girlfriend or friend-with-benes or dude-don't-label-us classmate.

The next crew would meet me in the computer center in thirty minutes. They'd get the remaining five snippets scheduled for today. I had just enough time to dash over to the studio project and check in. Working with Skye was a blessing. Control freaks rock. I need to find more control freak friends. After the initial design talks and project meetings, Skye took over the majority of the problem-solving. Since it was a joint project with her employer, she could sign off on many issues that came up in construction. At many other colleges, I'd recommended renovations, but after multiple meetings with the board or trustees or alumni sponsors, we'd end up scrapping nearly every project. Other than a few squabbles over the cost-splitting on this renovation, the recommendation for a three-set rotating studio, a news studio set with panoramic windows showing the university as the backdrop, and the combination university bookstore slash station gift shop and mini television museum was staying completely intact.

"Hey, Zoey," she greeted as I walked into the lobby of the remodel. She slid the last bite of a sandwich into her mouth as she turned away from talking to two of the construction crew on their way to a lunch break. For Skye, lunch on the go was her norm back in DC. I should feel guilty for bringing it back, but we both knew it was temporary.

"Anything come up today?"

Her hand flicked to some papers on the construction table. "Something with the specialty glaze on the studio's background window. They're saying the charge went up, and it's not in the budget."

My eyes rolled on their own. Contractors seemed to be the same no matter the country. "So basically, they broke something, had to replace it and reinstall it at their cost, and they're trying to make up for that loss with this extra?"

Skye patted my back and chuckled. "That's exactly it."

"We either sit them down for a line-item talk and see where we can help them make up the charge, or we stick to our budget and hope they don't cut corners when we're not around to make sure."

She set her hazel eyes on me, worlds of knowledge seemed to reside there. "When are you free for that talk." She could guess they'd cut corners if they didn't get this "extra work" charge handled. We'd have to negotiate a new amount. They could call it whatever they wanted, but we'd let them know we knew what the charge was for and it would be the last time or we'd find a new contractor.

"Want to come over for dinner Friday? The sheep miss you."

A soft snort escaped before I could pack it in. "Sure they do. It's not another night with Ainsley's colleagues, is it?"

"Thankfully no. I like two of them, but wow, the others are a lot to take. She doesn't see them often on campus, which is the only way they're still friends. I think if they all had offices on her floor, she might consider changing her specialty."

"That's kinda the impression I get with Celia's colleagues, too. Is it just academia? They're all so competitive about publishing and class size and popular scheduling slots that their default position is combative?"

"It happens in television, too, but you're right, some of her department get-togethers are so filled with tension I need an oxygen tank to breathe."

I studied my friend. She didn't seem changed and yet she obviously was. "How's married life?"

Her face broke into an elated grin. "Don't start. I get enough teasing from Dallas."

"She should be thrilled. You married her husband's cousin. You're officially family now." I gave it two beats and added, "Even though you said you'd never get married."

She cuffed my shoulder. "I said I didn't think marriages last, so what was the point of getting married?"

Okay, yes, she had said that. She didn't say she didn't believe in marriage. She said she couldn't imagine a marriage that would last, so it wasn't necessary. Until she fell in love with Ainsley. She either no longer believed that, or she felt her love was worth the risk that it might not last.

"And you? Still have the same views on marriage?"

"That it shouldn't be legal, yes."

She scoffed in amusement. "I hope you don't say that around our kind back in the States. That was their bright and shiny cause for decades."

"I don't think any marriage should be legal, regardless of sexual preference. Legality should have nothing to do with marriage."

"Probably best if you put it that way until the bright and shiny wears off."

"I don't put it any way, anymore. No one understands." Except people who are going through a divorce. They understand how unnecessarily complex a legal marriage is when they're trying to untangle themselves from the invisible contract they signed the moment they added their signatures to a simple marriage license.

"It is a hard stance to take. Believe me, I lived a similar attitude for my entire life. But look at me now." Her eyes went down to the gold band on her finger. A wide smile soon followed. She was happier, healthier, and with more family and a better job and a lovely existence. That was hard to argue with. "Have you asked Celia out yet?"

My eyes widened. "What makes you—"

"Don't even try it. I've seen the way you look at her, and you *talk* to her." She emphasized the word, knowing me well.

"She's pretty amazing."

"That she is." Her eyes caught mine again. I waited for the sure warning to come. We were both friends of hers, but Celia lived here and I was the occasional visitor.

"No warning?" I asked when it didn't come.

"Why would I warn you?"

"Warn me off, I meant."

"Why would I do that?" she repeated.

"So, you'd be okay if I dated her, even though you know I'm leaving."

Her eyes showed that world of knowledge glance again. She shrugged as if the notion didn't bother her, but it had to. It bothered me and Celia, which was why I hadn't mounted a full offensive to get her to go out with me.

"Friday?" she repeated her earlier invitation. "I can ask Celia to join us."

"You can ask, but I doubt it'll change Celia's no to a yes. Don't let Ainsley get any matchmaking ideas because I know that's where this is coming from."

She laughed and slid an arm around my shoulders. "We'd like to see you both happy."

"According to Celia, we're happier as friends."

Her eyebrows spiked. "Okay then."

Skye was like that. She didn't push or prod. She'd given it a try because her partner wanted to see if there was a match to be made. My response let her know I was on the right track. It might be filled with quicksand, but it was the right track.

CELIA

Nineteen

LOPING STEPS SOUNDED FROM BOTH AISLES as Celia's students clambered toward the exit at the front of the room. She liked to think they choose the front exit because it took them past her on their way out, rather than their laziness keeping them from climbing the three tiers to the back exit at the top of the theatre.

"Don't forget, we're to have a check-in on your projects next class. If anyone's having trouble before then, stop by during office hours."

"You're gonna love mine, Prof," Vera said as surely as she spoke all of her lines when in front of a camera. She was only one of four actors in Celia's classes this trimester. She'd been a favorite since the beginning. Not only was she smart and engaging, she took the time to learn every aspect of the media production world, rather than just concentrating on acting like too many of her classmates in the acting program.

"I'm certain I will."

"Not as much as mine," one of Celia's other favorites piped up as he passed behind them.

"You wish, Scotty," Vera, the Londoner, teased him. Only she could get away with being English in Scotland and still taking shots at the Scottish natives.

"I'm looking forward to both," Celia interrupted their sure bickering match. Many times, she'd mentally encouraged these two into a relationship. Their sexual tension had all the signs of something better than the usual student horniness. They probably wouldn't last, as he was going into television production and she, acting, but they could at least get over the constant back and forth their tension created.

"We're over to the café for lunch and a breakdown of our favorite series. We binged it last night. Join us, Prof?"

She shook her head at the offer. So many of her colleagues lamented their students' aversion to them on campus. Celia never had that problem. It probably had to do with the outgoing, unrestricted nature of the students in the creative media department. Boundaries were hard to maintain with creatives, and Celia liked that about her students. Their offer did give her an idea for another assignment, though. The psychology behind binge watching versus the traditional television series model. She could work out the details this afternoon before office hours. For now, she had a walk to get to.

Her plan got delayed as soon as she hit the first-floor lobby. Her friend and former flatmate, Damisi, came through the entrance with a determined look on her face. Upon spotting Celia, she raised a hand in greeting and flashed her beautiful smile. Damisi taught at nearby Edinburgh, and would often stop by for lunch. Seeing her now made Celia's heart thump. Not the giddy kind, the surprised kind. It wasn't raining; the early October day still showed sunshine and a touch of heat, exactly right for a walk around the park with her newest friend. Having one of her oldest friends cross her path first probably meant she'd have to forgo one of the last walking days of the year.

"Just the woman I was looking for." Damisi slung her arm around Celia's shoulders for a squeeze. She wasn't much of a toucher, but she made an exception for her closest friends, which always made Celia feel special.

"What's up?" Celia asked, hoping her disappointment at missing a walk with Zoey didn't sound in her tone.

"Time for another girls' night out. I'm in a rut and need some inspiration."

"What kind of a rut?"

"Publishing. I found out someone at Oxford is researching the same topic I'm considering. He's ten years younger and needs the paper to get an indefinite contract, so you know he's going to pound out something in a minute. I've got no chance of beating him to press. Now, I've got to find another topic that you-know-who hasn't already exhaustively researched and written expertly." She raked a hand through her loose black curls. They fell back into place impeccably, something Celia always envied about her friend.

You-know-who was Ainsley. Damisi rarely referred to her by name in a professional capacity since they were both in the same department with the same specialty, which made Damisi the second-best Scottish history professor at her university and well, the country, for that matter. She knew it and admitted it freely and usually didn't feel sour about it, but when she had to publish and couldn't settle on a thesis that Ainsley hadn't already written about, she could get a little shirty.

"You'll find something. There's a lot of years in that history."

Damisi laughed, making her impossibly gorgeous face even more gorgeous. Every proportion was precise and each feature seemed to highlight the next. Intelligent, funny, fit, and striking. Completely unfair. If she weren't so damn nice and fun to be with, many of their friends would have excluded her from girls' nights. She drew the attention of every available woman whenever the lesbian members of the group got together.

"Girls' night out?"

Celia nodded with a chuckle. "We'll get that sorted right away."

"Make sure to invite the dishy American."

Celia feigned ignorance because she didn't want any of Damisi's caliber of gorgeousness considering Zoey like that. It was entirely selfish of her to want to keep Zoey to herself, but she couldn't help it. Zoey had taken up residence in her heart and mind since their very first dance. A better friendship than she'd ever made so quickly in her life. A level of caring she hadn't felt in years. And these annoying feelings, so many feelings she didn't want to have for someone like Zoey—temporary, beautiful, delicate Zoey.

"She's still around, isn't she?"

Celia sucked in a breath. That's what it really came down to. Zoey was leaving. Not now, not in a month or two, but maybe three. And three months wouldn't be enough for the kind of feelings she already had for her. Three months was barely enough for their friendship.

"Aye, a few more months, I think. The branding is set for next term."

"Only till then? She's a friend of Ainsley's, yeah?"

"They went to Columbia University together. She and Skye were in the same program, but she knew Ainsley, too."

"Maybe she'll stay on."

"Not sure she'll have the choice."

Damisi's eyes narrowed before widening in realization. "Immigration issues?"

"I think her visa is tied to our employer. When the job ends, she'll have to get another employer to sponsor her, and the jobs she takes are usually short-term. It would be a lot of work for her to stick around."

"Maybe I should propose."

Celia coughed, surprise making it difficult to breathe. Just the thought of Damisi and Zoey married twisted her stomach.

Damisi patted her back and laughed. "I was kidding. Well, sort of kidding. She could make someone jump into marriage without looking."

Celia focused on her friend. She'd never heard her speak about marriage so recklessly before. Not with her history. Damisi had some trust issues and even kidding about marriage was a big thing for her. "That might be an interesting conversation to listen in on."

"Do you have time for lunch?"

"I'm done with classes for the day. You?"

"My last is at two. Let's eat." Damisi looped her arm through Celia's and tugged to get them moving.

Outside, Celia sighed, feeling the warmth of the noon sun touch her face, knowing it would have been perfect weather to join Zoey for her walk. She'd lost two dress sizes and a bra size since beginning those walks. They weren't strenuous. She never felt like she was exercising, but the movement in the middle of her day instead of sitting down for a high starch meal at a campus café helped keep her diet healthy. Her lung capacity was markedly better, she had more energy, and she no longer had any back pain at the end of each day. All these physical benefits and she enjoyed time with a lovely friend, too. She really couldn't ask for more.

"Talk of the devil," Damisi said, pointing across the way.

Zoey was walking toward them, her face turned away, minding the students on the footpath crossings. The golden-brown hair she'd been growing out since arriving in Scotland gleamed in the sunshine. She'd gotten it trimmed over the weekend, a razor cut to emphasize the shag style, which now reached to mid-neck. No need for a headband to hold back her fringe as it grew out to one length anymore. Sun-darkened lenses on her glasses shaded her expressive eyes. After getting to know her, Celia was surprised she didn't wear tinted lenses at all times. Zoey was a watcher and didn't like to be noticed doing it. Right now, she was watching the comings and goings of the students as they basked in the remaining heat of this beautiful fall day with a smile pursed on her lips.

She hadn't noticed them yet, and Celia couldn't help wondering how she'd react to seeing Damisi here.

"All right, Zoey," Damisi called to her.

Zoey stopped and swiveled her head to find them. Her expression went immediately to polite surprise, not her usual inviting warmth whenever they came across each other. She gave a wave in lieu of a verbal greeting and took the last few steps to reach them.

"Join us for lunch." Damisi laid her hand on Zoey's forearm.

"Can't." Zoey gestured toward the exit as if that explained everything. It did for Celia.

"You're entitled to a lunch, aren't you?" Confusion marked Damisi's tone.

"I like to walk." She glanced down at the hand on her forearm. She didn't seem to mind it being there, but she wasn't stepping into Damisi's space. Someone attracted to her would likely take advantage of the innocent touch to move in closer. No one usually needed encouragement to move closer to Damisi; she had a magnetic pull unlike anyone else.

"At lunch?" Damisi looked first at her, then swung her questioning gaze up to Celia.

"She likes taking a breather. It's a little time away."

Zoey gave her a grateful look. Others might be annoyed by someone trying to speak for them, but Zoey didn't seem to mind. It probably came with the whole not being very verbal. Celia wondered what it would be like, not to feel the need to talk all the time. Or really very much at all.

"When do you eat lunch?"

"Later."

"We were just talking about a girls' night out. Are you free Friday or Saturday?"

After a moment's hesitation, Zoey gave a hedging response. "I'll have to check."

Celia didn't think the hesitation came from not wanting to join them. Zoey often hesitated before speaking. It was minute, infinitesimal at times. The kind of pause someone uses in professional settings when speaking with clients. A careful choice of words to make certain they're all one hundred percent appropriate for that particular setting. She'd never before met anyone so careful choosing their words.

"If neither works, let us know. It won't be a night out without you."

"That's very kind."

"Enjoy your walk," Celia gave her an exit.

"Thanks. See you." Her brown eyes lingered on Celia for a moment before giving another wave to Damisi as she turned and headed on her way. Celia tried not to stare at her walking away, knowing Damisi would catch her and not wanting to give in to the indulgence.

"She's kinda shy, yeah?"

"She is." And that was just fine with Celia because Zoey wasn't shy with her.

Twenty

THE BABY CRADLED IN CELIA'S ARMS FUSSED momentarily as yet another family member pressed slobbery lips to her forehead or cheek. Along with the wet kiss was usually some sort of overwhelming scent, such as cloying perfume, spicy cologne, leafy cigars, and body odor. Poor baby, but it came with being part of this family.

Celia's cousin gave her a wink and a wide smile as yet another head bent over her baby. Greer went through months of them palming and patting her stomach during the pregnancy, this was the least Celia could do to give her a break.

"How she could choose you as the godmother, I'll never understand," her mother whispered when she sidled up and made a show of grooming the baby in her arms. "How can she expect you to guide this little pearl on God's path when you've turned away from the church?"

"Hello, Mother," Celia muttered on a sigh. She'd avoided her during the christening ceremony, which her mother presided over, and had hoped to slip away before being caught. "I haven't turned away from religion and

Greer knows that. She also knows I'd step in to help raise this child if the situation warranted."

"As would I or any other family member."

"Until she disappoints your rigid ideals and you kick her out, you mean," Celia snapped, surprised at herself. Zoey must be rubbing off on her. Normally she would have turned and walked away, but she was tired of her parents thinking she was less than just because she was a lesbian and no longer attended their church regularly.

"Don't backchat your mother," she reprimanded, as she always did. In her mind it was fine for mothers to snap at, cajole, and criticize their children, but a child could never speak out against the parent. "You've picked up some bad habits from that American. When is she out of your life? It's a short-term contract she's on, is it not?"

Celia's eyes narrowed. How had she found that out? She'd probably called her department's dean, demanding to know when the hired American would be out of the country.

"Are you talking about the American?" her father joined them, his current wife at his hip. This was wife number three, after the affair that ended her parents' marriage resulted in a short-lived second marriage for her father. Celia hadn't been invited to this wedding, so she didn't bother to learn her name.

"Excuse me," she said and turned to move away.

Her father's hand clamped down on her shoulder. "This has gone on long enough, Celia. It's time for you to admit your rebellion was a mistake and rejoin your family. We cannot allow you to be this baby's religious guide as you are now, without religion, without our support."

Allow her? Without their support? She hadn't had their support since coming out to them. In fact, it was worse than losing their support. She had to endure their scathing judgment time and again, and still be expected to keep up appearances as their faithful daughter whenever certain members of their church's hierarchy demanded an audience. This was the first full family event she'd attended in more than a decade. They knew nothing of her life. Of her religion. Of the fact that she'd found a much more accepting church and attended regularly.

"You have the magic touch, Celia." Her cousin stepped up and swiped two fingers over her daughter's head while smiling politely at her aunt and uncle. "If you weren't such an amazing professor, I'd suggest you open a daycare business."

Happy to have the distraction, Celia tilted the baby slightly, letting her be both shield and distraction. "She's an angel."

"Of course she is," Greer exclaimed proudly.

"Are you certain you don't want to include another choice as godmother?" Celia's mother suggested, her sweetest smile in place.

"Why would I? I have my best and first choice in place."

Celia couldn't help beaming, pride and a bit of smugness at the crestfallen look on her parents' faces. She handed the baby back to her cousin, leaned in and whispered, "I'm going to take my leave. Are we still on for later?"

Her cousin nodded as she cradled her child like an expert and not the novice parent she was. Her maneuver helped clear the path for Celia to escape the church without running into any other family members. She'd already spent enough time with her cousin's part of the family at this event, and tonight, they'd have their true celebration.

When the doorbell rang hours later, her home was ready for the visitors she expected. Her cousin was only in town for the weekend, and Celia wanted as much time with her and her aunt and uncle as possible.

"Are we early?" Skye asked as she stepped inside. She used her free hand to wrap around Celia in greeting. Her other hand gripped Ainsley's still, something neither of them seemed to realize they often did. Celia had known Ainsley for years and never seen her so smitten until her former college flatmate uprooted her life to move to Scotland to be with Ainsley. They had what Celia thought of as the ideal relationship: not too dependent but not too separate. They were supportive and cheering and loving above all else, even if they playfully bickered often.

"Hello, proud godmother. Where's the baby?" Ainsley asked as she slipped Skye's grasp to wrap both arms around Celia.

"Not here yet. They probably put the baby down for a nap later than usual after the christening."

"Was it all right?" Skye placed a comforting hand on Celia's back. She'd been privy to many encounters with Celia's family and knew the toll these events could take on her.

"They aren't happy I'm the godmother."

"Screw them," Ainsley said, sounding very much like her American partner.

"Damn skippy," Skye cheered her on.

The doorbell rang before she could get them into the living room. Ainsley rushed to the door, ready to get her hands on the baby. Loud chatter rang out as soon as the door opened. Her uncle's family adored Ainsley as much as Celia did and found Skye to be a breath of fresh air. Her cousin and Skye had hit it off immediately, so they were always included in any family gatherings.

"It smells amazing in here," her aunt praised as she sailed into the kitchen. "You've worked so hard. You always do that."

"It's good to have Greer back. I wanted to go all out."

"Reid is looking into a position in Glasgow, but don't mention it." Her aunt winked, glancing at her son-in-law in the other room. "He thinks it's bad luck to mention something before it happens."

Celia mimed running a zip over her lips, but inside she was giddy. It would be so great to have her cousin nearby again. She'd missed having her around. As one of only three family members who still included her in the family, she left a gaping hole when she followed her then boyfriend to Sheffield for his job transfer four years ago.

"Who is this American your parental unit kept mentioning?" Her aunt's eyes gleamed with delight. She'd never warmed to her husband's sister. She'd been just as supportive as her uncle after Celia had shown up on their doorstep during a break from graduate school when she'd finally had the courage to come out to her parents. Their closeminded reaction left Celia in emotional turmoil and without a place to stay for the remainder of her uni break. Her uncle and aunt had taken her in as if she'd always lived with them. Her aunt provided emotional support and her uncle was righteously upset at his bigoted sister. Her cousin ditched her shared flat and promised parties with uni friends in Glasgow to spend the rest of their winter break with her and show support before Celia could return to the University of Southern California to resume her studies. As awful as that school break had been, Celia was thankful for the opportunity to become even closer with this part of her family.

"Not Skye?" her uncle asked, joining them. He liked annoying his sister as much as his wife did.

Celia chucked. "Skye's friend, actually. They went to grad school together, and she's here on a contract with my employer."

"She's a special someone?" Her aunt introduced her to every single woman she could find, no matter her sexuality. Her aunt was one of her biggest champions and felt that someone was missing out by not being in Celia's life.

"She's amazing. She'll be here s—"

Her words were cut off by another doorbell. She was thrilled when Zoey agreed to drop in to meet her family. She assured her that it wouldn't just be family. Her cousin was inviting several friends who hadn't been invited to the family-only christening. Zoey finally agreed when Celia assured her that Skye and Ainsley would also be here.

"We could have picked you up," Skye was saying to her friend as they joined the greeting party in the living room.

"I like to walk," Zoey responded, her eyes darting around the living room until they snagged on Celia and remained. A smile tugged at her lips as her shoulders relaxed a fraction.

"It's raining and three miles away."

"Leave her be, darling. She likes to walk," Ainsley warned, then tilted the baby in her arms. "Look at this gorgeous baby, Zoey."

Everyone laughed at Ainsley's distraction tactic. Zoey followed her instructions and a sweeter smile came over her face, as it would with anyone looking at her beautiful goddaughter. Zoey's eyes lifted and found Celia's again, understanding in them. As if she knew without any words needing to be said how important this little girl was to cementing Celia's role in her uncle's branch of the family tree.

"You must be Zoey." Celia's aunt thrust out her hand, which prompted Celia to make introductions around. As everyone started conversing, Celia was again amazed at just how little Zoey needed to say to be included in the gathering.

"She's tidy, cousin," Greer whispered as she came into the kitchen to help Celia plate some appetizers. "Have you asked her out?"

Celia swatted her shoulder, her eyes peeking back at the living room where everyone had settled in to talk about the christening. She'd made the mistake of telling her cousin about Zoey's sexuality on one of their phone calls. Now that her cousin had met her, she'd probably never relent until Zoey left.

"Don't tell me she's not your type. She's smart and sweet. That's a rare combo these days."

"I know, but she's not staying and she's too..."

"Too what?"

Yeah, too what? Too gorgeous? Too sweet? Too skinny? Too smart? Too in demand? "She's not staying."

Her cousin shrugged. "So, have some fun while she's here. I should have had more fun before settling down. Now I barely get two hours of sleep a night and don't have the energy for that kind of fun anymore."

Celia smiled at her fatigued cousin. "That won't last forever. She'll start sleeping through the night soon enough, and if you move back this way, you could have loads of family members happy to take on a night shift here and there for you."

She smiled and held up crossed fingers. "I'm hoping Reid gets that job. I've missed this, being here, having you and my folks around. My friends in Sheffield just aren't the same, you know?"

After spending six years in the States attending school, yeah, she did know. She'd made some wonderful friends, but she never belonged. It wasn't just the accent or her upbringing. She'd chosen quite possibly the worst location to try to fit in. The greater Los Angeles area was inundated with people trying to make it into the film and television industry. For someone who'd never even thought of visiting a plastic surgeon and didn't spend three hours a day working out and actually enjoyed eating, she would never look or act the part. She was grateful for the experience and learning from the top school in her industry, but she'd been glad to return to her homeland.

"You took this photo?" Her uncle's surprised voice drew their attention to the crowd in the living room. He was holding out the framed black and white picture of Celia.

"You should see some of the other shots she took of our wedding," Ainsley bragged about Zoey's photographs.

"Her dad's a professional photographer and cinematographer. Taught her everything. We were so lucky she could make it to the wedding," Skye added.

"Could I get a copy of this? I meant to ask Celia the first time we saw it."

"That's on film, but I can make a digital copy for you." Zoey's face flushed at the attention. "Or I can take some photos of you all together right now, if you'd rather."

"That would be brilliant," Greer exclaimed. "We had a quick look at some of the photos the church photographer snapped today and they weren't great. If Reid's brother hadn't gotten everything on video, I'd be heartbroken. Are sure you don't mind?"

"Zoey," Celia interjected, trying to give her an out, but as Zoey flashed a smile and went to the hall closet for the handbag she'd brought with her, Celia could see this was what she'd planned all along.

"Get her christening dress from the car," Celia's aunt instructed her son-in-law. Apparently, they wanted to recreate this afternoon's ceremony, or at least have a decent picture of the sweetie in her dress.

Zoey started snapping photos before they even realized, which was probably what made her so good at what she claimed was a hobby. Before Zoey left tonight, she would have gotten every possible grouping among the guests. Whether she did it to keep from having to make conversation with strangers or because she really was that considerate, Celia didn't care. She seemed pleased to be able to do this, and it wasn't just to be polite. She wanted to do this because she knew these people were Celia's only true family, and on many occasions, she noticed the lack of family photographs. She was doing this for Celia, without doubt, and that caused an unstoppable swell of emotions.

Twenty-One

ZOEY POKED HER HEAD INTO THE OFFICE AS Celia was gathering her things to head home. It had been a long day with the added class she took over because Jenna was feeling ill. Jenna had felt ill consistently this trimester without looking or acting ill. Celia wondered if she was looking elsewhere for a lecturer's post. With the work Zoey was doing in their department, Jenna would be mental to walk away before those efforts shot them into the forefront of television programs outside the US. As one of the mixed media instructors, Jenna would reap the rewards at her next contract signing. Either way, this was the fourth time Celia had to take over her class and her early out day turned into a long one. Seeing Zoey brought a sense of calm to the frenzied buildup she'd been feeling at the unexpected turn to her day.

"Hi, Zoey. How was your day?"

"Good. Yours?"

"Long, but very glad to be done."

Zoey blinked, her eyes went to Celia's packed bag. "I don't mean to keep you."

"I'm always happy to see you."

"Thought you'd want to see the pictures."

Celia felt the invisible pressure of the day release all at once. This was just what she needed today. She waved her friend inside, eager to see what she'd done with the impromptu photo session.

Zoey brought out her iPad and let Celia flip through all the digital photos first. Then she reached into her bag and brought out an envelope, and they went through all the photos she'd developed from film. Greer would be thrilled with the results since the photos taken by the church photographer weren't much better than what a teenager could do with a mobile. These were as amazing as the ones Zoey had taken at the wedding.

"Thank you, Zoey. You didn't have to do this, but Greer will be so happy."

"I'm glad to be of service."

"You're more than that. My aunt is going to want to adopt you after seeing these."

"Your aunt is pretty great."

"She is. I'm lucky."

Zoey's eyes told her she understood the paradox of that statement. Celia was lucky to be so close to her aunt and uncle only because her own parents were so unaccepting.

"Would you—"

"What are your—"

They chuckled at the overlap. Zoey, of course, gestured for her to go first. "I was going to ask what your plans were for the night." She felt reenergized after seeing the photos and knowing how happy her family would be with them.

"I was going to ask if you knew of a place where we might enjoy a dance again."

Celia pulled in a surprised breath. That dance was something she'd relived many times since July. Dancing with Alastair and some of Ainsley's other male relatives had been fun, but the dance with Zoey had been divine. Surely, Zoey hadn't relished it as much. She barely said a word the entire time. Although, she barely said a word most times.

"Has this become uncomfortable?" Zoey took a step back.

"This?" she hedged to buy some time.

Zoey's eyes searched hers, trying for the answer without her having to ask. Celia wondered how many of her conversations went this way with people she knew well. For someone who didn't do a lot of talking, it was probably essential she learn to read people's expressions and body language. "My...asking you out?" Her hand waved between them. "I keep asking because you haven't told me to stop, but it puts you in a position to have to say 'no' or 'stop' and that's unfair."

It would be if she minded. Secretly, she relished the fantasy that Zoey desired her, even if it was more likely that Zoey enjoyed a chase. If Zoey actually caught her, would she really want to keep her?

"Be honest, Zoey. The only reason you asked me to dance was because you felt sorry for me after Ainsley's cousin was cruel." Her breath held as she prayed her guess was wrong. That everything she felt while they were dancing, how Zoey had looked at her, how much she didn't seem to mind twirling her around the dance floor was as genuine as Zoey had been their entire friendship.

"That's not true."

She pushed out a breath, relieved at the convincing tone. "Then why?"

Zoey looked away, gathering her thoughts as she always did. Celia had come to enjoy this about her. The longer she took, the more eloquent her words. "Because all evening you had this look that said there was no other place in the world you'd rather be than at that wedding." She smiled wistfully. "You could have been granted a wish to go anywhere, with anyone, at any time in history, and you would have chosen to be right there sharing in your friend's wedding. That was your demeanor all evening until you asked that jerk to dance. Then you wanted to be anywhere else but there. And I wanted to go with you."

"Why? You didn't know me. We hadn't even spoken because you were always flitting around the edges behind your camera."

She chuckled and shook her head as if Celia were crazy to ask. "You have a warmth that draws people in, and you're not stingy with it. You don't pick and choose. You share it with everyone, no matter how petty some people are." Zoey shifted her gaze to stare at her, and into her. "Call me selfish, but I can't get enough of it."

Celia felt her mouth nudge open and brow lift in surprise. How could someone who barely speaks be so riveting?

Zoey took a step closer, "You embolden me, and I've needed that for a long time. It's why I keep asking you out. But I can stop if you're—"

"Yes." The word came without thought from her lips, surprising not only her but apparently Zoey as well.

"W-what?" she blurted her own reply.

"Yes, I'll go out with you. Dancing, dinner, any of the other suggestions you've been making." All of them, even if it will crush her when Zoey leaves. The fleeting moments they'll get will just have to be enough.

"Yes?" Her eyes blinked rapidly. "Really? Yes?" More blinking. She'd shocked her, the look quite charming on the normally unflappable woman. "Great, good, yeah, good. Okay."

Celia grinned. "Now you're flustered? The only time you ever seem a little cocky is when you've been asking me out. I finally agree, and you get flustered? That's rich and so wonderful. Makes me sure I made the right decision." Even if it will end up breaking her heart because she knew it would be next to impossible not to fall for this woman, no matter how little time they had together. Unless Zoey was a lousy date. Should she hope for that? Oh, who was she kidding? She was already a little in love with her, one lousy date wouldn't change that.

"Okay, so dancing? Or dinner? No, I'll think of something good."

She was so damn attractive when she was flustered. Attractive when she was confident, too. Celia placed her hand over the one on her arm and squeezed.

"I'm up for anything," Celia told her, and for the first time in her dating life, because of this woman, she knew that to be true.

Twenty-Two

CELIA RAN HER HANDS DOWN THE FRONT OF her dress. She let out a nervous breath. It was just Zoey. They'd been out many times. Stayed in many times. This time shouldn't be any different. Yet her lips wouldn't stop twitching as she stared at her reflection. She reached up to pinch the corner of her lip, applying enough pressure to sting but not leave a mark. After ten seconds, she did the same to the other side. That seemed to do the trick.

Clear lip gloss added a subtle shimmer to the dusky pink. Her mouth was her favorite feature with its full bottom lip and finely bowed upper. Not too big or small, definitely better than her plain brown, boring eyes. Although, Zoey had beautiful eyes and they were brown. Honey brown with a dark chocolate border. She'd caught herself staring at them many times. There were times when she thought Zoey had been staring at her, but she was so subtle, about everything really, it was hard to tell.

One last brush through her hair. Should she wear it up? No, that was trying too hard. The strands fell to her shoulders, and with a little product, pushed out from her face just enough for a peek of her earlobes sporting drop gemstone earrings. They went nicely with the dress. Now for shoes. Zoey hinted they'd be spending time on their feet for this mystery outing. No matter how much Celia had tested, Zoey hadn't given up what they'd be doing. Thankfully it wasn't raining, so she could go with an open toe sling-back.

When the doorbell rang, Celia took one last look in the mirror. It was early for a date, but this was part of the mystery. She hoped she wouldn't be horribly overdressed for an afternoon at the karting track or something. Zoey was adventurous, but she would have warned her to dress casually if she'd booked something like that.

On her doorstep, Zoey stood looking only slightly less nervous than Celia felt. Her smile was full, a hint of relief, as if she'd been worried Celia wouldn't be home. Her eyes skimmed over Celia, down to her shoes, then back up and flared in appreciation.

A whirlwind of butterflies took off inside Celia's stomach. Her heart skipped into a steady beat, something she'd been trying to calm for weeks, or months, possibly since Zoey had stepped in and pulled her free of a humiliating moment. She'd been called worse before, and the guy had been drunk and an asshole to begin with, but it still hurt, as it always did. Yet Zoey disrupted those hurt feelings by asking her to dance without an ounce of pity in her eyes. Zoey asked her when she'd not danced with anyone else at the wedding, when she'd spent the entire evening looking at everyone through a camera lens. She put that aside to dance with Celia and gaze at her with the same appreciation she was showing now. Like it didn't matter to her that Celia was full-figured when Zoey would need to gain weight in order to qualify as model-thin. Her gaze during their dance said that Celia was the most beautiful woman at the wedding, which was crazy given how gorgeous the brides looked. All the same, Zoey danced with her and only her, and Celia forgot all about the asshole who'd called her a dumpy cow. It was likely then the start of this thrilling turmoil of sensations. Not knowing who Zoey would be in her life, allowing the friendship, craving it, deflecting anything more because it would all lead to this—these butterflies and heart palpitations and dry mouth and scrambled thoughts.

"You look lovely."

Celia let out a breathy chuckle. Zoey didn't speak a lot, but the words she chose were always impactful. "Thanks, so do you." And she did. Zoey wore a new set of trousers, adding to her brilliantly organized traveling wardrobe. She packed enough to fill out her week, but she'd gone shopping for this date, adding the trousers and a stylish scarf to the mix. Everything fit her trim figure perfectly, the benefit of being in the perfect size range for clothes shopping.

Zoey thrust a beautifully wrapped bouquet into her hands. Only no, it was heavy and clunky. She looked down at the cellophane with its bright lavender bow holding in the bulky contents. Instead of the flowers she'd expected to be peeking out, she saw the edges of DVD covers. Looking more closely, several DVDs were placed in a bouquet type arrangement. Her eyes shot to Zoey's in question.

"I...I," Zoey took a beat before continuing. "Flowers are so cliché." Her left shoulder rose up and dropped.

Damn, she was perfect. "What do we have?"

"Your job makes it hard to find shows you haven't seen, so I went with ones that only lasted a season in the States before being canceled." Thankfully, Celia had a universal player, as did most of the instructors and students in her department so they could watch shows from other countries.

Celia could see some of the titles through the cellophane, but what really drew her attention was the number of them. "This is too much, Zoey. You must have spent a fortune."

Her head was shaking, as she lifted a hand to wave off Celia's concern. "DVDs of canceled shows are always in the bargain bin, which we've agreed are always cheaper in the States." She took a step back, her hand waving again. "Not that I wouldn't spend a fortune on—"

Celia cut her off. "Thank you, Zoey. This is so thoughtful. And I can use them in class."

Her eyebrows spiked, a smile playing at her lips.

"Class assignments on why these shows were canceled so quickly. Many of my students hope to get jobs in American television, which as we've seen can differ quite significantly from British tele."

She nodded as her eyes went from the DVDs up to Celia's face. It was easy to read her expression. She was happy Celia liked the gift, relieved she'd accepted it so easily, and delighted it would be useful as well. And she had the same appreciative flare, the one that sparked the flutters in her stomach and drumming of her heart and desert conditions in her mouth.

Panda made an appearance, demanding Zoey's attention. Hemlock stayed out of reach, but visible, which still amazed Celia. He always hid when people came over, but with Zoey, he never felt the need to hide.

"Shall we?" Zoey asked after rising back to her full height from her love fest with Panda.

"Are you going to tell me what you have in mind for tonight?"

Her eyes cut to Celia's, a playful look drawing her in. She wanted to shock the playfulness out of her by grabbing her face and planting a kiss on those tempting lips, but she held back. She'd managed to stop the urge before, she could delay it again. It would probably startle Zoey into paralysis at this point. She'd been near paralyzed before. A question, a suggestion, a reaction she wasn't prepared for and she'd hesitate, long past her normal hesitation. It wasn't panic that made her hesitate. She just needed extra time to process and figure out how to react. It fascinated Celia, that pause in Zoey, made her want to explore what went on in her head during those lulls.

"I hope you'll like it." Zoey gestured outside.

Celia locked up the house and followed Zoey down the steps to the pavement. "Did you walk over? Shall I drive?"

Zoey shook her head and led them down the block. Celia spotted Skye's car tucked between two of her neighbors' cars on the street. She wondered if Zoey told Skye why she needed to borrow her car. Would she want her friend to know about their date? She hadn't told Skye herself, but maybe Zoey had. The idea pleased her to think Zoey would be proud enough to ask her friend for the use of her car because she landed a date that night.

Zoey opened the passenger door for her, which was sweet, or a mistake if she'd temporarily forgotten the right-hand drive of British cars. Either way, Celia smiled and slipped into the car, ready to start their afternoon and evening together.

Twenty-Three

AS THEY DROVE, CELIA TRIED TO GET SOME hints about their destination, but unlike the other times Zoey was quiet, this time she was deliberately tightlipped and seemed to relish Celia's prodding. They were headed toward Leith, and Celia wondered if they'd be doing something at the port. It was a little too nippy for water sports, and for that Celia was thankful. Perhaps a stroll along part of the Leith Walk before dinner. Based on the time of day, it would be a long stroll before tea time came around.

Zoey pulled off the A road on the outskirts of Edinburgh and down through the streets as if she'd made this trip many times. Celia knew she walked most places, took the train out to visit Skye, and a bus or rideshare occasionally. This crisscross through town made it seem like she was very familiar with the area, even though she lived more than five miles away. Knowing what Celia knew about her preferred walking trails, Zoey wouldn't be using these streets for her evening walks. She thought city streets were too loud with too much car exhaust. She preferred walking to a park or any of the public gardens and using the trails there.

Finding an open parking spot off the main shopping street, Zoey stopped the car. Celia's eyes roamed the nearby shop windows and still didn't have a clue as to what they'd be doing. Zoey flashed her a nervous smile before reaching into the backseat and pulling out a store bag. Maybe they would be returning something she purchased before getting to whatever she had planned. It was fun to wonder about all the possibilities. Celia's usual dates centered around where they'd dine, or if not dining, some activity that revolved around food, like wine and cheese tasting.

"Still no hints?" Celia teased when Zoey came around the front of the car to meet her.

Her eyebrow shot up above the rim of her glasses, just the one, a sexy move that Celia knew she didn't do on purpose. Not here, anyway. She might employ the sexy eyebrow hitch in a lesbian club, but with Celia, she was simply showing her playful side.

"Are we looking through some shops?"

Zoey laughed at the suggestion. She wasn't a shopper to kill time. Exploring historical sites was more her preference. "Before you said yes," she began, a slight blush cresting her cheekbones. "I forgot about the plans I'd already made."

Celia stopped walking, dread landing in her stomach. "I'm keeping you from something? You could have changed the night." She swiveled back toward the car.

Zoey reached out to keep Celia beside her. "I hoped you wouldn't mind joining me."

Celia's stomach unknotted. She released a breath and faced her.

"If you don't want to," Zoey started, her eyes darting away. "I can take you back and pick you up later or there's a nice coffee shop nearby."

Celia's hand came up to grip Zoey's arm. It helped stop Zoey's uncharacteristic bout of nerves. "I'm sure I'd love to join you for whatever it is."

She dropped the tablet back into the bag and gestured to get them moving again. After two steps, her hand reached over, not a long reach or a grasp, she held it there, letting Celia decide. Without hesitating, Celia slid her hand into Zoey's, clasping together as they matched strides down the bustling pavement. Zoey had taken her hand a couple of times before, once to keep her from walking into a cyclist who'd veered suddenly, and the other time when her brother had confronted her on campus. Neither of those times had been romantic. This most certainly was.

Before Celia realized exactly what street they'd turned onto, her eyes landed on the balloons tied to a street sign in front of one of her favorite places. She hadn't been inside in a few years, but she donated to the cat rescue every year in thanks for the two amazing cats she adopted from them. It looked like they were having an adoption fair today. How much arm twisting would she need to do to get Zoey to stop by for a look?

Apparently not much because Zoey led them right to the sign. "I signed up to help out for two hours."

Celia stared at her, not understanding. She'd looked into volunteering before getting her cats but found her varying teaching schedule always clashed with the level of commitment she'd need to give. Fostering was the best option, and after more than a year of fostering several cats, ended up adopting Hemlock and Panda. "Just for today?"

"I help out every week, but today's a special event. I told them I'd be bringing a cat-savvy friend along. You can play with the cats or help at the gift store or stick with me."

"You volunteer here?" Why this surprised her, she didn't know. Something like this was exactly the kind of thing she should expect from Zoey.

She shrugged. "I try to find a shelter or a Meals-on-Wheels program if I'm staying for more than their minimum time commitment. When I'm on a project, social opportunities are hard to find. Volunteering helps pass my free time and does some good."

"You volunteer here," Celia gushed, reaching to grip both of Zoey's hands. "My cats came from here. Did you know that?"

"I wasn't sure, no." Her head tipped toward the entrance. "Shall we?"

They'd barely opened the door when several women rushed to greet Zoey. Everyone seemed to know her, not that this was a large place with lots of staff, but they all crowded her like she was a rock star.

"Celia?" one of the women broke from the group and turned to her.

"Hi, Joan. Good to see you."

Zoey stepped over and pressed her hand to the small of Celia's back. "Everyone, this is Celia, and she's here to help."

"Wonderful," Joan said, looking overwhelmed. The place wasn't just crowded with volunteers. The fair had drawn in quite a number of potential adopters.

Zoey gave her a short tour of the new layout, ending back in the revamped lobby. Other than a paint job and a mounted television, all the furnishings were the same, just rearranged to include a greeting area and much larger shop that carried all the basic cat supplies along with t-shirts and hoodies sporting a new logo for the shelter and many new slogans. Zoey seemed to have worked her marketing magic here as well.

On the television screen, she spotted a familiar face. Vera, her best acting student, carried on a chat show with several of the cats from the shelter as her guests. Celia laughed out loud at the surprisingly funny "cat chat" as her student called it.

"You'll need to act as if you haven't seen that when she turns it in for her mid-term project."

Celia turned and looked at Zoey. "How did you...?" For once she didn't have all the words to ask the questions she wanted.

"Your lot is very welcoming. I asked if they had any ideas to help promote the shelter, and that genius came up with this chat show."

"And the new logo, the new layout, the expanded shop? Are those student ideas as well?"

Pink crested her cheeks, pushing her loveliness to a whole new dimension. "I do that stuff in my sleep. It's not a lot of work, and the students helped."

"Chat later, let's get to work," Joan urged when she came back with a t-shirt for Celia to wear as a volunteer.

Zoey pulled hers out of the bag she brought. "Unless you want to stick with Zoey, Celia, we could sure use your help in the shop."

She did want to stick with Zoey, but she'd have time later. For now, she wanted to be useful and not knowing anything about the cats in the shelter at the moment, helping new adopters with what they'd need for the cats they were taking home was something she could do easily.

Over the next two hours, she spotted Zoey walking back and forth from the cat cubbies to the viewing rooms with potential adopters. She always had a welcoming smile and seemed to be able to coax one out of everyone while steering them toward the perfect cat and not pressuring those who were clearly here just to look.

"How long have you known Zoey?" Joan turned to ask after she finished helping the last couple organize their kittens into a newly purchased cat carrier and placing a litterbox, food bowls, water fountain, and heated cat beds into carry home bags. They probably would have bought one of everything in the store, but Joan was decent about not overselling things.

"Met her at a friend's wedding months ago."

"She's lovely. Came in to volunteer, clean a few litterboxes, pet some cats, and we find out she's brilliant with marketing."

"She is that."

"Do you still teach at the uni?"

"Aye."

"She's had several students helping out here. Revamped the website, made it a simple task to add new pictures of cats, set up a cat webcam in the playhouse with a live feed, and made sure to get a video of every cat to add to the site. The effect is remarkable."

Celia's brow inched upward. Zoey always struck her as a remarkable person. To be remarkable to strangers, though, was an entirely different class of exceptional.

"It's a shame she isn't staying longer."

Celia's stomach dropped. It was a shame and the reason she'd held out for so long. She had to put that away for now and ride out her decision to just go with it. Enjoy her for now as she'd been enjoying her friendship.

"Just finished with my last, so whenever you're ready," Zoey said as she stepped up to them.

"You've done amazing things. I'll be surprised if we have any cats left by the end," Joan kidded with her.

"Unfortunately, some of my favorites are still here."

Joan reached a hand out to squeeze her arm. "That's because you like the senior cats and the skittish ones."

"They're the best." Zoey winked at Celia, obviously referring to her affection for Hemlock.

"I'm all set here," Celia told her as she finished restocking the cat toy basket.

"Thank you both for all the help. I wasn't kidding about running out of cats. We may have to stop the fair an hour early." Joan shook both their hands and then dashed off toward a viewing room where some kids were pounding on the window to get the cats' attention.

Zoey stepped close and placed her hand on Celia's lower back to guide her from the gift shop. She called out goodbyes to several people and wished them all luck. As they got to the reception area, her eyes took in the crowd still mingling around the cages set out and over to the viewing area. She came to a halt, her eyes landing on a couple with a young boy standing just inside the entrance. The parents clasped the shoulders of the boy, leaning down to talk to him as his eyes darted everywhere. It looked like they were trying to coax him toward the first table with the display cages.

Zoey turned to Celia and glanced back over at the family before lowering her voice. "Do you mind if I try one last adoption?"

Something about the way the boy appeared disengaged while all the other kids in the room were giggling or squealing with delight at whatever the cats were doing made Celia forget about her growing hunger and aching feet. She nodded and watched Zoey go to work.

"Hello," Zoey greeted them in a soft voice. "Are you just stopping in to pet some cats or were you interested in adopting?"

The father glanced down at his son before responding. "We were thinking of adopting."

"Duncan loves cats," the mother said. "He's enchanted with my sister's cat, but I think this might be overwhelming. We didn't think it would be this busy."

The boy's eyes had not lifted to either his parents or Zoey when they spoke. He rocked continuously onto the balls of his feet, burrowing deeper into the space between his parents.

"It is rather loud and bright in here, isn't it?" Zoey spoke to the boy. "Let's move somewhere better, and we'll bring the cats to you."

Her hand gestured toward the left hallway. The boy didn't say anything, hadn't said anything during the exchange, looked just as uninterested in being there as he'd been when they first spotted him, but Zoey acted as if he'd acquiesced and as soon as she started walking, he started to follow.

She led them to an office and offered them seats. The parents sat in the two guest chairs and Zoey indicated for Celia to take the seat behind the desk. The boy leaned back against his dad's knees, eyes darting around the office as Zoey clicked on the desk lamp rather than the overhead light. "Hi, Duncan, I'm Zoey, and this is Celia. We'd love for you to meet some cats."

She took a seat on the floor, crossing her legs and waiting patiently for Duncan to decide what he'd do. He rocked a while longer before sitting partially on his father's feet. The parents spoke about how he loved cats, drew pictures of cats, pointed out cats on the television, loved when the cat next door wandered into their garden. The whole time, Zoey nodded her head and smiled politely but kept her eyes on the boy. It didn't take long to figure out Duncan was special, even if his mother didn't mention his autism.

It was ten minutes of their constant chatter before Zoey spoke again. "How old are you, Duncan?"

When it seemed like his father would answer, she glanced up at him and gave a small shake of her head. It seemed to surprise him into silence.

"Seven, huh?" Zoey said to the boy.

"How did you—?" the father asked but stopped when Zoey's eyes shot to his again.

"Would you be all right with a cat your age? Or were you thinking of a kitten?" Again, Duncan didn't say anything or seem to give any indication one way or another, but Zoey nodded her head and smiled. "Good, there are three cats that might be perfect for you."

Celia watched the parents, their eyes growing wider as Zoey seemed to be having a conversation with their silent child. She could tell they wanted to jump in and respond, but it was clear that Zoey was focused solely on the boy.

"Are there any colors you don't like?" After a few seconds, her head twisted toward the bookcase beside her. "Orange or red?" She waited a beat, her eyes on Duncan, and nodded her head again. "Orange. That leaves out one cat. Now the big question. Do you want a quiet cat or a talker?"

Duncan's lips twitched, just slightly, and he rocked forward off his father's feet and closer to Zoey. His fists bounced once on his knees as he settled his legs in a mirror image of Zoey's pose.

"A talker, huh?" Her eyes found his parents before turning to look at Celia and back to Duncan. "Yeah, talkers are the best."

Celia's cheeks warmed as she realized Zoey had included her in that statement. It was one of Celia's main concerns about their relationship, how one-sided their conversations seemed at times, and yet she never felt like Zoey wasn't participating or interested. She was, she just didn't add much.

"Let's see if you want to make friends with Pinkerton." She got up and sent a questioning glance to Celia, asking if she was okay with staying behind, all without saying a word. She turned and disappeared out of the office, closing the door to keep the still noisy hallway out.

"What do you think, Duncan?" his mother asked. "Ready to meet a cat?"

"You did great, my boy," his dad said, laying a hand on his shoulder.

Duncan flinched and ducked out from under his hand. With any other child, Celia might think this was indicative of some kind of abuse, but she knew enough about autism to know touch could be difficult. Since he'd been sitting on his father's feet before, she knew he didn't have a problem with his dad.

A soft knock sounded before Zoey poked her head back inside. She eased into the room with a furry bundle in her arms. It was a mostly black cat, with splotches of white on his face around his nose and mouth, making the hot pink of his nose stand out all the more. She gracefully slid back to the floor and crossed her legs again. The boy's eyes flicked back and forth between something over her shoulder and the cat in her arms.

"This is Pinkerton." She let the cat stretch out of the cocoon of her arms. He stepped onto the floor, looked right at Duncan, and let out a loud meow.

Celia jerked back after all the quiet in the room. She cringed, worried that Duncan would freak out at the startling sound, but instead she watched in amazement as his hands reached out to land on the cat's back in a gentle stroke.

The cat bumped his head against Duncan, twisting this way and that, as cats do to get more contact in the right places. He meowed several times and it didn't take long for Duncan to make small sounds in reply. His mother had tears in her eyes as she watched her son play with the cat.

"How did you know?" His mother asked Zoey, wonder in her tone.

"Pink is great with kids, but most kids want kittens. He's verbal and that isn't always a desired trait, and he's six. He's been waiting a long time to find his perfect friend. Not to put any pressure on you."

"Oh, no," the father stopped her. "If Duncan wants him, he's got a home."

"What do you think?" his mother asked him.

He glanced up at her and back at the cat. That was it, but she seemed to read his response.

"It's a match, huh?" Zoey asked him with a smile. She looked up at the parents and said, "I can get the paperwork started while Duncan keeps Pink company."

She slipped out of the room again and was back in two minutes, clearly having gotten Joan or someone to fill out the paperwork when she'd gone to fetch the cat. Instinctively she knew making Duncan wait to get the cat wasn't a good idea.

They went over the paperwork and what the cat would need. Celia helped them get the basics from the store and Zoey set them up with one of the staffers who would follow them home for a home visit. Normally it was done before they could take the cat, but with the adoption fair, they were making simultaneous visits with the adopters.

Before they left, Duncan looked directly at Zoey for the first time. His fist hit his thigh twice, and he turned back to his dad, who was carrying Pinkerton in a cat carrier they'd brought with them.

His mother turned to Zoey. "How did you know he was seven?"

"My dad's a speech therapist. I've seen lots of communication styles. Duncan tapped his fist seven times against his knee. When I asked him about colors, his eyes landed on the orange and red books on the shelf behind me." She paused, considering her words again. "Could I make a suggestion?"

The woman's eyes misted over and she seemed choked up. She managed a nod.

"Have his speech therapist try sign language. He may not take to it, but it's often a stepping stone to becoming verbal. If you take away his frustration with communicating, he might ease into verbalizing."

She let out a soft sob before sucking it back in. Her eyes watered and she nodded vigorously. "I wish we'd thought of that."

"You already know how to talk with him, so it wouldn't occur to you."

"You're wonderful, Zoey. Thank you so much."

"You're welcome." She watched them leave and turned back to Celia, pointing toward the office and starting back that way to shut out the lights and close the door.

Celia followed automatically, the whirlwind of feelings she'd been keeping at bay crashed through her barriers coming dangerously close to spilling over as she watched this amazing woman deal with a special child.

Zoey reached over the desk to turn off the table lamp. Celia entered and shut the door behind her without thinking. Zoey turned and smiled at her as she went to turn off the floor lamp. Celia caught her hand and tugged her forward. In the next instant, she was in her arms, her eyes widening a touch before pleasure took over. Her face lifted and Celia couldn't stop the lean down to brush their lips together. A soft sound escaped her mouth before connecting again with Zoey's kiss. Her heart thundered and her hands flexed, aching to grip Zoey's hips as tightly as their lips were clasped in a concert of movement. Celia knew if she took hold of Zoey right now, she'd never let go.

When Zoey's tongue skimmed across her bottom lip, her own reached out to meet it, tangling together in a dance as perfect as the one they shared at Skye's wedding. Another sound came from inside her as their lips glided and clung and shifted in exploration. Her hands contracted again, moving to slide up Zoey's torso. Not allowing herself to take hold, she took a tiny step back, savoring one last lip lock, and pulled away. Her eyes slowly opened, meeting the flare in Zoey's gaze.

"I couldn't wait till later to do that," Celia told her.

A smile pulled at the lips she'd just been kissing. "I'm glad."

Celia's hand swept through the air beside her head. "I hope there aren't any cameras in this office."

Zoey's cheeks flushed, and Celia thought she'd never seen anything more beautiful. "It would be a good show."

The best kind of show. One Celia wanted to repeat, many, many times.

Twenty-Four

BY THE TIME THEY WERE FINISHING DINNER on their fourth date, Celia couldn't help wondering again about Zoey's persistence. She had her pick of several women, and yet, she'd held on and on and on until finally Celia said yes. They'd had a perfect first date, something so unusual but fitting for both of them, and Celia had seen how wonderful Zoey was, not just to her friends, but to strangers as well. And the patience she'd shown with several adopters, especially the last family, it made her heart thump. Even as pressure mounted through their dinner and afterward toward the end of the date, she hadn't become overly familiar or assumed she'd be invited in. She'd been happy with a goodnight snog and asked for another date. The second and third were just as spectacular. She was everything Celia had always wanted in a date, a girlfriend, a partner. Everything.

"Did your cousin's husband hear back about the job in Glasgow?"

And she remembered things and asked about them and checked in and stayed entirely in the moment. How had no one snapped her up yet?

"Reid got it. They're moving back in two weeks. They'll stay with my uncle until they find a place closer to Glasgow, but I think they're going to do what Ainsley did and get a place somewhere in the middle."

"You must be thrilled."

"I am. We've always been close, but especially after...anyway, I've missed her, and it'll be so great to have her and my goddaughter nearby." Celia studied her date. "Are you close with your cousins?"

Zoey nodded before answering. "On the Thais side, yes. My dad's an only child, but he has multiple cousins from his five uncles and one aunt and the cousins all have kids in my age range."

"Five uncles and only one aunt?"

Those beautiful lips pulled wide, teasing Celia with a desire to kiss her again. As much as she appreciated Zoey not assuming they'd sleep together on the first few dates, she could have braved another hour or four of kissing.

"That's a Thais tradition as well." Zoey's response snapped her out of the haze of desire, forcing her to focus, as she should be focusing on getting to know Zoey more intimately than their friendship had allowed thus far. "One girl per generation, until mine with two. Goes back seven generations."

Neither of her parents could even name their great-grandparents much less know facts from their grandparents' era. "Are you the older girl?"

"My cousin's a year older."

"So, she's born and everyone in that generation thinks, 'well, damn, now I have no chance at a girl,' and then you come along a year later. That must have surprised them."

There was that smile again, all light and warmth and unknowing seduction. "It took five years, but yeah, they were surprised and thrilled."

Celia frowned. "I thought you said she's only a year older?"

Her usual hesitation lasted ten seconds this time. "I came to live with my dads when I was four."

Celia covered her mouth with her hand. She felt stupid for her assumption, and she'd probably made Zoey really uncomfortable. "Forgive me. I assumed you'd been adopted as a baby."

"I was. Just not by my dads."

She stared at her, watching the surprise cross her face, clearly indicating she hadn't meant to share that. And the answer made Celia want to ask so many more questions, but she'd already put her foot in her mouth. Yet she couldn't let it go. She wanted to get to know this side of Zoey. She already knew she was an excellent friend. She wanted to know so much more. "Did something happen to your original adoptive parents?"

Zoey hesitated so long Celia almost let her off the hook. "I was returned."

Celia shook her head; not sure she'd heard her right. Returned? How can that happen? Zoey wasn't a television, she'd been a baby. "They returned you?"

She shrugged. "That's what I call it. It's a long story, but basically, they sent me to a specialized boarding school when I was three and some of the staff, including the speech therapist who came in once a week, raised some questions for social services. After some probing, my original adoptive parents decided to relinquish their parental rights rather than justify their decisions to a state agency."

So many questions to ask, but Celia started with a guess. "The speech therapist was your dad?" At Zoey's nod, she wanted to launch into so much more, but she could wait to hear the full story some other time. "Do you remember them?"

"Yes."

No malice in her tone. But even at the age of three she remembered a set of parents who were no longer in her life. "What was the specialization of the school?"

Zoey looked away. "Most preschools aren't boarding schools in the US."

That wasn't all, at least Celia didn't think so, but she wouldn't press. "Your dad saw you and fell in love, did he?" She was starting to think it was inevitable with Zoey.

"He said he always wanted a little girl."

There was a lot more to the story, and Celia hoped to get all of it in time. For now, she could settle for more comfortable topics. "Then he shows up with the first second girl in any generation. How did the Thais family take to that?"

She chuckled, relief and amusement deepening her tone. "It still amazes me, really. They're sometimes so stereotypically Greek, and being Greek is so important. Every birth is celebrated as if it's the only one ever in the family. Then my dad comes back to the family homestead with a child who is not a baby, nor is she likely Greek, but that family of his, my family, did not care one bit. I was my dad's and had his name, so I was as Greek as any of them."

"And a girl."

"And a girl. My dad was a hero, and my cousin Hedy and I have had the men in the family bending to our will since we became a team."

"Sounds just about perfect."

"It is. I'm very lucky."

Celia wasn't sure she'd feel that way if her original parents had given her up. Then again, she wished her parents would give her up now. But that was an adult perspective. She wouldn't know how to feel as a four-year-old, yet another remarkable thing about Zoey. "What about on your other dad's side?"

"He's also an only child. His parents never seemed to get past him being gay. They'd use it as an adjective for everything. They'd say things like, 'Our son is gay married and he and his gay boyfriend adopted a child who will probably turn out gay and he works in a gay photography studio.' They weren't the most cuddly people to begin with. Very different from Dad's family."

Celia's eyebrows rose. "Hard to believe Warner turned out so sure of himself."

That dragged a chuckle out of Zoey. She'd probably describe him as full of himself, but in the best, most amiable way.

"He somehow charms a variety of his colleagues into providing talks at least once a month. It's remarkable how he's able to do it." But not so remarkable, given his daughter was just as charming.

Zoey's head tilted, a frown burrowing between her eyebrows. "What?"

"He's been arranging for someone to speak to my class once or twice a month since his first visit. Surely, he's told you?"

Her eyes blinked the confused glaze away. "Seriously?" She gave an amused snort. "Just when I think he's lost himself to the self-involved environment he works and lives in, he goes and does something like this."

"It's been a lovely surprise. He'll just call out of the blue and tell me he's got someone on the crew or production team all set to make the trip, on their shout, by the way. Are you saying he hasn't told you?"

She shook her head. "That's one of the things I love best about him. He could have made himself look good by telling me about this, but he doesn't. It shows me how much he likes you and how much he loves me." When she spotted the flicker of confusion on Celia's face, she explained further. "He knows how important you are to me."

Celia felt the heat rush through her body. She knew she was blushing. Like with so many other compliments Zoey had paid, this one felt so very honest. Zoey was just as important to her.

As if she could tell she was embarrassing Celia, she changed the subject. "That dress is killer, or what do you say here? Smashing? A triumph?" Zoey's teasing tone made her smile, but the compliment and appreciative flare in her eyes sent another lick of heat through her. She was easy with compliments. Easy, but genuine. Celia had never met anyone like her.

"Either, and thank you. We've already established how good you look." She had, when she'd gone to pick up Zoey to bring her back here for a homecooked meal and noticed yet another new date outfit. The effort Zoey was making took her breath away at times.

"Are they custom made? I haven't seen anything similar in stores, not that I do a lot of clothes shopping, and never dresses."

Celia grinned. She couldn't imagine Zoey in a dress. A skirt, maybe, but she definitely didn't carry herself as a person who would be comfortable wearing dresses. Not a tomboy or butch, she was definitely feminine, she just moved with the efficiency of a panther, and material that didn't mold to her would only get in her way. "I like to sew."

Her eyes widened and swept down slowly over the top half of the dress visible above the table. One she'd made just last week. "You're a designer?"

She chuckled and grabbed Zoey's hand, drawing her to a stand. Together they walked into her workroom. Unlike on their first tour through the house, she hadn't bothered to put everything into the wardrobe to keep this part of her life hidden.

"A seamstress." Her hand indicated the sewing machine sitting on the work table, the material draped across the worktable, and bare dress form waiting for its next fitting. "I follow patterns for the most part."

The tip of Zoey's tongue made an appearance at the corner of her mouth, giving her a sly look as her eyes landed on all the sewing accoutrements in the room. "But not always? That makes you a clothing designer. Do you have a name for your label?"

Celia laughed again, stepping in close to wrap her arms around her. Zoey was always so quick to bestow credit and build up her friends. She could so easily fall for her. If not for that pesky living on two different continents thing. "I would have to share the name with the cats. They won't let me put anything on the dress form without first inspecting it thoroughly."

"I'd expect nothing less." Zoey's mouth brushed kisses against the crook of her neck, raising gooseflesh on Celia's arms. Her eyes flipped up to meet Celia's, an unspoken question for more information hanging there.

"I started when I was sixteen. It was hard to find dresses made with quality material and sewn durably on the clothing allowance I had." She remembered the frustration of split seams with barely more than a tug of the fabric, of clingy, cheap material that wouldn't hang correctly, of styles that did nothing for her body type.

Always full-figured, she liked the way dresses didn't spotlight her waist or her thighs or her bum as trousers would. Shirts with buttons in the wrong place would gap open unflatteringly. Dresses were fun to wear and not at all restricting. So, when the material got cheaper and cheaper in the teen sections at shops, she dusted off her grandmother's sewing machine and taught herself to follow a pattern. Since then, she'd upgraded her equipment and become proficient enough to piece together something from a sketch or an image in her head. The hobby helped her unwind and left her with a wardrobe no one else could copy.

Zoey's head pulled back from the magic she was creating with her lips. Her fingers coasting over the lines of her dress. "It's beautiful, all your dresses. You're very talented."

Celia felt heat touch her cheeks and kick off in her stomach. Half the time, she didn't know if she wanted to rip Zoey's clothes off or cry with joy at the wonderful way Zoey treated her. "Thank you."

Lips pressed against her throat again. "Really talented," Zoey repeated.

She swooped down to capture those teasing lips. Her hands pulled Zoey closer as Zoey's hands roamed her back. The temperature in the room seemed to rise to a level of discomfort. Her clothes felt too hot, her hands needed to feel skin. Zoey seemed just as desperate to get to more of her.

"I need you," the words slipped easily from her lips between kisses. "All of you."

Zoey pulled back, eyes flaring. Her kiss-swollen lips stretched wide. A single nod of her head was all the response Celia needed before gripping her hand and tugging her toward her bedroom.

Twenty-Five

STUMBLING THEIR WAY TO THE MASTER, Celia didn't have time to overthink what they were about to do. That had always been her problem. Overthinking sex. Worrying that their lust would die down once the clothes came off. This time, with her mouth and hands attached to Zoey as they moved down the hall, she didn't feel her mind click on. All of her senses were doused with emotions too strong to let trivial thoughts bother her right now.

Moonlight broke through the storm clouds outside the bedroom window giving off just enough light. Her eyes would adjust to see more, she wanted to see more, but she also knew that would mean Zoey would see more of her. All of her. Zoey's perfect petite body and her not petite or perfect body.

Her bedside lamp clicked on, startling her lips off the jawline she'd been following. Her eyes blinked in the sudden brightness and her hand reached of its own accord to click the lamp off. A short burst of breath puffed against her cheek as a reaction to the lamp going out. She gripped Zoey's face, plucking her glasses away to set them on the bedside table, and placed a soft kiss on each corner of her mouth to distract her from not having light in the room.

Zoey tilted her chin up when Celia kisses her way onto her neck. Her hands clutched and released at Celia's waist before becoming more purposeful, sliding around to the zip at her back. She felt the dress loosen around her shoulders and her waist. Hurriedly, she dug her fingers under Zoey's shirt, eager to divest her of the garment. Of all her garments. With frantic movements, she slipped Zoey's shirt over her head and unhooked her trousers to drop at her feet. Her own dress soon followed. They wasted no time pulling off their undergarments.

A nudge had a naked Celia dropping onto the bed. Her hands reached out to drag Zoey with her and she moaned at the slight weight covering her. Zoey's skin was hot and smooth. "You feel so good."

Zoey dragged her mouth down the column of her throat and onto her chest. Her hands worked just as magically, moving up to cup her breasts, thumbs flicking her nipples to life.

Celia gasped and squirmed, her legs falling open to trap one of Zoey's between her thighs. What she thought would be a calculated move to make Zoey crazy backfired. She was so close to the edge already, and now Zoey's thigh brushing against her center, she wouldn't last. So not what she wanted. She wanted to savor, to memorize, to marinate in these delicious feelings and sensations.

"It's too soon." She yanked her pelvis away from Zoey's leg.

Zoey leaned down and blew cool air across a nipple. Her mouth closed over the sensitive tip, lips soft yet insistent. Celia bucked up against her, seeking more friction. She warred between wanting both more and less contact to make this last forever.

"Keep doing that, and you'll make me come," she warned her.

Zoey's response was to add her teasing tongue to the heavenly suction of her mouth. The tongue lapped and slid and lashed, pulling another loud groan from her.

She skated her hands up Zoey's sides, fingers bumping over her ribs. Their prominence should bother her, but she was too eager to get her hands on Zoey's breasts. When she felt the small orbs fill her palms, all concerns about Zoey's too slim frame left her mind.

Zoey stiffened momentarily, but no sound escaped. She redoubled her efforts on Celia's breasts and slid lower, her mouth dropping wet kisses down her torso. Celia grasped her waist before she could move lower. Zoey hadn't said a word, hadn't even moaned, could she not be enjoying this as much as Celia? Then her mouth was back, attacking her breasts, sliding up, nibbling her collarbones, and taking control of her mouth in a searing kiss. Her hand skated down, burning a path toward her center. It slipped over her mound and fitted perfectly as if she'd been making love to her for years instead of the first time.

"Right there, yes, Zoey," Celia breathed out, panting and moaning as she rocked forward and back to match the rhythm of Zoey's fingers.

She positioned her leg for Zoey's undulating hips, tried to give her the relief she'd soon experience, but Zoey was determined. Her teeth pulled at the skin below her ear as her fingers pushed inside. Celia held on, gripping Zoey's hips to bring her closer, trying desperately to sustain this feeling of reckless exhilaration. Zoey pumped in and out, swiping her thumb and nipping her neck, and Celia lost control, shouting and moaning and succumbing to the months and months of repressed lust she'd been feeling for this incredible woman. Her body shuddered and swayed as Zoey continued to wring everything it could from her.

"God, Zoey, so good." Celia wrapped her arms around her, heart pounding, breath panting, and sated beyond anything she'd ever known.

Zoey continued to press soft kisses to her neck and jaw and face and mouth, letting Celia calm and recover when she must be dying herself. Zoey moved to roll them over, but even with blitzed thoughts and rubbery bones, Celia stopped the move. She knew she wouldn't be strong enough to hold herself up, and Zoey was too fine boned. She'd be too heavy for her. She'd save being on top for the next time when she had the strength to stay up on her arms.

Celia ran her hands down Zoey's sides, thumbing her nipples on the way and drawing a shiver from her. "You like that, don't you?" Her voice was still hoarse from the moaning and shouting and panting.

Zoey's pelvis pushed forward, sliding against Celia's thigh. Celia's hands gripped Zoey's bum to urge a more forceful grind. It seemed like Zoey was holding back, taking care of Celia first, keeping herself in check. That stopped now. She was going to make Zoey feel everything she'd felt, make her scream, if she was the type.

"I want so much with you, Zoey," Celia whispered, brushing kisses onto the jaw that rocked next to her head.

"To touch every part of you, to make you come, to be inside you, to be everything for you."

Zoey's head jerked into a nod as she increased the thrust of her pelvis against Celia's thigh. Celia shot a hand through her legs, cupping Zoey's swollen sex. She groaned at the wetness she found. Her fingers circled as her leg added pressure. She pushed inside, moaning at the feel of the tight, slick channel. Zoey's hips moved faster, and Celia matched her every stroke. Zoey's breath hitched as she went rigid above her. Her channel fluttered and contracted through her climax.

"You're so beautiful," Celia whispered as Zoey collapsed on top of her. She could feel Zoey's heart beating against her chest as her lips skated lightly over her throat.

Exhaustion overwhelmed her. They'd been working toward this moment since the first time Zoey asked her out. She'd held off, not trusting she was anything more than a passing fancy for this beautiful visitor, then not wanting to ruin the beautiful friendship, and finally not wanting to fall in love with someone who wouldn't stay. The effort fatigued her. To finally give in and have it be so much better than she expected, she could slip into a three-month coma and have no regrets. Other than not being able to do this all over again tomorrow and the next day and the next until Zoey had to leave. She wouldn't, couldn't think about that now. Now, she'd pull every bit of pleasure from this moment and others to come.

"A quick kip, and I'll be ready to go again," her voice slurred slightly with the sleep pulling at her.

Zoey's faint laugh pushed through the haze as she settled at her side next to her. One arm wrapped over her, a thigh slid on top of hers. Before Celia fell into oblivion, she realized Zoey's chuckle was the first sound she'd made since they'd started kissing in her workroom. She wondered about that. Would have to think more about that. As soon as she got some sleep and could think clearly again.

ZOEY

26

SOMETHING WOKE ME UP. IT TOOK A SECOND to orient myself. Not my landlords shutting the door on their way out of their house above my garden apartment. Not Skye's sheep bleating a good morning. But not a warm body brushing against me or even an arm slinging over my midsection as would have been my preferred way to be woken up. Prying my lids open, I glanced over to discover what I already knew, even as tired as I was. The other side of the bed was empty.

The noise sounded again. A soft clank, then one more. Celia was in the kitchen, probably making breakfast. It would have been so much better to wake up in her arms, but I'd slept in and I couldn't fault her for foraging for food like a normal human.

Still, since it was her house, I probably shouldn't presume it was okay to use her shower without first seeking her out. Plus, I only had last night's clothes with me and putting them back on after taking a shower didn't appeal. I stretched my arms up, letting my body get used to the idea of being awake. Finally, I was able to push myself up, slip into my discarded clothes, and shuffle into the bathroom. A splash of water, a swish of toothpaste, a hasty finger comb and it was as good as I'd get. Hopefully, she'd still find me sexy the morning after.

Celia was standing at the stove, her back to me, fully dressed and put together. She must have used the guest bathroom because, surely, I would have woken to her taking a shower. I came up behind her and slid my arms around her middle. She stiffened momentarily, almost making me draw my hands back, but then, one of her hands gripped mine as she relaxed into my embrace.

"You're up. I was going to bring you breakfast in bed."

My eyebrows shot up, and I bit my lip. She turned in my arms before I could say anything and leaned down to brush a soft kiss on my mouth.

"Good morning." Her minty fresh breath puffed out as she pulled back. "Did you sleep well?"

I smiled and nodded, happy she seemed so easy with me being here. A couple of my former bed partners could go from being Jekyll at night to Hyde in the morning, as if they'd never invited me to stay over. I hadn't been worried about that with Celia, but given the few hesitant moments last night, I wasn't sure if she'd be shy this morning.

"Coffee or tea? And do you want the full Scottish or are you a toast and fruit kind of lass in the morn?"

I pushed out a breath, deciding whether or not I should lie. She'd gone to so much trouble, and she was used to cooking for me. I could probably eat something and just suffer the consequences later, but I'd have to suffer on every other morning because this wouldn't be a one-time thing. "Actually..."

Her face fell. "No, come now, don't say what you're going to say. You have to eat."

"I'm sorry." And I truly was.

"You don't like breakfast food? I can make something else?"

"I can't stomach it. Sorry. It takes two, sometimes three, hours before I can eat anything in the morning."

"You get queasy?"

"More than just queasy."

Her hand fluttered to her stomach as if envisioning being sick. "Oh."

"But please, don't let me stop you. I'm happy to join you if I can get a glass of water."

"Water?" She scoffed involuntarily, but she walked it back with a bright smile. "Of course. I should have asked before assuming."

"Celia?" I reached out to grab her hand. "Please, eat what you've prepared. It smells wonderful. I'll sit with you."

Her eyes bounced between mine and the food. She was hungry, and why wouldn't she be? Most people are starving for breakfast. Add in the workout we'd had last night and she'd be ravenous. I reached for a plate and handed it to her. Her stomach made up her mind for her.

I filled a glass with water and poured water from the kettle over a tea bag in the cup she'd laid out. By the time I sat at the table, she finished putting her breakfast together and joined me.

"This feels strange."

"Don't let it, please. I'd eat with you if I could." Not for the first time, I cursed my strange eating habits. It was almost worth trying again to ease her discomfort, but knowing how I usually reacted to ingesting anything before my stomach has settled in the morning, I didn't want to risk ruining my Sunday.

"This means you'll have to do the talking while I tuck in." She grinned before taking her first bite and letting a blissful sigh escape. She'd given similar sighs last night, prompting a spike in my pulse rate.

"Haven't seen the kitties this morning." My eyes scanned the usual hideaways.

"They like a lie-in every morning."

"Me, too."

Her cheeks flushed, and I wondered if I could convince her to go back to bed after she finished breakfast. Forget that she was already put together for the day, I could be persuasive.

She glanced up, eyes studying mine. She had wonderful table manners. Even as hungry as she must have been, she was taking small bites and dainty sips. I'd sat across from some pretty atrocious eaters in the past. When I wasn't eating, table manners could become a deal breaker.

"What?" I asked after several long moments of silent glances from her.

"Was...did you...were..." She paused, reminding me of how hard I tried to start unrehearsed speeches. I never knew she was afflicted by the same hesitation. "Did you enjoy yourself last night?"

I let out a relieved laugh. "You couldn't tell?"

Her expression grew serious. "No, actually."

I started forward. "Really?"

"Well, not entirely. What I'm trying to say, or ask, well, say," she hemmed, setting down her fork and turning fully to face me.

My stomach knotted at this sudden somber turn in our morning conversation. Had I done something to upset her last night? Tried something she didn't enjoy? She had stopped me from going down on her, but I thought it due to a fevered passion to kiss me, rather than interrupt me from something she didn't like.

"This is not a critique at all," she couched whatever she was about to say. "Are you always so...so quiet, or was it because it was our first time making love?"

My brow furrowed. I was quiet always, but I didn't think it came through when I was having sex. Certainly no one else had mentioned it.

"You're quiet, I know that. It's just...you were virtually silent."

My eyes lifted to meet hers. Concern met my gaze. Concern and something else. "I see." I used one of my pat replies to figure out how to respond.

Her hand reached forward to grip mine. "You were wonderful. I had an amazing time. I just worried that you didn't enjoy yourself as much as you could have. If maybe you were holding back?"

Holding back? Like insisting the room stay pitch black? Or keeping herself from rolling over on top of me? Holding back by not talking during sex? How could I be chatty when lust blanked my mind? When I was barely chatty otherwise?

"Zoey?" Her entire expression was concerned now. "This isn't in any way criticism. Truly."

Of course, it was. She clearly liked her sexual partners to be verbal. "All right." Another pat answer.

"I'm sorry. I must be feeling insecure this morning. I started thinking about last night and realized perhaps you didn't enjoy yourself as much as you could have."

I swallowed and tried to grasp what she was telling me. "Because I was quiet?"

"Almost silent. I never realized I needed feedback, but I must. It lets me know if I should keep doing something or move on to something else." Her cheeks went pink.

Silent. Quiet. Nonverbal. All things I'd heard in the past from other girlfriends. Never in regard to sex, but in the relationship in general. It was often the last criticism thrown at me during a breakup.

"I dis-dis—" I couldn't bring myself to say it. Even if it was true. "You were disappointed."

"No, never." She squeezed my hand harder. "You could never disappoint me."

Yes, I could. Easily. "You like talking during sex?"

"Communicating, yes. It doesn't have to be sexy talk, although, that's a load of fun, too." Her eyebrows fluttered, and my heart sank. Of course, she would think that. "You don't?"

I shrugged. Other than one lover, no one had ever gotten too raunchy with whispered words or utterances. It didn't do anything for me, one way or another. Clearly, it did for her, which was just my luck. She'd want me to try. Not right away, but sooner or later, she'd ask me to try, and I knew I wouldn't be able to do it.

"It's not important. Really, it's not." Her hand came up and patted the air between us, trying with a gesture to emphasize how something clearly important to her wasn't. "I let my insecurities wind me up this morning. Now that I know you had a good time, that's all that matters."

My lips pulled tight, doing the best imitation of a smile. There's nothing like hearing you're lacking when it comes to sex by your new sex partner. "Did you?" I had to ask. I'd thought she had a good time, but this conversation was taking me by surprise.

"Yes, absolutely."

I should let it go at that. I should, but I knew it would become something bigger later on. "Not as much as you could have."

Her slight hesitation told me everything I needed to know. Talking during sex turned her on. Made her hotter than hot. Was a crucial addition. Would always be the missing piece between us.

"I see," I repeated, collecting my thoughts. "You thought the sex was fine, not great, not even good. Just fine."

"No, no," she began, clutching at my hand again. "It was wonderful."

A romantic description. A polite assurance. No doubt she had a good time. She'd climaxed, of course, she had a good time, but between her climax and mine, she realized she wasn't sure I was enjoying myself, which made her second guess herself and her technique.

"I should let you get to your church thing." I said, remembering she had plans for later this morning. Somewhere in the back of my mind, I'd secretly hoped she might consider blowing it off to spend the whole day with me. That was no longer my hope for the day. I stood, taking my glass to the dishwasher.

"What?" She jerked forward, confusion and upset clinging to her expression. "Zoey, please. I didn't bring this up to point out anything wrong."

I gave a derisive laugh. "You just wanted to know if I'd continue to make you uncomfortable during sex if we carry on with this relationship."

"Zoey!" She couldn't hide her shock.

I was a little shocked myself. I almost never say exactly what's on my mind, but finding out I disappointed someone in bed threw off my usual verbal stoppages.

"I-I," I started and took a deep breath before saying anything else I might regret. "I get it. Really. I do. I'm sorry this wasn't as you expected."

She stood, taking two steps after me as I turned toward the door. "Please don't leave like this. You're upset, and I didn't mean for you to be. I've made a mess of this. I really just wanted to find out what you liked, see if I could do anything special for you."

To make me react to what she did for me. To make me more effusive. To make me more verbal, so she could get what she needed. What she deserved, and as someone who wanted to give her everything, she should get all that and more. "It's fine. I told my landlord I'd help her today, and you've got that church bazaar to get to."

She shook her head, eyes misting. I hated upsetting her, but I needed to get out of here before her disappointment cut straight through my heart and it was too hard to move. She opened her mouth and closed it a few times, rejecting the many things she probably would have said eloquently, but was afraid I'd take it the wrong way. As she seemed to be insisting I was doing about not being able to perform as she liked. So instead, she asked something random. "How do you remember about the bazaar? It's been a month since I mentioned anything about it."

I plucked my jacket off the stand by the door. My eyes met hers and the one consistent truth in our relationship spilled out, "I like listening to you."

She brought a hand up to her chest, probably touched by what I said. And yet, it wasn't enough to stop me from leaving the home of the woman I'd pursued for three months but who'd found our intimacy lacking.

27

MY LANDLORDS' DAUGHTER WAVED TO ME AS I got out of the taxi in front of their home. She didn't resent me for taking over the ground floor flat that used to be her domain through college and a year beyond. But after she'd scampered off to Manchester for her career, she persuaded her parents to rent out the space as a vacation rental to keep it open on the occasions she returned to Edinburgh for a visit. That I'd gotten her parents to rent it out for a much longer term didn't bother her at all. She'd already thanked me for being a good tenant and helping her parents in the garden from time to time. She liked knowing they had extra income and someone around to keep an eye out, even if they did that more for me.

For the third time today, my phone buzzed with another text. Probably from Celia. Probably asking when I'd be home. When we could see each other again. When we could talk. The trip to Glasgow had been a mix of perfect timing and good fortune. Skye's bosses asked me to take a look at the station setup in Glasgow. Since I'd manipulated them into paying for a new studio buildout in

Edinburgh to be equally beneficial to them and my employer, I thought it was the least I could do.

Skye and I spent the week in Glasgow at Ainsley's parents' house. She had full days getting the station organized under the same structure she put in place in Edinburgh and conducting a few interviews for a replacement station director. I had talks with everyone in the station and at the associated university to see what they needed most. As with my current employer, this school could take advantage of their unique partnership with the network. I could put in the same kind of branding efforts there, but highlight their journalism program. Or at the college I'd put off in London to come to Edinburgh. My inbox also had a few new requests from colleges in the States and one in British Columbia. A stint at home might be nice right about now. It didn't matter that I'd been having the time of my life here. But after months of warm fuzzy wonderful, culminating in a spectacular night with an amazing woman who couldn't hide her disappointment in me, the time of my life came to a screeching halt.

Setting my suitcase next to the washer, I headed into the living room and read the latest text from Celia. Was I busy tomorrow night? I didn't get it. She basically told me our night together was lackluster, and yet she seemed to want to give it another try. I'm all for giving someone another chance, but when that person tells you she can't provide what you need, why bother?

I sent a quick text back. The phone rang before I set it back down. I heaved a sigh and answered. "Hi."

"Hi, Zoey. You're back! Was it a successful week?" She sounded so excited. So like her usual self. My heart clenched at how warm and welcoming she sounded. If only I'd listened to her from the beginning and stuck with being her friend, this ache wouldn't be so persistent. It felt like it might never go away. I'd been kidding myself that I could have this amazing but brief affair with Celia and not have it change me forever.

"Good, thanks. How was yours?"

"Fine, but I missed you. Have you eaten? Want to come to mine for tea?"

I did. I wanted to see her beautiful face. I wanted to feel her hands on me again. Luxuriate in her kiss. Bask in the sound of her voice. Listen to all the amazing things she had to say. I wanted all that and more, but it would lead to a second night together, which would go no differently on my part. Then the morning after would be even worse than our first. So, no. I didn't want to go over there.

"I'm dead on my feet tonight. Another time?"

"Oh, aye." She hid her disappointment much better this time. "Will you be on campus tomorrow? Stop by my office or go for a walk?"

"All right," I agreed finally because I wouldn't be able to avoid her while working. She and her department were the focus of my work efforts over these final six weeks.

A breathy exhale sounded in my ear. "Brilliant. See you soon."

I set the phone down, made a quick trip to the bathroom, and then started to tackle the dirty clothes in my suitcase. As I reached for the zipper, a knock sounded on my front door. It was too late for the landlords to be inviting me to dinner. They ate at five every day. Skye left me at her train stop a half hour ago, and I just got off the phone with my only other friend in the city. Maybe someone was selling something.

Two people I didn't recognize stood on the doorstep. Both in suits, both looking official. "Miss Zoey Thais?"

I nodded, biting my tongue to keep from correcting his use of a sexist title. These suit types wouldn't appreciate me correcting them.

"We're with immigration. May we come inside?"

What was this about? I'd gone through customs when I first arrived and when I'd traveled back from Greece. Neither time did I have anything to declare. Still, two officials on my doorstep, I had no choice but to step back and let them inside.

"We'd like to have a look at your passport and visa."

"Of course." I wanted to ask why, but thankfully, I'd been trained not to blurt whatever first came to mind. They took a seat on the sofa in the living/dining/kitchen area as if they owned the place. My head shook as I headed into my bedroom to grab my papers. This wasn't my first trip abroad. Not even my first extended trip abroad, but it was the first time I'd run into an immigration official outside of the airport.

Handing over my passport and the separate document granted with my visa application, I studied them as they studied my papers. They were both frowning and probably would have whispered if they were in their own offices. Instead, they looked up at me.

"This is a Tier 2 visa."

"Yes." Always best to keep responses short with official types.

"Not, as we've been led to believe, an academic visa."

Who would have led them to believe I was here on an academic visa? For that matter, who would have told them anything about me?

"Do you have your sponsorship letter?"

"Yes."

"Who is your supervisor?"

"Vice Chancellor Marsh."

"Fine, we'll check that out tomorrow. Thank you for your time."

Wait, that was it? What was this about? "You were led to believe by whom?" I asked before I lost my nerve.

The taller of the two agents flitted a small smile my way. If we were on an elementary school playground, he'd be saying, "That's for me to know, and you to find out."

The other one responded. "It was an anonymous tip."

I bet it was. If it weren't for the academic guess, I'd say it came from one of the professors who objected to an American coming in to tell them they weren't the most important focus in their university. But they'd know not to say I was here on an academic visa. They'd try to get me in trouble for holding an unauthorized second job with Skye's network. I'd been very careful in dealing with them. Even with the meetings over the past week, I was careful not to take a consulting fee and continue working on the university project while in Glasgow. Who else would object to me being here? Did I piss off someone at Skye's network? Threaten their jobs?

Closing the door behind them, I leaned back and sighed. Maybe this was a sign. Everything coming to a head at once. Good friendships reignited. Job project winding down successfully. Failed attempt at a relationship. Immigration alerted to my presence.

A whole boatload of signs. Should I follow them?

28

THE EXECUTIVE PRODUCER OF THE NIGHTLY news show did not look happy that we'd stolen the backdrop for her set to hide the construction still going on in the new studio. Skye was an expert at calming all kinds of onscreen prima donnas and was applying those efforts to dial back the snittiness of the EP. We were only borrowing the curtain for a couple of hours this morning to take videos and photos of the new studio spaces without all the tools and construction materials still present for the finishing work on the new building.

Three of Celia's students, my favorite three, strode into the space chatting, laughing, and jostling each other. They were giving up serious study time on their finals to be involved in these shots. Not that it was a hardship for these kids. Their photos would be part of the website showcasing the media program. Another twenty or so of the program's students would be showing up in the next ten minutes. Along with all of the professors and lecturers.

My stomach twisted with unease at the thought of seeing Celia again. My trip to Glasgow gave me some processing time after our disastrous morning-after. It allowed me to consider my other sexual encounters. Not every experience could be categorized as great or even good. I hadn't wanted to repeat those performances, but they could have been chalked up to first-night anxiety with someone unfamiliar. It was different with Celia. I was already so emotionally involved, and I wasn't the one who thought we lacked something together in bed. She was. So, how to handle it? That was the question of the week.

When she walked in with two of her colleagues, my mouth went dry. Another pretty dress, another warm smile, another hearty laugh, all things that made me want to go out with her in the first place. Now those things just served to feed a yearning ache I'd never felt before. My plan to suppress any romantic feelings until she decided we could date seems to have failed miserably. Once I allowed the feelings to flow, they burst out with the ferocity of an erupting volcano instead of my usual slow build up.

She caught my gaze and smiled. Skye stepped close and looped an arm around her waist while greeting her other colleagues. I scampered up a ladder to secure one end of the backdrop curtain, blocking out the unfinished portion of the studio. One of the students took the other end before I could and put it into place, ending my excuse to avoid interaction with the group.

"All right, Zoey?" One of the other television instructors snuck up on me as I put the ladder behind the curtain.

"Yes, you?" I responded. Everyone in the media department had warmed to me over the past couple of months. A few of the more traditional academic departments still harbored holdouts, annoyed with any changes, jealous they weren't chosen as the spotlight, but the media folks were happy with my efforts.

"All sorted. Where do you need us?"

I got the professors to mobilize their students and set up the just unpacked television cameras as if this were a working studio. My camera bag was stashed behind the news desk. Two of the students would be taking photos as well, but I was the fallback if their shots didn't get what we needed.

A hand touched my back, brief but recognizable. Her touch would forever be detectible, no matter how brief. "Hi."

"Hey." I turned to face Celia. She stepped back, staying a respectable distance away to go with our professional setting.

"You're busy, but chat later?"

No, but what else could we do? I nodded as one of the students called for our attention. It went that way over the next hour as they posed in our model studio, taking the places they'd take to run the shows while I and two students snapped photos to use in the brochures, in social media posts and ads, and on their website.

The executive producer left us at some point, taking her anxious energy out of the space. Left with just the students and their professors, the atmosphere became more convivial. The instructors and students naturally fell into their roles even without the benefit of a fully functioning studio. Snapping pictures was easy, easier than at Skye's wedding because there was no pressure to get those specific moments. Here, if the student producers didn't show what I needed, another set of students would take over the booth in ten minutes. Same for the kids on the set working the cameras and sound equipment and the ones on screen. By the end of the hour, without glancing at any of the shots first, I knew we had what we needed in my camera alone. Whatever the other two students got would be a bonus.

I'd almost forgotten that my personal life was waiting just off stage, literally, at the moment. As soon as the students and instructors cleared out to get to their last week of classes before finals week, I'd have to deal with something uncomfortably personal.

"Thanks, Zoey. I almost forgot this wasn't a class. It felt so real, and the students really got into it." The professor who took advantage of Celia's good nature most often spoke up. The number of times Celia took over this woman's class was alarming. She had excuse after excuse. Celia thought she was looking at other universities, but her excitement today didn't belong to someone searching for another job. She was likely one of many professors who lost her passion for teaching halfway through her career and either needed to move on or reinvest herself. She was using Celia and any of her other colleagues until possibly today when she again looked jazzed to be doing a job she should love.

I nodded and smiled, keeping my thoughts to myself. Three of the other lecturers came over to comment favorably on the process this morning before leaving. All of the students made a point of saying something before leaving, seeing what many of their professors couldn't in the value of my services.

"You have a Scottish fan base, now, you know?" Celia kidded as she stepped up close to me.

Her scent washed over me. A scent I could now name thanks to those brief moments in her bathroom spent trying to make myself presentable on the morning-after. She used an after-shower powder, not a baby powder scent, something clean, not overpowering like perfume or scented deodorant could be. I focused on the pleasant scent rather than looking up at her because I'd forget myself and want to touch her or to lean forward and kiss her.

"The students had fun and the shots are going to be great, however you use them. I've been telling the dean we needed new photos for the past few years."

Not anything I hadn't heard before. Often it takes someone from outside the system to make suggestions stick.

Her hand came up to squeeze my shoulder. A beautiful, hopeful smile tugged at her lips. "Do you have some time before your next meeting? I feel like we haven't been able to chat since I handled things so poorly."

My head shook, trying to negate her assessment of the last time we really talked. "You were honest. I prefer that to false politeness."

She sighed and pulled me along with her to sit together. Her eyes took in the space. She paused listening for the construction crew. I'd made them take their lunch early today so we could work with the students in peace. We had another ten minutes alone.

"I'm sorry for pouncing on you first thing. It was bad timing. You know how my gob runs away with itself."

"Celia," I started and pulled in a breath to collect my thoughts. "You should never hold back. I happen to like your gob, but you know that."

She smiled, her beautiful mouth tantalizing in its fullness. "I shouldn't have let my insecurities rear up, especially not first thing after such an amazing night."

"It wasn't just your insecurities. You were being honest about what you liked and what you needed."

"I blundered the question. I only wanted to make sure you had as good a time as I did."

"Because I didn't let you know while we were together, and that's something you need."

"I don't need it." She shook her head, a hand reaching out for mine. "I don't. I just needed to know how to interpret your responses. Now that I know, there's nothing to be insecure about."

My eyes locked onto hers. She was convincing herself as much as she was trying to convince me.

"I know you had to travel this week and were doing double duty. I know how busy you were, but it feels like you've pulled back. Like you've decided to walk away from this. From us. And I know it's because you think I was criticizing you."

"I know you weren't." Not really criticizing. She was merely stating what she wanted in a sexual relationship and asking if I could accommodate that.

"And yet, here we are. A week later, very little contact, and no dates."

I could get defensive and point out I wasn't in town, but if I'd wanted to be in town, I could have been. I could have already had a date set for tonight. I could have come back three days ago for a date night and gone back the next day. Glasgow was only an hour away. I commuted farther to work at colleges in my home state and be able to live at home.

"Why does it seem like you're giving up on us?"

I released a long breath. "I don't want to, Celia. I fought hard to get to where we were, if you'll remember."

"I do," she said, a blush cresting her cheeks.

"But you're not being honest with yourself. This isn't just an extra technique you consider to be a nice addition in our normal lovemaking routine. You told me what you need. How much you like it. How it makes you feel if you don't get it." I could feel the frustration building inside me, frustration at her for making this already hard thing that much harder, frustration at myself for not being able to give her what she needs, frustration for already feeling too much for her when I shouldn't and couldn't feel those things anymore. I had to cut this short or my heart might shred into more pieces than can ever be mended. "And not only did I tell you that I don't do that, but I can't."

Her eyes widened as I spoke, realization seeming to dawn. I didn't want this to end, but I couldn't see a way through, either. "It's not something I need, Zoey. I just have to learn to interpret your responses. I don't expect everyone I sleep with to be auditioning for a porn video. There doesn't have to be constant moaning and screaming and talking. I'll learn to listen for a change in your breathing. For a desperation to your kisses."

"S-stop...settling." I pressed a hand against her chest. My breaths were coming in rapid bursts now. My mind felt like a tornado touched down, twisting up all my thoughts, making it difficult to say what I needed. "What you want is the equivalent of saying you like using toys or you love going down on someone, and what I said was, 'yeah, I don't do that. Deal with it.'"

Her head shook again, more vigor this time. "It's not the same."

"You're fooling yourself if you think it isn't. Talking, feedback, responsiveness, it's what you crave. You might be able to go for a while without it, but can you really tell me you'd be okay if you never got it again?" Because even though we'd only slept together once, the connection we shared convinced me we were in far deeper than a short affair. I held up my hand to cut her off. "No, don't answer right now. Really think about it. If we do move forward, can you imagine a sex life without something you've needed in the past? Do you really want to deny yourself that pleasure just to be with someone you were already so reluctant to date?"

Her eyes grew misty as my truth hit home.

I swallowed hard and stood, breaking our contact. "I don't want to give up on this, but I want to make you happy, and I'm not sure I'm the one to do that anymore."

Her gaze was like a heavy weight I carried across the room and out the door. Being noble never felt so awful.

29

GERMAN FLOWED STEADILY FROM BOTH sides of the camera, too fast for my college level courses to follow. I'd held my own for a while, listening and adding a few words here and there, but they'd been switched off to anything but the language of their homeland for the past five minutes. I only hoped the video was capturing what we needed as we'd done with the Costa Rican, Brazilian, Pilipino, and Japanese students before. A last-minute brainstorm hit me with all the extra non-dating time I'd had over the past two weeks. International students added diversity and money to the university. Appealing to more of them with videos narrated by their countrymen showing the favorite places on and off campus seemed like a good idea. The chancellor agreed, especially since it didn't cost him extra. Over the next two days, I'd be dealing with the English-speaking international countries.

I looked at the cameraperson. He was in his last year. Nice kid, transferred in from Heidelberg University to go into the television program. Unlike most of his classmates, he was a quiet one, or stoic, as his classmates always teased him about. With a single nod of his head, he told me we'd gotten everything we needed. For the Europeans today, he recorded three and a French student with a penchant for languages filmed the rest.

"How did it go?" The chancellor met us at the campus studio as we were checking in the video equipment.

"Smoothly," I replied.

He clapped his hands together and then clapped the student on the back as he was making his way out. "I love this idea. It may be your best. If the department you've chosen as the marquee for your branding campaign ends up generating the most income, all the regents will be very happy."

And he'll look like a genius for hiring me, but that was all part of my job. With budgets so tight at most universities, hiring a branding specialist, took a lot of justification. One of my goals was to exceed their return on investment expectations.

"Are the students giving you what you need?"

"They are. Tomorrow we'll be filming students from English speaking international countries. Then we'll edit and get them ready for the new website launch. We still need to discuss the school outreach program and college fair options. Students are highly influenced by personal interaction with college representatives."

"It's something to consider, and I'll discuss it at the next board meeting." He glanced over my shoulder to the closed door and back at me. "We had a second visit from immigration this afternoon."

My gaze shot up to meet his. "Second?"

"I confirmed your employment and provided the paperwork, but this is the first time we've ever gotten a second visit about the same employee."

My head nodded and thoughts swirled. I'd shown them my passport. They'd confirmed with my employer. Why the need to visit again? Was it intimidation? Was this the move they made to pressure non-UK citizens to leave? Or more specifically Americans to leave? I couldn't really blame them. It didn't seem to matter which administration was in office these days, the US had a knack for antagonizing any country, even the friendly ones.

"A different pair of officials. It was strange. Acted like they didn't know someone had already checked on your paperwork." He gave a hearty chuckle. "Government officials, you see. No one ever talks to each other."

"I'm sorry for the inconvenience."

"Not to worry. It was just odd."

Yes, odd. Distressing as well.

* * *

Skye's concerned gaze hit me harder than usual. She'd insisted I come over for dinner, and I couldn't say no. "You've lost some weight."

I tended to lose track of time in the push to the end of every project. Finding time to eat was often forgotten, but people didn't usually notice.

"Darling." Ainsley's voice was a soft warning before she turned to me. "You look wonderful, Zoey. You always do."

Heat crawled up my neck. Compliments from beautiful women always made me blush.

"Right, I didn't mean," Skye stopped herself and gave us a chagrinned look. "I was worried you were working too hard and forgetting to eat."

"Which is why you're subtly pushing food down my gullet all night?"

"And being subtle about it," Skye kidded.

"And subtly trying not to ask about your plans once the new station opens," Ainsley added, batting her pretty cornflower blue eyes.

A thud dropped in my stomach. I was torn about what to do next. Since striking out on my own, I hadn't been able to put a halt to forward movement. Knowing exactly where to go next was as necessary as eating to me. My eyes dropped to my still full plate. Okay, maybe more necessary than food to me. Four offers were waiting. Four very good offers, for four different reasons. Which one would be the most important?

London for a bit of nostalgia and another country on my references. British Columbia for an extended stay at home after the recent emotional tides I'd waded through here. St. Louis for work with the largest university in my portfolio to date. Or Glasgow for more time with these wonderful friends in this lovely country. Of all the offers, it paid the least. It wouldn't be as challenging since I'd be replicating a lot of the word done in Edinburgh. Variety was the reason I enjoyed my job. For that reason, Glasgow should be last on my list.

"I spoke with my boss. We'll sponsor your work visa and split your salary with the university if you go with

Glasgow. No pressure, but I know you were worried about those immigration visits."

"That's very unusual," Ainsley mused, her eyes searching the distance for answers. "Two different sets of agents and both could have confirmed your work status without a visit."

"What are you thinking, sweetheart?" Skye asked.

She shook her head, the wild mass of curls bouncing this way and that. "It's just weird. We've had guest lecturers before who've never had so much as a glance, and you get two visits, even after the first confirmed your work status? I don't get it."

I didn't either, and it still made me queasy thinking about it. Was I now marked on some list at the UK government? Forever to be checked and hassled if I stayed within its borders? Surely, they could look up my collegiate career and see I spent an entire year in their country because I liked it that much. Or maybe they were thinking I liked it too much, and they didn't want any more asshat Americans storming their borders or, more accurately, beaches. Skye made it in to stay. Of course, she had Scottish ancestry, not to mention she just legally married a UK citizen. I could qualify for EU citizenship through my Greek grandparents, which might make me more palatable to the UK government than being a US citizen, but my tax situation was complicated enough without adding another country to the mix.

What was I thinking? I really should take that college in southern Vancouver. It would allow me to commute from home and be surrounded by my dad and hometown friends. That would be the wisest decision, and yet it hurt my heart to think about it.

"If they visit again, let me know. I'll get our news magazine to do some investigating and see if they're abusing their power."

"Don't antagonize them, Skye," Ainsley warned. "Your citizenship is not yet finalized."

"Yes," I agreed, wanting to say more. How she shouldn't screw up her own citizenship chances to help me. There was so much more on the line for her. The idea of anything even tilting the life she'd built here scared me to the point of getting emotional. I couldn't form enough words, even in my head.

Skye looked like she was going to argue but recognized my panicked look and spotted something similar on her wife's face. She sat back against the chair, defeated. She was a champion and used to dealing with problems to which she'd always find a solution. The idea of not jumping in with her sleeves rolled up to knock out everything standing in our way aggravated her.

"Let's talk about more pleasant things," Ainsley suggested. "How're you going with Celia? She's so lovely. Did she have other plans tonight?"

The small lump forming in my throat at the thought of Skye putting her existence in the UK on the line for me grew to bolder sized. I couldn't think about Celia without getting choked up, which made it difficult to find the right words. My mouth opened to come up with some excuse for her absence without having to tell them that I'd failed at my attempted relationship. As usual, nothing came out.

Skye snapped her fingers. "That's right, she's helping her cousin move this weekend. Well, they're cooing over the baby while the husband deals with the movers."

"I'm so glad Greer is moving back." Ainsley smiled fondly. "She's lovely, too, and knowing what we know about Celia's family, it's wonderful she's such a support system for her."

Skye was nodding her head as she reached over and automatically took the hand of her own support system. They were the lovely ones. Such good counterparts for each other. Like Celia and I could have been, if I hadn't screwed it up. If I were capable of being what she needed.

30

DAD'S TONE WAS HESITANT. HE WAS NEVER hesitant with me. I should have insisted on a video chat to see if it was a product of my imagination.

"Dad?" I hoped my tone indicated a plea for him to drop whatever the hesitation was. He was always so patient with me. Always so encouraging.

He blew out a breath. "You know me so well." He took another breath. "I'm thinking of moving to Bellingham."

My eyebrows spiked. We'd lived in Seattle my whole life. His home now was the one we'd moved to after the divorce. He liked stability and wanted to provide it for his family. I owned a condo less than five miles away. His office was even closer. His office assistant had been with him for nearly twenty years. His clients stayed with him for many years. At two hours away, Bellingham wasn't a commuting distance from Seattle. He'd have to give up his office and assistant and all of his clients. It was a massive change, and aside from all the work to relaunch his business, one that could lend itself to him slowing down a little. Something I'd been trying to get him to do for years.

"You need a change." It was a guess, but the long break he took this summer must have influenced this idea.

"I'm considering it. There are a lot of advantages to moving, but I don't want to feel like I'm abandoning you."

"Dad," I scoffed, letting some of my anxiety out in a chuckle. "I'm the one always running off to jobs."

"But you always come back to home base. And now I'm thinking of moving part of that home base."

My heart started beating faster. He would be, and yet, it wasn't about me. "I like the idea of you being in a smaller DSHS region. Fewer emergency calls, and you can stick to the once a week commitment." Social Services has been taking advantage of his emergency assistance for years. With more demand for his type of services and not enough therapists willing to help, it fell to him most often. Working with a much smaller regional office, he wouldn't get nearly as many requests for help.

He chuckled. "I'll forever be glad I didn't stick to that commitment, you know that."

Heat pulsed through me. I was glad, too. Without his willingness to come in and help out on Social Services cases when needed, I might never have gotten him as my dad.

"I'm just at the thinking stage. I wanted to let you know so you can think about it for a while. Then we can talk about it when I see you next."

Another great thing about my dad. He instinctively knew when I needed extra time to process things. He also knew it would be best for both of us if we spoke in person, and thanks to Alistair's wonderful invitation to spend Christmas together at his house, we would be able to do that. I'd normally go home for the holiday, but with a contract end date in the first week of January, it seemed ridiculous to fly home, then come back to finish up, only to possibly fly home again if I took one of the US or Canadian jobs next.

"Stop worrying, Dad. Things always work out."

"Thanks, sweetie. See you in a few weeks."

I clicked off and slumped back on the couch. Things would be different not having my dad a few miles away. We had dinner together at least once a week whenever I was in town. This was almost too much to think about on top of the changes I was going through. Less than five weeks before I was done and still no commitment to my next job. I was dragging my feet, which should tell me to go home and take stock. But home would be different if Dad moved two hours north.

A knock on the front door brought me out of my contemplative mode. My landlords sometimes dropped by on weekends. They were a sweet couple just entering retirement, used to having their daughter living in this space. They'd invite me to dinner more than they should, and I'd make sure to help with anything I saw them trying to accomplish on the grounds or in their house. Since I talked them out of taking this flat off the more lucrative vacation market to live here longer term, I felt I owed it to them. Today would be a struggle to stay bright and cheery, not when I was struggling with so much already.

But it wasn't the landlords. It was Celia, looking beautiful in a long wool skirt and cowlneck sweater. On a weekend, she looked dressed to kill, putting my jeans and thermal shirt to shame.

"This is a surprise," I managed after the shock wore off.

"I should have called but didn't think about it. I just wanted to see you."

"Okay." I gestured her inside. She'd only been here once before. We always hung out at her house to take advantage of the full kitchen, the home theater, and to love on her cats.

"Is it okay?"

I stalled, spotting the tentativeness in her stride as she entered my home. I'd made her unsure of herself. That didn't feel good. "Of course, Celia."

She let a breath push out, indicating her nerves. Her eyes bounced around my small all-purpose living area, glancing at my open laptop and the phone still on the couch cushion. "Am I interrupting work or a call?"

"Just talked to my dad."

Her smile was bright. "Priam? Because I just talked to Warner."

I matched her smile. Ever since she'd told me that my other dad was coordinating his colleagues for her class, I couldn't help feeling proud of him. And happy for Celia. She got plenty of talent through her affiliation with Skye's network, but Dad worked on Hollywood blockbusters and award winners. Her students would have little chance of speaking to people who worked with that kind of budget and equipment and personnel without someone like him to coax them in.

"I need to call him," I said of my other dad. Thank him again. Arrange to meet up with him before his next shoot.

"Is Priam well?"

"He is." I could go into the decision he was considering, but she must be here for a reason. Deflecting wouldn't help. "Can I get you some tea or coffee?"

Her hand fluttered to her stomach before waving off the offer. I took a seat on the couch, waiting for her to join me. She looked and smelled amazing. I'd missed her. Missed being able to gaze into her eyes and listen to her wonderful voice and lilting accent.

"You said I should think about what I wanted. What I needed. I've thought about it." She drew in a breath, and my pulse quickened. This wasn't at all how I thought my afternoon would go. How she'd handle our next conversation. When I'd said those things, I thought it was a convincing argument. One that ended the topic. More rhetorical than thought provoking. But here she was, opening the topic again. "I want you."

Three simple words, and yet, so weighty. When I'd given up on the idea of continuing our close friendship for something more casual, she was here, telling me she wanted me. Seemingly ready to push aside some of her proclivities to accommodate me, because she wanted me.

"I had a wonderful time that night." She brushed a hand through her chestnut hair. My fingers ached to follow the motion, but she was bringing up that night again. The one that put an end to further exploration of romance, yet it couldn't stop me from craving all the luxuries that came with romance.

"So did I," I assured her again.

"Then, I stupidly let my insecurities take over."

"They aren't stupid."

"They are if they convince a wonderful woman I'm more trouble than I'm worth."

"Never," I whispered.

"If I hadn't said anything, we would have continued to have an amazing time together. No doubts or questions." Her eyes searched mine to see if I agreed. She didn't need to search long. Of course, we would have continued if she hadn't made me aware I couldn't give her what she needed. "And maybe it would be all right for me to..."

I edged forward, heart in my throat. "To?"

"I don't have any right to ask this, and it's unfair, but I can't help what I want." She took a long moment, teeth pulling at her bottom lip. "You've become so important to me. From that very first moment when you asked me to dance. Your smile, your kindness, your smarts, every bit of you. You said I was reluctant to date you." Her hand reached out to take mine, shooting tingles all up my arm. "I was and I wasn't. I knew if I agreed to act on these feelings, I'd be so very hurt when you left. I wanted to save myself that heartache."

I swallowed hard and gripped her hand. She always said she wanted to stay friends. Perhaps, deep down, I knew she meant it was a way to guard her heart. I should have felt the same. Did feel the same, but didn't let it stop me. Because, well, Celia. It was as simple as that for me. She would be worth any amount of heartache.

"When I finally relented to my feelings, we were everything I'd ever wanted." She pinned me with her gaze and repeated. "Everything. All of it, every moment. And I don't want it to stop. So, I'm going to do something I never thought I'd do. I shouldn't, but I can't help myself."

Anxiety swirled inside of me. I had no idea what she was going to say and didn't know if I wanted to hear it. I could only handle so much emotional turmoil that led to heartbreak.

"Stay. Please," she whispered. "Give us a chance. You said at one point you had an offer from London, and you went to Glasgow, perhaps there as well? Would you consider taking something here in the UK again?"

Her beautiful brown eyes tore through me, expressing hope and also a tinge of shame at trying to influence me to make a career move that might be contrary to my best interests. I wanted to agree immediately. Felt the emotions churning and hope and happiness taking over. Yet, I knew what came between us before.

"I-I," I stopped and tried hard to concentrate on what I needed to stay, otherwise I'd blurt my agreement without resolving anything. "The way I am...was...that night, it won't change."

Her hand left mine, waving in front of us. "I only need to know my partner is having a good time. Is satisfied. It doesn't have to be verbal. It wasn't until the following morning I started to doubt myself because you hadn't said you enjoyed yourself like I had."

"But it's so important to you. It's a turn on."

She exhaled loudly. "It is, but so is reading my partner's responses. I was waiting for verbal cues when I should have been watching and listening for the nonverbal ones. That is just as exciting to me."

She sounded so convinced. I didn't know if I could believe her. If, after a few more months together or a year together, she wouldn't start to resent my nonverbal cues as nearly everyone else in my life had.

"Your pleasure is all that matters, Zoey. I'll learn to read your cues. I want to learn, and I hope you want to learn to read mine. It's all part of the fun of getting to know a new lover." Her fingers landed on my cheek, stroking lightly. "We need time for that. I shouldn't interfere with your career, but my heart is already lost to you. Will you give us more time together? Are those universities still hoping to hire you?"

They were. Both of them, and Skye's offer to carry the employment contract would make things even easier. It was a good solution and one that would allow this relationship to continue. All the hope I'd been stifling, all the happiness I'd been holding back, all the love I'd wanted to soar, rose up, overwhelming every part of me.

"Are they, Zoey?" Her face drew so close to mine.

"Yes," I managed through the tide of thoughts and feelings muddling my mind.

"Will you stay? Will you give us time to learn more about each other? Enjoy each other? Love each other?"

We already know each other. We already enjoy each other. We already love each other. I could say any of those things. I could say so much more. I would say those things and more.

"Stop thinking, and just say what's on your mind." Celia's frustration and pleading and desperation strained her tone.

I jerked forward, startled she'd lost patience with me for the first time. Anything I'd planned to say, dropped right out of my mind. I had to collect my thoughts again.

"Zoey, please! You always consider what you're about to say. You choose your words so carefully to avoid hurting someone's feelings. Stop it. Just stop." This time the finger comb through her hair was more forceful. "You don't need to contemplate with me. You can tell me anything, even if you think it will hurt. I need you to be honest. Talk from your heart. Stop trying to say the perfect thing. Please. I've put my whole heart out in the open for you, don't hesitate. Just say what you feel."

Tell her you want to stay. Tell her you've never felt this way before. Tell her she's everything you've ever wanted. Tell her she means more to you than a home or a career you've always known. Tell her she's worth everything and more. Tell her.

A shuddering breath pushed from her mouth while I was trying to get my mouth to follow my mind's orders. "Or maybe I'm the only one with anything to lose here. Maybe you were happy with how that morning went. Maybe it gave you the excuse you need to leave the country guilt-free."

My heart squeezed painfully with every one of her voiced suppositions. None of them were true. A clamor started to blare loudly in my head. My limbs grew heavy with the ache to move, to speak, to touch, to love. I couldn't think clearly, but I knew for the first time since I was a child, I had to say the right words. Had to or I'd surely stop breathing and collapse lifeless where I sat.

Celia rose from the couch, staring down at me. Pleading with me to say something, anything. Pleading with me to place my heart in her very capable hands. She'd been so patient with me for as long as I'd known her. Given me all the time I needed to find the right way to say the things I needed to stay. She'd finally lost that patience, and I couldn't blame her.

Staring up at her, my head pounding, my ears clanging, my heart thumping, my lungs constricting, I knew the words. I could see and hear them in my head. They were so easy and yet so hard. *I love you, Celia. I want what you want, and I'll do whatever it takes to get it.*

She turned away from me and started walking to the front door, shoulders slumped. My silence convincing her I didn't have anything invested in this relationship. She was hurt and disappointed and heartbroken, and I had to stop her.

Say the words. They're right there in your mind. Open your mouth and tell her you love her. Stop her from walking out of your life.

"I sst-stut-t-ter."

31

CELIA FROZE IN PLACE, THEN WHIRLED TO face me. Her eyes found mine, a jumble of emotions running through them. Her mouth nudged open and her posture slowly straightened. She took one hesitant step toward me, then another.

My heart raced, making me dizzy. The loud clamor grew louder as I realized what I'd admitted instead of saying the words I should have said. I didn't mean to say those words. I never said those words. *I'm quiet. I don't like to talk. I don't have much to say. I'm better at listening. I never know what to say.* All of those, all of them, I'd said in the past when friends or girlfriends grew frustrated with me. All of those, but never that. Never the truth for why all of those applied to me.

I couldn't look away from Celia, even as the shame beaten into me from the moment I learned to talk sifted through me again. How ironic the word to describe the condition was one of the most difficult to say for people with the condition.

From the very beginning, my speech pattern stalled. As far back as I could remember, I stuttered. It was an embarrassment to the parents who originally adopted me. Parents who pinned all their legacy hopes on an adopted baby whom they expected to be perfect. It became their sole focus to fix about me. Reward and punishment were tied to how badly I stuttered and in front of whom.

Therapists were thrown at me at first, then placement in specialized daycares, and finally, when they gave up hope that I would grow out of it, an institute for autistic children to hide me away. Until my dad. Until his patience in using every tool and technique available to speech therapists. Until his and my other dad's love and acceptance. I no longer disgraced everyone in my life. I could stutter until I learned how to manage it and not be punished. I could take years, if needed, and I did, but I'd be loved the entire time by a man who always wanted a child and another man who loved his husband enough to learn to want to be a dad.

"You stutter," she whispered the words as she sank down next to me. Her hand reaching out to caress my cheek. No judgment, no teasing, no disbelief. It was as if those two words, words I never used, never intended to use, hence the stutter in speaking them, explained everything. "You're not editing or holding back or only saying what you think I want to hear. You're, what? Crafting the words in your head?"

My eyes filled with tears as I nodded. "Rehearsing."

"Your dad taught you?"

"And to mimic."

She let out a breathy laugh. "The accents. Of course, that's why you're so good at them."

Yes, but no one knew that, and for her to make that leap told me she understood more about speech therapy than most.

Her thumbs swiped at the tears that had dropped onto my cheeks. "Everything you say?"

Everything. Always. Forever. "Unless I blurt before I think, or I'm unable to think."

It took a few seconds for that to sink in, then her eyes widened as she realized why I didn't talk in the throes of sex. Why I'd never be able to talk then. And it wasn't just then. If I get overwhelmed with emotions or feelings or pressure, I can't properly rehearse what I need to say. If I drink too much, it happens. If I rush to say something, like my earlier admission without thinking, it happens.

"You could have told me. However you say something or choose not to say something will never bother me."

I let out a wet laugh, swiping at the wetness still on my cheeks. "You say that, but it always comes up. Almost every close friendship I've had, and every relationship, they all demand I talk more, contribute more, put in more effort."

"You say enough."

Instinctively I couldn't believe her about this. Based on history, I couldn't believe her. And yet, I think I did. "They withheld my food until I asked for what I wanted to eat in complete sentences." Apparently today was a day for confessions.

"What?" she screeched, moving her hand to grip my nape. "Your adoptive parents? They starved you?"

"Telling them I was hungry wasn't enough. I had to say things like, 'Could I please have some peas with my chicken, Mommy Kate?' Or, 'I would like some applesauce,

Mama Jennifer,' before they'd place it on a plate for me. It would take five minutes just to get the words out. And they'd tell me to try again and again and again while I ate. They were so disappointed their child couldn't speak properly. I saw it in everything they did and said around me. Finally, I just stopped speaking, which meant I didn't get breakfast or dinner. They couldn't withhold lunch because the daycare would have reported them, so I got to eat lunch at school and would save some of it for dinner."

"Zoey, that's horrible. How can some parents be so awful?" She looked stricken, even with the experience she had with her own parents. This seemed to be far worse to her. "How did you end up with your dads?"

"One of the daycare providers was concerned when I stopped speaking and my stomach made constant hunger noises. She spoke to the adopters, who immediately took me out of school and found what they thought would be a solution to everything."

"The boarding school you mentioned?"

"It was an institute for autistic children. Since I'd stopped speaking, they convinced themselves I was autistic." Or that was how I chose to think about their drastic move to place me in a special needs institute. When a child doesn't speak, it's often the first diagnosis.

"I can't even imagine how scary that must have been." She shook her head, distressed and compassionate and so loving. "Is that where you met your dad?"

"He spends two days a week working on state social and health services clients. The institute falls under his jurisdiction."

"And how quickly did he figure out you shouldn't have been there?"

I grinned, proud of my dad, remembering that day again, even though I was only three and a half. The memory was so vivid. How wonderful my dad was to all the kids and me.

"About five seconds." Which was true. He had so much experience with autism and speech impediments he could spot one or the other without looking at times. Even without me speaking, my direct eye contact, my clear understanding of his words and instructions, my comfort with touch, he knew in seconds I wasn't autistic. Once he got me to speak, he understood. Once he got me to speak more, he got DSHS involved in assessing my home situation, which prompted my original adopters to give up their parental rights. Within a month, he was granted emergency foster care status to take me in. Just after I turned four, my dads applied for adoption.

My dad worked one hour a day with me on speech therapy. No more, no less, and only after he asked me if I wanted to try to learn to speak without a stutter because he and my other dad would be fine if I didn't. He tried some of the usual techniques my earlier speech therapists tried. Singing, dropping the first consonant, or rolling into a word to get it started never worked. He taught me sign language to communicate when I couldn't verbally. Then we discovered my ear. How I could repeat something that was just spoken. We watched television and listened to audiobooks to expand my vocabulary, and he taught me to remember the most used phrases so I could always have them run through my head before speaking them. Filler words to allow for time to rehearse other words. Some of the complete sentences I speak come directly from audiobooks or movies or television. In fact, the first words I said to Celia came from a movie. A Disney movie, no less. The scene and words ran through my head before I said them to her.

"I am so happy you found your dads."

"Me, too." Even my other dad who wasn't too sure of himself around preschoolers at the start was a blessing.

I'd learned to forgive my original adopters. As a lesbian couple who were both willing to carry a child, they had twice the chances of most couples to have a biological child. When they went through all their options and were left with adoption, they needed her to be more than just healthy. More than just ahead of the developmental curve. They needed her to be perfect, and when she stuttered, no matter how much therapy she was given, and then stubbornly refused to speak because their reward and punishment system wasn't worth the effort, they were baffled and frustrated and regretting the adoption process. If I'd been their biological child, they could have made excuses, but being adopted, they seized the opportunity to displace blame onto my birth parents. Being investigated by social services because a therapist at the institute where they stashed their kid was one thing too much for them to handle. They didn't know what they were getting into with adoption, but because their poor decisions placed me in my dads' care, I couldn't hold it against them.

"I'm very glad you told me."

"I'm very happy I found you."

Her eyes brightened. "Are you?"

"I am. I-I," I paused, pushing out a breath.

"You don't have to rehearse with me, Zoey."

"It's automatic now." It was, even with my dad, I rarely even stammered anymore.

"As long as you know I'll listen to whatever and however you want to say something."

I pushed forward and kissed her beautiful mouth. Soft accepting lips danced across mine, relishing the touch as much as I was. When I pulled back, the tension knot in my stomach released. "I want to stay. I want to be with you. I love listening to you. I love that you don't mind how quiet I am. I love that you always have something to say. I love that you'll accept me as I am. I love you, Celia."

One hand pressed against her chest as the other reached out to cup my cheek. Tears filled her eyes. "My heart is so full right now. You're everything I've ever wanted. Are you able to stay? Choose another university in the country?"

My head nodded as my heart thumped hard enough to be heard. "Skye offered to sponsor a similar joint branding project with the station in Glasgow and its affiliated university. I want to take it. I want to stay for what we have together."

"I love you. You've made me so happy. I tried to hold back, tried to resist, but it's impossible with you." She leaned forward to kiss me again. Longer and more involved this time. Filled with all the love and promise we had for each other.

32

SKYE PULLED THE CAR INTO ONE OF THE LAST spots allotted to her station. She glanced over and grinned at me. "I'm torn between being glad we'll have our own car park and sad that it takes away my usual evening meet up with Celia or some of her colleagues."

"You needed your own parking lot." My eyes landed on all the cars that didn't belong to anyone in her station. They were supposed to have an entire section of the staff parking lot reserved for them, but no one on the security staff could be bothered to monitor the lot. She might like bumping into Celia and the rest of the television department as they made their way to their cars each evening, but not being able to find a place to park anytime she leaves the office during the day is a pain.

"And the extra income for the college is a good thing too. Nice work there." Her eyes jumped across the street to the new parking garage set back behind the station building. Lines were being painted today. It would open for the grand showcase of the amenities in the new building. They'd have an entire floor of the garage only accessible to station personnel. The rest of the garage could be used for overflow university staff and paid public parking.

I reached for the door handle but stopped when Skye's hand grabbed my forearm. I turned back, noticing a concerned look cross her face.

"I didn't pressure you into this, did I?" She gestured to the paperwork we'd just completed in conjunction with the university in Glasgow where Skye's sister station was located. "Ainsley and I were talking the other night, and I just want to make sure you staying here wasn't because we kept badgering you."

I thought about how to respond. She was a large part of the reason I was staying. A good part, and her offer to carry the employment sponsorship made it easier to stay. At the mercy of an employer with zero stake in my personal interests, I could be dismissed from the contract and expected to leave the country immediately. That wasn't a worry with Skye's employment. Even if the university, who would technically be the authority on my next project, decided they didn't like the direction I was taking them, Skye assured me she'd keep me on to brand some of her station's shows. Not my preference, but if it kept me in the country legally while I got the funds into place to apply for an entrepreneurial visa, I'd do it.

"You like it here, right? You wanted to stay?" Her eyes flicked to mine. "I was in a different place when I made my move. It might have colored my attempt to influence you. Ainsley reminded me how different our situations are."

Most definitely different. She had been in a high stress job for which she was severely underappreciated and overworked. She'd liked being an executive producer of her friend Dallas's news magazine show, but once she was promoted to news director, the amount of work and type of work wore her down. By the time she became reacquainted with Ainsley, she was at her wit's end with work, and the raw emotions Ainsley evoked in her made the move very easy for her.

I wasn't at my wit's end. I didn't need to escape my job. But I was emotionally involved with several people here. And falling hard for Celia. Staying on was the right move for me.

"I do want to stay."

"Okay. Good." She let out an audible breath. "You know, when I came here last year, it was to ask Ainsley to move to the States. She had offers from three universities in DC, she was a dual citizen, she'd lived in the US already, it seemed logical."

My eyebrows shot up. She hadn't told me she planned to bring Ainsley back to the US.

"I was in the middle of this long speech I prepared about how we belonged together, and she offers to move. Hardly thinking about it at all, she just wants to be with me. And in that moment, I think what a selfish ass I am to take her away from all this." Her hand waved along the windshield, indicating the whole of Edinburgh. "She is the leading authority on Scottish history in the world. She has a permanent contract at a prestigious university and a lovely house near her parents who are her best friends, and it was stupid of me to even suggest she walk away from any of it. And yet, she offered. So, I did the same. No thinking, no consideration for what I might do or how I could get citizenship or anything. Just went with my feelings for the first time in my life, and it was the best decision I've ever made."

Again, not much like my situation, but I could understand the just-go-with-your-feelings part. It was the best explanation for my decision to stay on.

"I'm thrilled you're staying, but even more happy about you and Celia."

Still giddy whenever I heard her name, I couldn't stop the blush. "Me, too."

She nudged me and laughed at my understated agreement. Inside I was doing cartwheels, still amazed at how the last few days had turned so beautifully. How brave Celia had been to come to my door. What I'd admitted to her and her immediate acceptance. We'd barely spent a moment apart since, until today when Skye and I had to make a trip to Glasgow to finalize my employment contract.

"Should we grab our Scottish lassies and head to a celebratory dinner?" She was sounding more Scottish by the day. Car park, lassies. Definitely cute.

"I'm not sure what she has planned for tonight." I didn't think we'd make it back in time for dinner, so we planned on our first night apart since getting back together. The misinterpretations we'd had during our first night of making love and the morning-after together hadn't surfaced even once. Only the fun and heat and lust. Celia would whisper sexy words, ask rhetorical questions, and give compliments because she loved being vocal. I tried to vocalize a little more, not words, but sounds of pleasure and excited breathing. As we became more comfortable making love, she became more confident and I became less muted. And neither of us could get enough.

"Let me drop this off in my office, and we'll see if she's still on campus. Or am I butting into a private celebration?" She accepted my head shake as a reply and stepped out of the car. "You want to check her office while I run this upstairs? Or we can go together?"

I pointed toward the path to campus in reply and started walking that way, eager and hopeful to catch Celia. Not that we couldn't call and run by her place to grab her for dinner if we had to, but this would be a nice surprise.

My search didn't take long. Celia was standing just outside her building talking to someone. As I drew nearer, I recognized the other person as her mother. What was wrong with her family that they'd continue to stalk her like this?

Seeing her standing quietly while her mother talked and gestured made me want to rush over and wrap her in my arms. I'd want to do that anyway, but on campus, we made sure to keep a professional distance. Enough of her colleagues were upset I'd chosen her department as the branding effort, they didn't need to believe my decision was due to a personal entanglement.

"...in consideration, and the other members will expect the family to represent the Kirk's values and beliefs," her mother was saying. "The caterers will leave by half five. I'll expect your help in placing everything into serving dishes."

Celia scoffed, then looked away and caught my approach. Her face broke into a lovely smile before her mother's words dimmed her elation.

"Keep talk of your profession and unmarried status to a minimum, and under no circumstances will you tell the GA about your lifestyle choice. That would take me right out of the running." Her mother was still oblivious to me standing close enough to overhear. She wasn't even focused on her daughter or she would have noticed Celia looking at me.

"Hello, Celia," I spoke over whatever her mother was starting to say.

"Hi, Zoey." Her tone reflected the relief she must feel at this interruption. Clearly, her mother was trying to get her to attend an important church dinner when her mother never invited her to attend anything unless it would be of benefit to her.

Her mother whirled around, a ferocious look on her face as she regarded me. "What are you still doing here?"

"I work here," I responded calmly, stepping in beside Celia. I had to fight the urge to rub her back in soothing circles.

"You should be gone by now," her mother insisted, a furrow managing to crease her tightened face. She looked genuinely perplexed by my presence.

"Mother," Celia got her attention back. "Zoey's project isn't complete yet, and that's not why you're here."

"No, well, no, but this is exactly what I'm talking about, Celia. If you so much as mention your 'friendship' with this woman," her fingers formed quotes around a word that almost never needed quotation marks.

Both Celia and I waited for her to finish her statement, but nothing else came. Her breathing came in rapid puffs, features pinching in consternation.

"Mother," Celia started again but was cut off.

"No, Celia, this is unacceptable. Any mention of you and this woman will ruin my chances of being considered for General Assembly. I've worked for this my whole life. They cannot know you think you're homosexual."

"Wow," the word escaped my lips before I could help it. Think she's homosexual? Not she is homosexual, but she thinks she's homosexual. This lady was a piece of work.

"That will be quite enough out of you, young miss," her mother scolded me. "You shouldn't even be in this country anymore. Immigration should have taken care of this problem."

The way she said it, with certainty, caused a tightening in my chest. She couldn't...no, that would be both difficult and unnecessarily nasty.

"What are you saying, Mother?" Celia knew about my immigration visits and how they'd been worrisome enough to make me hesitate in my decision to stay in the UK. "Did you do something to place Zoey in jeopardy here?"

"I have many loyal congregants. Some of them work in official positions. I might have mentioned how unfair it is that foreigners are taking spots at universities and jobs away from good members of our church."

"You did not," Celia insisted, her own breaths coming in faster spurts.

Her mother's smug smile said enough.

"What were you thinking? This is Zoey's life you're trying to ruin."

"She's ruining your life. I will not allow her to taint you further."

My hand reached out to grip Celia's. Her usual reaction of staying silent and walking away whenever family members accosted her sounded like a good plan at the moment. We should leave.

"So, you had a couple of your congregants examine Zoey's visa status?" Celia's voice rose, and my hand gripped firmer in response.

"What's this?" Skye's voice called out from behind us. Despite being closer to me, she stepped around to flank Celia. "Did I hear correctly? You used your position in the church to force some of your members to check on a legal visitor to this country?" Her arm slipped around Celia's waist, solidifying the wall of defense.

"I didn't force anyone. And someone should look into you, lass." A finger poked into Skye's face.

"You know, our news magazine show is short a story next week." Skye's eyes twinkled. She never had a problem with confrontation, and at the moment, I was her biggest cheerleader. "Perhaps I should send them over to investigate ministers using undue influence on congregation members to illegally exploit their government positions for the purpose of intimidating people. That sounds like an award-winning story to me."

Celia's mother grew pale. Her smug announcement had turned against her.

"Truly, Mother. If anything, you getting immigration involved might have pushed me to make a rash decision to keep Zoey in the country by any means. Be thankful your ploy didn't work or you might have gotten a wedding invitation."

Her mother sucked in a shrieking breath. Eyes wide with shock, she pointed her poking finger in Celia's face now. "I will not hear of such a thing. Be at the house by five tomorrow."

Celia gazed down at me and took her hand from mine to slip around my waist. She looked back at her mother. "No. If you think I'd do you any favors after what you've done to Zoey, you're mad. I can't believe you'd stoop this low."

"Celia!" her mother shouted as we turned as one and started off toward the parking lot.

"Good for you," Skye encouraged. "You were brilliant."

"I can't believe her. Zoey, I'm so sorry." She stopped once we moved into the parking lot, out of her mother's sightline.

"As long as my papers stay in order and I don't piss off Parliament, she can't do anything to me." I tried to sound reassuring because Celia needed it, but inside I was trembling. An influential woman wanted me out of the country enough to break all sorts of rules with her congregation.

"I can't believe I'm related to her. To any of them really."

"Hey," I reached up to cup her face. "You're beautiful and kind, and nothing else matters. I'm glad you won't have to go to her dinner party."

"I'm done. No more favors to keep up the appearance of happy families."

I smiled and tapped a finger against her sternum. She automatically looked down, and I pushed up on tiptoes to capture her lips. I'd risk getting caught kissing this wonderful woman on campus after such a stressful encounter. She deserved a reward after that encounter. It wasn't at all for my benefit. Not at all.

33

MY ARM AUTOMATICALLY REACHED TO TUCK around the warm body next to mine in bed. When it snuggled back against me rather than stiffening like it had the first few times we woke up together, I smiled widely. Hopefully, this would be the end of her insecurities about her body. About me touching every part of her luscious, curvy, sexy body.

"Happy Christmas," Celia murmured as she rolled over to face me.

"Merry Christmas," I replied and leaned in for a soft kiss.

"This is the best Christmas morning ever."

I chuckled. "You're easy. Should I take back the pony I got for your present?"

She laughed and smooched me again. "Where would the pony live? In my tiny back garden?"

"Panda and Hemlock can share their kitty beds."

"How big do you think ponies are? Do they come in kitty sizes in the States?"

A knock interrupted my reply. "Come on, lovebirds. Elspeth cooked a feast, and there are presents." Skye's voice came through the door of the guest room Celia and I were sharing.

"Who knew she was so chipper in the morning?" Celia gripped my waist and brought me over her. We were clothed out of respect for our status as guests, and I fought the urge to grind against her. My slow morning wakeup was already trashed by Skye, and now I couldn't even take advantage of the lovely treasure underneath me. "Think if we're quiet, they'll leave us alone?"

I grinned and dropped a kiss onto her lips that quickly became heated. Her hands skated over me as mine slipped under her shirt and up to palm a full breast. She groaned into our kiss and pushed up against me. My lips popped off her mouth, trailing down along the column of her throat. We rocked together until we both skittered close to the edge.

"We shouldn't," she whisper-moaned. "We're guests. Your dad and Alastair are in the house."

I groaned my frustration, knowing I'd started it, but she was right. We weren't animals. We didn't need to screw like bunnies every time we slept together, especially with my dad, friends, and Ainsley's parents all in rooms on the same floor. Celia wasn't exactly quiet when we made love, something we both really liked, but she was right. Decorum was in order.

I rolled to the side and forced myself to get out of bed. It was too tempting to just stay there all day, but Skye had a point. There were festivities and presents and people to enjoy.

After showering and dressing, I met Elspeth and Ainsley in the kitchen while Celia finished getting ready.

My eyes searched the living room, but no sign of my dad or Alastair. Skye was likely out with Elspeth's sheep herd, although she could easily be assembling whatever extravagant gift she no doubt got for her partner. Celia and I agreed on spending the holiday together as our gift to each other, which took the pressure off, but I still had a few surprises she would enjoy.

"Good morning, love," Elspeth sang from the kitchen. "Did ya sleep well?"

"Yes, thanks." My eyes flicked to the sliders for a view into the backyard. Alastair and my dad were practicing their golf swings, picking up on their friendship as if they'd seen each other last week instead of three months ago.

"You'd think he'd be tired of golf, but he loves it. They'd be on the course right now if we didn't have other things to do this morning." Elspeth pulled one pan off the stove as Ainsley poured tea and coffee into a line of mugs. They looked like they had an entire short order grill going with all the food they were producing. I rubbed my stomach, loosening the tight muscles. Skye was familiar with my no breakfast habit, having hosted me as a guest in her home over the years we'd known each other. She assured me she'd already warned Elspeth, so I wouldn't have to worry about offending her or make excuses for why I wouldn't be eating any of this scrumptious food. My dad would also be there to smooth things over.

"Happy Christmas, everyone," Celia greeted as she came down the stairs fresh from her shower. She wore a new dress, one of her own, easily identified by the figure-enhancing tailoring.

"Happy Christmas, Celia," Mother and daughter said together.

"It smells divine in here." She slid a hand across my back, leaning down to plant a quick kiss on my cheek. "What can I do to help?"

"A hand with carrying some of these plates, if you please. Zoey, call the lads in from the cold. And where is that wife of yours, Ainsley?"

"You have to ask?" Ainsley murmured, knowing how much her partner enjoyed the small sheep herd her parents kept on the farm.

"I'll get her," I volunteered, stepping outside to call to my dad and Alastair. Skye appeared through the shrubs forming a fence line between the back garden and the barn just as I finished my chow call.

We settled around the table with lively chatter. I accepted a mug of tea while everyone else helped themselves to the food.

"Tell us about this new house," Alastair asked my dad.

He smiled wistfully, his eyes finding mine. He'd found what he thought would be the ideal work-live location. On his second walk-through, we had a video chat so I could take the tour with him. He wanted a second opinion and for me to be comfortable with it as well.

"It's a big lot in north Bellingham. The house is a recently renovated turn of the century Georgian. It has a detached two-story garage that I'll redo to use as my new office and convert the upstairs into an apartment for Zoey and Celia when they visit."

My heart swelled at how quickly my dad went from thinking of me as me to thinking of me as a couple. Celia made a small joyful noise, her hand reaching out to grip my father's. It wasn't like this was a surprise announcement for us. As soon as I'd told him of my plans to stay on here, his house search expanded to include either a bigger place or something with a guest suite so I could sell my condo and still have a place to stay in the States. Still, for my dad to clearly accept her role in my life and cement it with a renovation, meant the world to Celia.

"You're not keeping your condo, Zoey?" Skye asked.

"I'll need the funds from the sale to put into a UK bank account to apply for an entrepreneur visa. Since Dad's moving and I hope to stay here without needing to find new employers to sponsor me, it made sense." I squeezed Celia's thigh next to mine. We may still be new, but I was certain of her permanence in my life.

"This is so exciting," Ainsley declared. "We've converted another, Mum."

Elspeth laughed. "Go Team Scotland!"

We all laughed at that. Alastair pointed at my dad. "You next, Priam."

He smiled and winked at me. "Perhaps when I retire."

I beamed, thrilled he'd even consider it. My other dad was also planning more film projects in Europe so he could drop by more often and continue to coordinate guests for Celia's classes.

Celia caught my eye and matched my grin. This was the first holiday where one of her parents hadn't made a demand on her time today. Well, they had made the demands to help out at their church or be seen but not heard at a brunch for the church committee members. They conveniently forgot Celia wasn't welcome in their family when they were trying to keep up appearances. She was expected to respect their family wishes or she'd be hounded by various family members until she acquiesced. This year, she was done, not just with the way they mistreated and berated her, but with what Celia's mother tried to do to me. Like me, Celia was more forceful when standing up for someone she cared about. I couldn't be prouder. She assured me she didn't mind missing her own church's service this morning to come to Glasgow and spend Christmas with our friends and my dad. Her uncle's family would be joining us at Elspeth's for dinner tonight, which was the perfect celebration for her. Dad, Celia, and I would head back to Edinburgh tomorrow while Skye and Ainsley went to the States to visit Skye's mom and Ainsley's cousin. My dad would set his sights on making Celia feel welcome in our little family unit and spend more time with his newest friend, Alastair. I was looking forward to every minute of it.

"Having a good time?" Celia leaned in and asked.

I nodded and ran my hand down her shoulder to grip her hand. Last Christmas, it was just my dad and me. I hadn't even been able to get my other dad on the phone because he was on a behind budget film set with a twenty-hour shooting day in a time zone many hours ahead. We always made due, my dads and I, but this, spending the holiday with my dad, my best friends, their family, and the love of my life, this could never be equaled. I hoped every Christmas holiday could be spent the same way. And the look in Celia's eyes told me she hoped the same.

Epilogue

"WE NEED TO BE OUT THE DOOR IN FIFTEEN minutes," Celia said as she rushed into our bedroom.

I caught her as she tried to scoot by, lifting my face for the hello kiss she normally gave freely when she wasn't so harried about being home late. She smiled and dropped a kiss on my lips, increasing the pressure when my hands pulled her hips close.

"Hello, my darling," she whispered as she pulled away. "Good day today?"

We'd spoken earlier when she told me her dean called a late meeting for their department. He'd been doing that almost monthly since my branding efforts went into effect. Her department had expanded so rapidly, he kept holding meetings to brainstorm ideas for staying ahead of the demand.

"Very good day. I don't need to go back to Berlin for two weeks." After working with several colleges in the UK and Ireland these past couple of years, I finally ventured out farther to find a European university where I could hold my own with the language. My German had improved greatly over the past three months, even with their excellent grasp of English, but the best thing about it and the other colleges I'd worked with in the UK was their complete lack of neediness. No handholding was necessary. After the initial two weeks on campus evaluating departments and making my recommendation, I could work remotely on the branding efforts, checking in on campus once a week or so. This one in Germany seemed fine with me working off campus for most of the project. Whatever it was that let them not micromanage their contractors unlike their American counterparts made me very happy.

"That's wonderful!" Celia exclaimed, wrapping her arms around me again. "They're so impressed they don't even need to see you to know your work is brilliant."

I laughed and kissed her again. "Fifteen minutes."

She squeaked and jumped back, rushing into the closet, giving another squeak of pleasure at the size of the space. We'd been living in this house on the outskirts of Edinburgh for four months, and she still sighed or squeaked or commented on how much more room we now had. Three bedrooms, one for her sewing room, one for my home office, and one for us, a much larger kitchen for Celia's love of cooking, a second bathroom to use as an occasional darkroom, and a lot of green in the front and back gardens. Her townhouse served us well enough for more than a year after I gave up my rental, but I wanted her to have a sewing room separate from the home office I needed, and the closets in her townhome wouldn't have satisfied a newborn.

As many times as she assured me she didn't care about making the commitment we'd made to each other legal, it wasn't until we bought this house together that the last of her worry lines vanished. She truly believed our union was more powerful than any legal claim could make. I made sure to reinforce those feelings for her whenever I could. Never again would I have to worry about being sideless. She understood me and loved me.

"Can you believe they're having twins?" her excited voice called out from the bathroom now.

I chuckled. We'd had this discussion several times since learning Ainsley was expecting twins, but it made Celia happy, so we brought it up over and over. Tonight was the baby shower. Celia made the tiniest kilts I'd ever seen, good for a girl or a boy, since Ainsley and Skye were waiting until the birth to find out. They'd been surprised by the news of twins, even knowing Alastair's side of the family had a few sets of twins in generations past. Skye was overwhelmed, but Ainsley's parents would be at their beck-and-call for babysitting duties. Celia and I were happy to help as well.

"I hope they like the kilts."

"Th-they'll love them," I assured her.

Her face appeared in the doorway with a wide smile at recognizing my stutter. My speech impediment always gave her the biggest clue I wasn't just saying something she wanted to hear. "They are pretty adorable. The kilts, I mean. Skye and Ainsley, too, but the kilts are cute."

They'd make the historian in Ainsley ecstatic. Her dad, the proud Scot would also love the thoughtful touch of a tartan in both his and Elspeth's family clans.

"W-w-would you…" I started and blew out a breath while thinking about what I wanted to ask.

Celia came into the room, now in a beautiful yellow print dress of her own still unnamed label. She looked at me curiously, not used to me having trouble with my speech pattern twice in one night. "What, darling?"

The words ran through my head and when I could hear them, I began. "We've talked about kids before."

"Aye, we did." Her tone was encouraging as she came close and reached out to cup my hips. "Kids, no kids, either is fine with me as long as I have you."

"Same here," I told her and brushed up against her. "Now that our best friends will have kids, I've started thinking about it more."

"Yes?"

"Would you be okay with adoption?" I searched her expression, nervous about what I might find. "We'd have to wait for my citizenship to come through first. If-if it's something—"

"Yes!" she cut off my halting question with a searing kiss. "A baby or toddler or what are you thinking?"

"A little girl, four or five. Skye's kids will be about that age by the time we'd be eligible. It would be fun to have kids the same age."

"It would, and unless one of your other cousins breaks the Thais tradition first, you'd bring a second girl into this next generation, just like your dad did."

Not the reason I wanted a daughter, but the immediate acceptance by my family would be one of many benefits to adopting a little girl. My thoughts had cycled around to adoption many times over the years, make some kid as lucky as I'd been, but until I found Celia, a life partner to love and parent with me, I didn't allow myself to think past the concept. Now, I'd be free to plan every step we'd need to take. My heart thumped happily.

Celia's hands drew up my sides to cup my face. She covered my lips with her own, kissing softly. The leisurely thump of my happy heart accelerated to a ferocious pounding. She pulled back with a breathy sigh. "You, my dear, are brilliant."

I beamed at her compliment. "Only because I chose you as a partner."

"Luckiest choice of my life."

My fingers traced the smile on her lips. I'd noticed this smile before anything else about her. Loved seeing it on her and loved even more being the reason it was there so often.

"Best choice of mine," I told her.

"You sweet talker." She tapped a finger against my chin, eyes lingering on my lips. Her head shook and she stepped back. "Baby shower tonight. Help our best friends with the bairns. Get your citizenship, and add a little girl to our family." She ticked off each on her fingers, a cheeky smile on her face.

"Good plan. You make all the plans from now on."

She laughed and pulled me back in for a tight squeeze. "You are so good for my ego."

"And you're so good for my everything." Every possible thing. Now and for the rest of our lives together.

About the Author

Lynn Galli has lived in the Pacific Northwest for so long she doesn't know any better. Yet during every political season, she contemplates buying a private island (based on her budget, it would have to be a very small island, probably densely wooded and filled with bugs that will poison her, which is also slowly sinking into the ocean to make it affordable) to set up her own government and not be unsettled by American politics anymore.

Connect with Lynn Galli Online

Email: gallilynn@yahoo.com

Website: lynngalli.com

Facebook: LynnGalliAuthor

Twitter: @lynngalli

Other Publications by Lynn Galli

SCOTTISH CHARM

One-Off (Book 1) – Weddings have never been Skye MacKinnon's thing. When she's put in charge of planning her friend's big event, she's less than thrilled. Finding out she'll have to work with the bane of her college existence, Ainsley Baird, may push her right over the edge. Knowing there's nothing she can do to change her circumstances or the company she'll have to keep, her only plan is to make it through the happy occasion without setting fire to the whole show or one person in particular.

Speak Low (Book 2) – With a unique view on legal marriage, Zoey Thais tends to have a fleeting relationship with relationships. It suits her chosen roving career path, even if she wishes she could find someone to put up with her quirks. Celia Munro is sensible about love, even if she wishes she had the courage to take a risk on a wanderer. Will the marriage cynic and the reluctant romantic set aside their ingrained hesitancy to take a chance on love?

VIRGINIA CLAN

At Last (Prequel) – Willa Lacey never thought acquiring five million in venture capital for her software startup would be easier than suppressing romantic feelings for a friend. Having never dealt with either situation, Willa finds herself torn between what she knows and what could be.

Wasted Heart (Book 1) – Attorney Austy Nunziata moves across the country to try to snap out of the cycle of pining for her married best friend. Despite knowing how pointless her feelings are, five months in the new city hasn't seemed to help. When she meets FBI agent, Elise Bridie, that task becomes a lot easier.

Imagining Reality (Book 2) – Changing a reputation can be the hardest thing anyone can do, even among her own friends. But Jessie Ximena has been making great strides over the past year to do just that. Will anyone, even her good friends, give her the benefit of the doubt when it comes to finding a forever love?

Blessed Twice (Book 3) – Briony Gatewood has considered herself a married woman for fifteen years even though she's spent the last three as a widow. Her friends have offered to help her get over the loss of her spouse with a series of blind dates, but only a quiet, enigmatic colleague can make Briony think about falling in love again.

Forevermore (Book 4) - M Desiderius never thought she could have a normal life filled with love. She gets all that and more when she marries Briony, including an amazing foster daughter named Olivia. Every wish she'd never allowed herself to voice became real. When someone from Olivia's past threatens M's newfound family, can she carry on in the face of loss or will it push her back into a life of solitude?

ASPEN FRIENDS

Mending Defects (Book 1) – Small town life for Glory Eiben has always been her ideal. With her rare congenital heart defect, keeping family and friends close by preserves her easygoing attitude. When Lena Coleridge moves in next door, life becomes anything but easy. Lena is a reluctant transplant and even more reluctant friend. Their growing friendship adds many layers to Glory's ideal.

Something So Grand (Book 2) – A designer for the wealthy, Vivian Yeats doesn't have time for relationships, yet she longs for romance. She's had to settle in the past when it comes to women but won't be doing that again. If romance is going to happen for her, it'll take someone special to turn her head. Natalie Harper, the new contractor on her jobsites, might just be the woman to make that happen.

Life Rewired (Book 3) – Two years ago, Molly Sokol decided she wanted to get serious about finding that special someone. She can picture her ideal woman easily: petite, feminine, excitable, adoring, and ultra-affectionate. When the opposite of all that comes along in the form of Falyn Shaw, Molly never thought they'd be anything more than friends. Being wrong has never felt so good.

OTHER ROMANCES

Uncommon Emotions – When someone spends her days ripping apart corporations, compartmentalization is key. Love doesn't factor in for Joslyn Simonini. Meeting Raven Malvolio ruins the harmony that Joslyn has always felt, introducing her to passion for the first time in her life.

Full Court Pressure – The pressure of being the first female basketball coach of a men's NCAA Division 1 team may pale in comparison to the pressure Quinn Viola feels in her unexpected love life.

Clichéd Love – As a journalist, Vega spends her days writing other people's stories. For her latest assignment, she's taking down LGBT love stories and worrying that her eyes might roll right out of their sockets during every mushy interview. Only the help of her new friend, Iris, who also believes romance stories are worth mocking, prevents her from finding ways to make her subjects mysteriously disappear to save her from having to listen to more clichés.

Out of Order – Lindsay St. James spends her days fixing political problems. No problem too taxing, no issue too complex to resolve for someone who dedicates herself to her career. When she stumbles into a judicial bribery scheme affecting her political candidate, she has to rely on the help of the newest and most distracting member of the judiciary. For the first time, her personal interests are keeping her from focusing on her profession, and she doesn't seem all that bothered about it.

Winter Calling – As a human resources coordinator for a ski resort, Tru's biggest challenge is finding people to take the job seriously. The new CFO definitely fits that characterization. A little too well, according to Tru's colleagues. Her stoic demeanor makes them believe she's a cold, unfeeling android. Always willing to think the best of people, Tru sets out to discover if Renske is really as imperturbable as she seems.